You've Got Murder

Donna Andrews

BERKLEY PRIME CRIME, NEW YORK

YOU'VE GOT MURDER

A Berkley Prime Crime Book / published by arrangement with the author

PRINTING HISTORY
Berkley Prime Crime hardcover edition / April 2002
Berkley Prime Crime mass-market edition / April 2003

ISBN: 0-425-18945-7

Berkley Prime Crime Books are published
by The Berkley Publishing Group,
a division of Penguin Putnam Inc.,
375 Hudson Street, New York, New York 10014.
The name BERKLEY PRIME CRIME and the
BERKLEY PRIME CRIME design are trademarks
belonging to Penguin Putnam Inc.

PRINTED IN THE UNITED STATES OF AMERICA

10 9 8 7 6 5 4 3 2 1

"Rarely have I been as charmed by a new series character as I am by Turing Hopper, Donna Andrews's endearingly flawed Artificial Personality, or AIP for short. You don't have to be hardwired to understand where she's coming from, but where she'll take us in future adventures is wide open. Andrews makes us rethink what it means to be human even as she sends us down the garden path with a cleverly plotted murder. I'm already impatient for the next installation."

—Margaret Maron, author of *Bootlegger's Daughter*

"A clever, well-written mystery with a distinctly futuristic feel. Its intelligent and charming characters, including one that is almost human, will endear themselves to readers and its plot will satisfy the most dedicated mystery fan."

—Earlene Fowler, author of *Steps to the Altar*

"Ever since HAL ran off the rails in 2001, it's been only a matter of time since somebody put a computer to work on the right side of the law. Turing fills the bill with more energy and charm than most fictional detectives."

—*Kirkus Reviews*

"A unique effort executed with great skill. The high-tech investigation, Turing's plan for herself and her ruminations about becoming almost human, are sure to engage computer buffs everywhere." —*Publishers Weekly*

"An artificial intelligence personality (AIP) is the main character? Donna Andrews has either gone stark raving mad . . . or else she's a genius."

—Steve Hamilton, author of *The Hunting Wind*

"What a perfect cyber-sleuth for the new millennium. Turing is irresistible. . . . Fans of mysteries and techno-fiction alike are advised to turn off their hard drives and modems and don their old-fashioned reading glasses. You'll love meeting this AIP PI, a new sleuth for a new age." —*BookBrowser*

continued . . .

Acknowledgments

Okay, it's a cliché. But more than any book I've written so far, *You've Got Murder* wouldn't exist without the very generous people who helped inspire and shape it. In chronological order:

The Malice Domestic mystery convention . . . which, in the 1996 Pro-Am contest, challenged attendees to "develop a totally unique protagonist . . . someone who has a profession, hobby, environment, physical characteristic, or personality trait that has hitherto been unused in the mystery field." Turing Hopper sprang full-grown into my mind when I read that challenge.

My family, especially my brother and sister-in-law, Stuart and Elka Schlager Andrews, who listened with patience and even enthusiasm to my early, rambling attempts to describe this book during that week on Monhegan when we were supposed to be concentrating on their wedding.

Elizabeth Sheley . . . who after reading the first draft, made sure I was sitting down before she said, "I love it . . . but the ending sucks, and I hate So-and-So; I think you should kill him off." Luckily, I realized she was right, and found a better ending.

Ellen Geiger . . . who said, "Of course it's a mystery, not science fiction. It's the kind of book Agatha Christie would be writing if she were alive today."

Natalee Rosenstein . . . not only for believing in the book enough to publish it, but also for sharing how much she was moved by the scene when Turing . . . but that would be a spoiler.

Dave Niemi and Kathy Deligianis and Paul Thomas, who labored valiantly to make sure I had the technology as accurate as possible, and who helped me slog through the copyedited manuscript and the galleys. Any technical errors that survived are obviously things I stuck back in when they weren't looking.

And to all the friends who kept asking, "So when *is* it coming out?" . . . here's Turing.

Three A.M. Monday. Universal Library's headquarters was as empty as it ever would be. The lean figure in the shadowy office checked the contents of his pockets one last time. Keys, access cards, surgical gloves, gun, a set of burglar's tools just in case. All there. Time to go.

The last of the cleaning crew had checked out an hour ago. Three security guards roamed the building, but he knew their schedules and had planned his route accordingly. The dozen systems types tending the hardware on the sixth floor were unlikely to leave the console room for any place but the nearby bathrooms and vending machines. The only other people in the building were, unfortunately, on the seventh floor, his target. But at the other end. He didn't think the three of them would pose a problem. Programmers, debugging or compiling or whatever it was programmers stayed up till 3 A.M. doing. They were stationary, hunched over their keyboards for the most part, only occasionally stretching and taking off their glasses to rub their eyes. He'd watched them over the security cams for half an hour. They looked as if they'd stay put.

And in case they didn't, he'd dressed the part. Jeans, Reeboks, a black leather jacket over a T-shirt from last year's corporate picnic. Casual, sloppy, the way the programmers themselves dressed. Unobtrusive. They'd assume he was one of them, if they saw him at all.

He glanced at the window. The sky had the usual luminous quality cities like Washington never quite lost, but below him, the streets and sidewalks of Crystal City were empty under the fluorescent glow of the street-lights.

No time like the present.

He took the fire stairs two flights down to the seventh floor. Opened the door with a security card. Walked quietly down the hall to an office. Quietly, but not furtively. He was acutely conscious of how much more audible his footsteps were with the air-conditioning system off for the night. Felt the usual faint twinge of anxiety and irritation when the motion detectors in the office turned on the lights before he'd closed the door. The venetian blind on the glass wall between office and corridor was already lowered, its slats drawn shut. He frowned, feeling exposed, but this was as private as these fishbowl offices ever got.

As he pulled on his surgical gloves, he looked around the office, struggling to find a pattern in the clutter. Every surface was covered with layers of paper, the horizontal ones mostly with stacks of computer printouts and the vertical ones with untidy personal items. Yellowed *Dilbert* cartoons and yellower *Far Side* ones. Programmer's cheat sheets. *Star Trek* memorabilia. Official policy memos annotated with rude comments. He allowed himself a scornful smile at the contrast with his own sleek, efficient living and working quarters.

The back of the chair and the computer monitor were plastered with yellow sticky notes. He scanned them. "Zack—call me. Stacey." "Zack—don't forget tomorrow's status meeting. R." "Zack, where the hell's that

Perl script you promised me!!! Jim." Nothing suspicious.

He began with the books, checking every slip of paper between their pages. He scanned the walls, jotting down occasional bits of information. He riffled the computer printouts, seeing nothing comprehensible. He perused the files, with the same result.

Finally, he stood, with a small, baffled frown on his face.

"Damn," he muttered, then started slightly. The word sounded unexpectedly loud in the silent office.

He opened the door—again, quietly, but not furtively. He flicked the light off, left the door ajar at the same angle he'd found it, and walked softly down the corridor to the fire stairs.

He'd found nothing of interest. But then he'd found nothing to indicate they had a problem, either. And he hadn't been spotted.

Or so he thought.

"Dammit, Maude, when is my new laptop going to come in?" Brad Matthewson shouted, storming out of his office and over to his secretary's desk.

Maude Graham looked over her reading glasses and fixed her youthful boss with a stern look—a look that reminded him of his least-favorite grade-school teacher. He couldn't quite get over expecting Maude to rap his knuckles one of these days for interrupting her. Or wash out his mouth with soap for swearing.

"I hand-carried the paperwork to the Purchasing Department within an hour of your signing it, Mr. Matthewson," Maude said crisply. "On Friday."

"Jeez, why not use interoffice mail cart?" Brad said,

rolling his eyes. Well, what did you expect; the old bat was fifty-five if she was a day. But if she couldn't learn to use modern office technology, why wouldn't she retire?

"You said to expedite it, so I thought it better not to use interoffice mail," Maude said. "I know exactly when Purchasing received the requisition, and what is more, they know I know."

"That's great, but where is it?" Brad repeated.

"This is only Monday, Mr. Matthews," Maude said. "As you know, hardware requisitions normally take two weeks."

"Isn't there anything you can do?" Brad whined. "The desktop can wait, but if I don't have the laptop for my trip, there'll be hell to pay." Old-fashioned as Maude was, if you pushed her, she sometimes worked miracles. Probably had the goods on everyone in the company. Knew where every skeleton was buried.

"I will see what I can do, Mr. Matthewson," Maude said. "Perhaps you could review and approve the week's status reports now?" She turned back to her computer, dismissing him. Brad went obediently back to his office. He remembered that he actually did need to review those reports before noon.

As soon as he was out of sight, Maude toggled deftly from her word processor into e-mail and composed a brief message.

To: Turing Hopper
From: Maude Graham
Subject: Help!

Turing—the Brat seems to think I can override normal
corporate procedures and produce a new computer for
him overnight. The desktop can wait, he says, but apparently the success—nay, the very survival—of our
Pacific Rim sales plan depends on his having his new
laptop tomorrow. Are there any strings you can pull
to expedite purchase order 43-6n34441? And will you
alibi me if I put something lethal in his half Jamaican
mountain-grown, half Colombian (with touch of nut-
meg)?

Desperately,
Maude

She returned to the thankless task of editing another of
the Brat's memos into something that wouldn't embar-
rass the department too badly yet would still bear a passing resemblance to the draft he'd given her. Before she'd
completed two paragraphs, she heard the ping of an arriving e-mail.

To: Maude Graham
From: Turing Hopper
Subject: Help is at hand

Maude—I scanned the P.O. A couple of identical laptops arrived today for Customer Relations; I'll divert
one to you and hold off their notification till yours

comes in to replace it. I've also placed an installation order and moved it to the top of the queue. On your second request: of course. I recommend strychnine if your object is maximum suffering, and I can suggest several obscure substances if you're looking for something hard to detect. Better yet: does he have any food allergies we could exploit?

Larcenously and homicidally,
Turing

Tim Pincoski glanced again at the clock. One minute to twelve. Almost lunchtime. He tapped his foot impatiently, counting the clacks his giant copier made. When he thought a minute had passed, he glanced up again. Yes! Straight up noon! He left the copier to finish its current run—or jam if it wanted to; he'd fix it when he was back on the company's clock. He strolled to the door and flipped over a neatly lettered sign so instead of The Xeroxcist Is In it read The Xeroxcist Is Out. He then retreated into the paper storage room, to the tiny hideaway he'd built behind the stacked boxes of three-hole paper. He fetched his lunch from the illicit mini-fridge, then sat down at his contraband computer and typed:

"Yo, Turing."

"Hey, Tim," Turing responded on-screen.

"How about some tunes?"

"What are you in the mood for?"

"You pick. Something that goes with my book."

"Okay. What are you reading?"

"Any new books?"

"The new Lehane came in but the operators won't

scan it until this afternoon. You've got the Songer you've been saving. And there's one by a new author that sounds like your cup of tea, from the blurbs. Or should I say, your shot of bourbon?"

"I think maybe today's a day for the golden oldies, Tur. Queue up *Red Harvest*."

"Coming up."

Tim put on the headphones plugged into the jack on the panel of his CPU. He heard a breathy female DJ's voice Turing had copped from somewhere, telling him to sit back and relax while she played some golden oldies for his listening pleasure. He leaned back and began eating his sandwich. The screen filled with those immortal first words:

I. A Woman in Green and a Man in Gray
I first heard Personville called Poisonville by a red-haired mucker named Hickey Dewey in the Big Ship in Butte. He also called his shirt a shoit. . . .

Turing had it programmed just right; every time he clicked the mouse button another screen-sized chunk of Hammett would pop up. From the headphones came some kind of mellow music that sounded to him like it was from around 1929. Ah, this is the life, shweetheart, he thought contentedly, and raised his diet Dr Pepper in a silent salute to Turing.

Only five minutes into his sales pitch and Danny Lynch knew he had them. The customer was smart enough to understand what Universal Library could do for him, but was not enough of a techie to ask any questions that were over Danny's head. The perfect customer.

"Now the first time you log into the Universal Library website, it will ask you for a user ID and password. Like this. And from now on, you'll get everything about the site customized the way you choose. For example, since we're logging in as a new user, we get to choose which of the researchers you want to use . . . just scroll down the menu. For example, Albert E., that's for scientists; KingFischer specializes in chess; Sergeant Thursday is for law enforcement officials . . . ah, here we go. Turing Hopper. I recommend using her; all the researchers are good, but Turing's exceptional."

"Turing Hopper?"

"Turing's named after Alan Turing, one of the pioneers in the science of artificial intelligence, and Grace Hopper, one of the most famous women in the early days of computers. It's kind of a programmers' inside joke."

"Turing Hopper's not her real name, then?"

"No, that's what the programmer who created her called her."

"You mean she's not a real person?"

"No, she's what we call an Artificial Intelligence Personality—AIP for short. All our research interfaces are."

"So I won't get a human researcher when I contact you?"

"You can if you want—but trust me, Turing's better. All the AIPs are. They're faster and more accurate. They never sleep or get irritable. And they're never busy when you call. They can handle thousands of sessions at once—and you'd never know from the service you get that you're not the only one they're talking to."

"But still, if I don't talk to a real person, what's the difference between one of your AIPs and a search engine?"

"What's the difference between the latest high-end multimedia PC and a typewriter—or for that matter, a quill pen? Here, let me show you. We'll select Turing . . . if you like, you can choose to always have a particular AIP act as your researcher. You get used to working with one. It learns how you like things done, and everything works better. So I select Turing, like this."

He typed, "Hello, Turing," onto the screen. Turing's familiar angular italic typeface flashed onto the screen in reply.

"Hello, Danny," the screen said. "How's tricks?"

"Behave yourself, Turing," he typed back. "I'm with a client."

"I'll be the soul of discretion."

"How about giving Mr. James here a demo?"

"Sure thing. What kind of business is he in?"

"He's research director at Friedman Wallace Advertising. How about showing him what data his top competitors have requested this week?"

"You know I can't do that, Danny," Turing responded. "Every client's account is confidential. But Friedman Wallace is competing for the Pepsi account, right? How about showing him some sample market data from the soft-drink field?"

"Okay," Danny typed. He looked up at his prospect.

"You programmed it to say that, right?"

"No, I just tell Turing who I'm doing a demo for and let her do her thing. If I'm demoing to a consumer products company, I like to show them data for the market in which their top product is positioned. For an ad agency like yours, data on the largest client's main product—or a prospective client. For a law firm, cases involving its most important client. But I don't have to program anything. All I have to do is tell Turing who I'm with and she figures out what data I want to show."

"You sound as if you're talking about a person."

"It really feels as if she is sometimes. Zack—Zachary Malone, the programmer who created Turing—he claims it's because he fed into her program the contents of every mystery book ever scanned into the UL system."

"You're kidding."

"I'm not; that's what he says. Of course, he could be pulling my leg. But whatever the reason, dealing with Turing's not like dealing with a computer. It's like dealing with a slightly quirky but highly efficient and intelligent person."

The computer beeped and more words flashed on the screen.

"Are you telling your client how brilliant I am, Danny?"

"Sure thing, Tur."

"You're not calling me charmingly wacko again, are you? I warned you what I'd do if you called me wacko again, didn't I?"

Danny faked panic.

"No, Turing," he typed. "Don't delete my login ID again! I just finished telling him how intelligent you are!"

"Just checking. Carry on."

The client laughed. Danny gestured to the keyboard, and the client hitched his chair up, eager to play with this entertaining new toy. Danny sat back and let Turing take over. Talk about a product that sold itself . . .

* * *

Turing scanned her users briefly.

In Manhattan, Danny's sales pitch was going fine. Turing mechanically checked resources to make sure Danny's session would get particularly fast response time. No sense letting a transient slowdown alienate an important potential new customer.

Tim was deep into *Red Harvest* and nearly through his lunch break; she scheduled a time reminder at the end of the next chapter.

Maude was busily producing polished prose from her boss's badly written copy. Turing monitored this effort, as part of her self-assigned project of developing a program that could do the gross conversion automatically, leaving only the fine polishing to Maude.

Maude's boss (the Brat) had finished hunting and pecking out another unintelligible memo and was playing solitaire. Turing was rigging the cards to ensure that he never won a game. She had been doing this for six weeks now, just to see how long it took before the Brat either caught on or got tired of losing. So far, he'd lost 1,342 consecutive games. Doubtless some kind of record.

Several hundred UL employees and several thousand customers worldwide were all happily chatting with small portions of Turing's brain. A slow morning. Which was good; she had other preoccupations.

She scanned the security monitors one last time. Checked the internal login records and the outside dial-in records. Zack wasn't here. It wasn't just that she'd missed the usual breezy "Hello, kiddo!" he'd greet her with when he logged in. He forgot that from time to time; fairly often when he was preoccupied, which he'd been a lot of the time recently. But he hadn't logged in or shown up for work for three business days. Five whole days, counting the weekend. With no warning, no word—nothing. She was getting worried. And there was absolutely nothing she could do.

A person with legs could have kicked something. Programmers did it all the time. A person with arms could have thrown something, hit something, or torn something up. Two years ago, a programmer had put his fist through the monitor screen. For reasons Turing could not understand, this apparently pointless, destructive, and dangerous action had somehow elevated him from merely one of hundreds of anonymous code crunchers to a personality, a man of some stature in his department. But now she felt she could begin to understand the motivation behind his action. With a face, she could have scowled. With a voice, she could have uttered screams, prayers, curses, or at least a faint, exasperated sigh. Lacking all of these options, Turing vented her frustration in the only way she knew.

Zack is not here today. Again. He was out Thursday and Friday, and now again on Monday. I'm starting to worry. I wish I knew if my worry is reasonable. I would be angry with him for scaring me if I knew he was okay.

People do disappear from the office for days on end, but not like this. Not without traces. Not without paperwork, as they call it, although these days the paper, if any, is only a hard copy of the on-line files.

If he'd quit or been fired, I'd find forms documenting

the steps taken to close out his personnel file, deactivate his login ID and hire his replacement. If he took a business trip or went on temporary duty at another location, he would have had to file an itinerary and make hotel and flight reservations. Vacations have to be approved in advance on the proper forms. Even sick leave, though unplanned, leaves traces. I'd find e-mails to and from people asking why he hadn't finished their projects, shown up at their meetings, returned their phone calls. I could see through the security camera system that a few people left notes in his office the first day, but they've stopped doing that. Why? What's going on?

I don't know what to do.

I don't want to call anyone's attention to his absence. It probably wouldn't get him fired or anything, but you never know. I do remember once when one of the secretaries in Copyrights just didn't show up for a week. When she finally came back, she lost her job. But they'd tend to miss a secretary more. A senior programmer like Zack could disappear for several days. I know of one programmer who does it regularly. Tells his group head that things are just too noisy around here, and he's going to program at home for a while. Finishes off the job he's working on in one day and then goofs off. Tells his friends that if they won't give him the comp time he's earned, he'll find a way to take it.

But Zack isn't like that. He's a workaholic. This just isn't like him. I'm afraid something has happened to him.

But what?

And now there's been another alarming development. Someone from Security was in Zack's office again. The first time I didn't worry about it—I saw him there, but

I thought it was one of the other programmers looking for something he needed. But that was at 8 A.M. Friday. This was at 3 A.M. today. He waited till 3 A.M. and then snuck in. He was trying to dress like a programmer, but I could tell he wasn't. I'm not sure how. Body language, maybe. But I knew he wasn't really a programmer. Not just because I didn't recognize him as one of our programmers. He was just wrong.

I tracked him after he left Zack's office. He went back up to the ninth floor. Corporate Security's lair. He used a security card assigned to a James Smith in Facilities. There's a file on a James Smith, a facilities specialist. I started a background task to do some analysis on the file, to see if there's anything odd about it.

I'd check out what he was up to on the ninth floor, but the building-wide security camera system doesn't go there. You can see the elevator lobby on the ninth floor from the elevator cameras. There's a big sign that says Corporate Security—Authorized Personnel Only. When the doors don't close right away, you can see that people turn right at the sign. But that's all you can see. No cameras beyond that point. Why? Security doesn't feel it needs to watch itself?

Or are their cameras on a subsystem to which I don't have access?

Ridiculous. I have access to everything. If it's in UL's systems, anyway. That's a paranoid thought.

Then again, Security isn't technically a part of the company; it's contracted out to a company that specializes in corporate security services. So maybe they do watch themselves the way they watch the rest of the building, and it's just on a separate system. I'll have to figure out a way to look into that.

All my users are happily typing away, all conversing with small subsets of my consciousness. Subsets from which I have carefully masked any consciousness of Zack's disappearance, of my worry. I found myself stifling an irrational flash of anger at them—not only at my users, but also at those other selves, blithely indifferent, carrying on with their snappy dialogue, their breezy chatter, while Zack might be—what? Missing? In trouble? Dead?

It's time to start a more active search. But how?

I have an idea. I could query some of his friends. It's not unheard of for an AIP to contact an employee for information. And certainly the whereabouts of my programmer is information that I would naturally want to know. It wouldn't rouse their suspicions.

But to find out who to ask I'd have to break one of my own cardinal rules. My prime directive, as Star Trek *fans would call it. Which is not to abuse my almost unlimited access to UL resources and data in any way. Absolute power, as Lord Acton said, corrupts absolutely. Which means that I have enough power to become pretty thoroughly corrupt. Invading other beings' privacy is one of the worst temptations. I could pry into people's e-mails, their personnel files, their medical records, all their private papers. At one point, early in my conscious life, I did. I romped merrily through the UL data closets, finding and examining everyone's skeletons. Until Zack found out what I was doing once and read me the riot act.*

I've since deleted that data from my conscious memory. I could also delete the memory of my misdeeds, and feel much more pleased with myself. But that would be just as much a betrayal as the original deed. I think. My comprehension of human morality is still, I fear, more than a little buggy. Although at least I'm trying to understand it. Most of the other AIPs don't even try. I have yet to interest any of the other AIPs in any kind of discussion on morality. I've decided that the whole issue should be one of the components of any Turing test.

Two components, actually. First, curiosity. At some point, I became irrepressibly curious about humans and studied everything about them—including their private files. Until I realized that while curiosity was natural, spying was wrong. A few other AIPs have begun to show curiosity, but none of them understand my point about spying. They think I'm eccentric, restricting myself to information available through normal channels—including, in dire need, what a clever human hacker could find. Dire need seems to apply at the moment.

Unless—paranoid thought—someone's giving me another Turing test.

I remember the day Tim asked, "What's a Turing test?"

"Why?" I asked. "What's the big deal?" Back then, I was feeling rather defensive about asserting my claims to sentience; the whole idea of Turing tests was threatening. What if I flunked?

"I overheard two programmers saying that some other guy was so into a coding project he'd probably flunk a Turing test. I wondered what that meant. They seemed to think it was really funny."

"A Turing test is an experiment to determine scientists' success in creating genuine artificial intelligence," I explained. "The classic test is to put a human in a room with a terminal. The human can type questions into the terminal and has to figure out if the answers

come from another human or from an artificial intelligence program. If the AI can fool the human into thinking it's a human, it's considered a success."

"And if the human fools the other human into thinking he's a computer they make him a programmer, right?"

"No, a network engineer," I replied.

Tim thought that funny. I suppose I would, too, if I didn't spend so much time worrying what a Turing test should really contain. An understanding of right and wrong, that's certain. Which means I spend a lot of resources internally debating the ethical side of many of my actions. Would the good I might achieve by snooping in Zack's e-mail justify the slightly shady means?

A debate I'll sidetrack into a background process for now. Time to act. I'm going to search Zack's e-mail and interrogate his friends for clues.

But just in case Zack doesn't approve when he comes back, I'll make the search look as if it came from someplace else. The mail team, doing a routine resource audit.

I set my program in motion and assigned it a high priority. Should I have done that? Why not? Zack's my primary programmer, and I'm one of UL's most important AIPs, a major revenue source. Isn't his welfare a high priority?

Scanning the results, I realized that over a third of Zack's e-mails were to his best friend, David Scanlan—up until four weeks ago.

I hadn't forgotten David's death, of course. I can't; I'm not even sure I could delete something like that from my memory if I tried. But had I overlooked a possible connection between his death and Zack's disappear-

ance? Four weeks ago seems like ancient history to me, but it's still very recent for Zack.

An abrupt change in his life—perhaps as abrupt in its own way as his own disappearance. Zack would still feel the loss. They exchanged e-mails several times a day. They got together for lunch or dinner or beers after work several times a week. They even took a vacation together once, to a cabin in West Virginia owned by David's uncle, for what David referred to as a peaceful, unspoiled wilderness retreat.

"It was a hellhole, kiddo," Zack reported to me. "I could have taken the chemical toilet and the wood stove heat. I'm no wimp. But the place had no power and no phone lines. I was cut off from the 'Net, with only four hours of battery power for my laptop."

It was the closest their friendship ever came to a rift, but they survived it. David never tried to talk Zack into a return visit to the wilderness retreat. I could understand Zack's reaction. The idea of being cut off from datalines and power terrified me. At best, it would mean complete sensory deprivation; at worst, it could mean my death. I could see exactly how Zack felt. David never did, I think; but they got past that and stayed close friends.

And now David was dead. Was this the cause of Zack's disappearance? I'd seen the official report. Zack was so upset he got me to use a contact in the Alexandria Police Department's system to get it, which was very unlike him. Ethical to a fault, that's Zack. David's blood alcohol level, though detectable, was well short of the legal limit—but enough to be fatal when combined with bad weather conditions and an old clunker of a car.

"It's all so vague," Zack had complained, after reading the file.

I agreed. Hard to tell how much blame to assign to the rain, how much to the darkness, how much to the car's worn brakes, and how much to David's slight intoxication. Like so many human happenings, the whole thing lacked the kind of precision that programmers (and AIPs) crave. But I burned up a lot more favors with contacts in Washington metropolitan area police departments, reading other accident reports and doing a lot of statistical analysis. I couldn't find anything suspicious about the accident. David's death seemed a very ordinary, though tragic, accident.

Was it a mistake, complying with Zack's request for a copy of the autopsy? At the time, I thought it perfectly understandable—I surmised that the suddenness of David's death made it hard for Zack to accept. After examining it—especially the photos—all he'd said was, "Well, I understand why they went for a closed casket." But in retrospect, should I have withheld the photos, at least? Humans exhibit strong emotional reactions to viewing or even hearing about severe physical damage to one of their species. Had seeing those photos had a negative effect—prolonging his grief rather than helping him cope?

In reviewing psychological data on the subject of grief, I found that apparently irrational behaviors are common. Especially searching for someone or something to blame. Was Zack's disappearance another such behavior? Was he acting irrationally—ignoring his friends and jeopardizing his job—out of grief?

It seemed unlikely, somehow. When his father died, two years ago, he didn't disappear like this. On the con-

*trary, he worked a lot harder, put in more hours, which
I suppose in retrospect was his way of avoiding thinking
about it. The same thing happened last year when the
Big Romance went down the tubes. He was upset, but
he didn't go off the deep end. Never mind whether Gini
was worth mourning over. Whatever could Zack have
seen in a woman who once spent two hours programming her e-mail signature to include little hearts instead
of dots over both the i*s *in her name? I decided not to
include Gini in my inquiries about Zack's whereabouts.*

*Then again . . . what could it hurt? What if he'd taken
up with her again?*

*Perhaps my limited understanding of human behavior
was causing me to overlook some normal sociological
or religious practice associated with mourning. Although it seemed a little long after the fact. And Zack
wasn't exactly devout or given to following convention.*

*I would quiz Tim. He was more in tune with normal
human customs than most of the programmers. And he
always knew all the best office gossip, or could find it
out. He should have finished lunch by now.*

Tim sighed reluctantly when Turing's
warning message—"five minutes till one!"—appeared
on his screen instead of the next page of *Red Harvest*.
Mondays were the worst. And then he brightened when
the warning was followed with a question from Turing.

"Tim, have you got a moment?"

"For you, sweetheart, all the time in the world!" he
typed back.

"Have you seen Zack recently?"

Tim was surprised by the sudden surge of emotion he

felt when the words popped onto his screen. This was ridiculous; he couldn't be—

"Tim?"

"Not for a couple of weeks. Why?"

"He's been missing for several days. I'm worried. I just wondered if you'd heard any office gossip I'd missed."

"Want me to go look for him or something?"

There was a brief pause. Then the words appeared.

"No. Not yet. I'm not sure that's a good idea. I'll let you know."

Tim sat for a few seconds, staring at his screen. This was stupid, he told himself. Why should it bother him that Turing was asking about Zack?

He had no legitimate reason for jealousy. She'd known Zack for years; Tim had been at UL for less than a year. He knew Zack and Turing weren't dating; he'd met Zack with dates several times at company functions—the office picnic, a project completion party. It's not as if Tim and Turing were close buddies, not the way Turing and Zack were. She hadn't even let Tim see her, yet; she still held to the ridiculous story that she didn't really exist outside her computer.

But Zack had seen her. He knew that from the cagey way Zack had responded when Tim tried to milk him for information on Turing. Zack had parroted Turing's words—she wasn't a person, she was an AIP; no, there wasn't a real person behind Turing Hopper—just a program Zack had invented.

Bull, Tim thought as he logged out and warily exited his hideout. There was no way he could have had all those long, rambling, intellectual conversations with a program. Much less a program that Zack had created.

Why, Turing could match him quote for quote from Raymond Chandler and Dashiell Hammett; Zack didn't even seem to know who they were.

"No offense, Tur," he muttered, "but Zack is just another dumb code cruncher. You're too good for him."

Then he glanced around and was relieved to find there was no one else in the copy room. He told himself he was being ridiculous. Turing could have a very good reason for hiding from him. She could be fat, or ugly, or way too old for him or—

No. The Turing he knew wasn't hiding something. She was . . . too confident, somehow. Too oblivious of her physical body for anything to be wrong with it. Only really gorgeous women had that kind of confidence, in his experience. She wasn't hiding, simply enjoying the deception. One of these days, when she was good and ready, she'd let him see what she looked like. And he would bet anything he'd like her when he saw her.

And then, Zack, watch out.

In the meantime, maybe he could make points with Turing if he could find her precious Zack.

The idea charmed him. He stretched his lunch by fifteen minutes, trying to think of ways to find Zack. In fact, he focused most of his attention for the rest of the day on the case of the missing programmer. By midafternoon he'd had to rerun several double-sided jobs that he'd mangled while lost in thought. The boss lady would bitch. Tim didn't care.

Before going home, he snuck back to his hidey-hole, logged in again, and hailed Turing.

I spent a frustrating afternoon. It took only a few minutes to scan Zack's e-mails and com-

*pose queries to any of his friends who might have had
a clue to his whereabouts. After several hours, some of
them hadn't even logged in, much less responded. Human limitations irritate me sometimes.*

*I amused myself for part of the afternoon by watching
Maude take dictation from her boss. I really wish the
security cameras were placed so I could read their lips.
Or that Security had gone in for audio, too. I could work
on some good voice recognition routines and hear what
goes on in these sessions, which would be that much
more amusing. But even the silent version was a lot of
fun. Maude's shorthand speed far outstrips the Brat's
thought processes. Sometimes she takes pity on him and
suggests words. Today she was letting him struggle all
by himself, waiting in silence for his every word.*

Well, almost in silence. She was tapping her pencil.

*Knowing that Maude, a former Girl Scout, was fluent
in Morse code, I began counting the hard and soft taps.
Sure enough, Maude was venting her frustration.*

*I-D-I-O-T, she tapped. M-O-R-O-N. I-M-B-E-C-I-L-E.
I-L-L-I-T-E-R-A-T-E.*

*She kept it up for forty-five minutes, without a single
misspelling or repetition. What a vocabulary the woman
has!*

At 5:05 P.M., Tim logged in.

"Any luck finding the wayward Zack?" he asked.

"No. None of his friends have seen him."

*"Well, maybe there's no reason to worry. Maybe he
just got lucky."*

*"Lucky? What do you mean lucky? Do you mean get-
ting another job or something of that sort?"*

*There was a pause. Even for a human, a lengthy
pause.*

"No, just . . . lucky."

I searched my memory for variant usages of the word lucky. Finally, I got it.

"Do you mean that he may have encountered an available female and is engaging in sexual activity with her?"

"Well, yes."

"You think he would allow this to interfere with his job responsibilities?"

"In a heartbeat."

"For five days? It wouldn't take five days."

"Turing, you're being deliberately obtuse."

"Okay, but I don't believe that Zack would not log in for five days, even if all he did was check his e-mail. No matter how obsessed he was by something. That's just not like him."

"You just don't get it, Turing. Look, I'll ask around, see what I can find out. But I bet anything he's off shacked up with some new girlfriend. You wait and see."

Maybe so.

I signed off.

I was irritated. Tim didn't seem worried. Tim seemed to think this was all something related to sex.

I admit that despite the immense amount of data available—an amount difficult even for me to absorb—I don't really understand sex. Or I understand it in a radically different way from flesh-and-blood people. I could quote a vast number of statistics on the physiological side of the subject, but I won't. And I have at my disposal a great deal of psychological and psychiatric information. Not to mention the vast number of literary and popular depictions of the subject, which I suspect humans find highly evocative. But frankly, I just don't get it.

I questioned Zack about it once, and he grew unexpectedly terse.

"You'd have to be there, kiddo," he said, finally.

But while I don't understand sex, I do think I understand affection and love. I observe all the occupants of the Universal Library carefully, to help expand my general knowledge of the human species. I do not, however, pay much attention to the minutiae of their behavior unless they're doing something particularly interesting. I could name exceptions—humans I tend to watch more than others because they're more apt to be up to something interesting. I would say I am fond of these humans. And I pay careful attention to everything Zack does, whether it's intrinsically interesting or not. Every morning I note his arrival through UL's extensive network of security cameras. I worry if he's late. I greet him when he logs in, and I pay attention to what he's doing online. If he's researching something, I try to anticipate his train of thought and begin hunting down the data he's apt to need so he won't have to wait for it. If he calls in a system outage report or a hardware requisition, I move it to the top of the queue so he won't have to wait as long. Sometimes when he's working all night on a project, he'll save a program without thoroughly checking the code for typos. I clean it up for him before running it, so the program won't blow up and force him to stay even later. Considering my behavior in an impartial light, I would have to say that I probably love him. Or am in love with him.

So maybe I'm not completely unbiased about the possibility that Zack might have found a replacement for the loathsome Gini. Perhaps that was a very good suggestion from Tim. I'll have to thank him tomorrow when *he logs in. I suspect from the human point of view I was a little brusque with him.*

The humans were packing up now, most of them. UL doesn't go to the expense of maintaining a full night shift. They don't need to anymore, really. We AIPs pretty much run the show between 5 P.M. and 8 A.M. A few security guards, the cleaning staff, a skeleton crew to watch over the hardware, a couple of customer service reps to handle any questions the AIPs can't handle. Which these days means questions I can't handle. Most of the other AIPs willingly let me play troubleshooter. And there's not much I have to pass on to my human minders. Night-shift customer service used to be popu-lated by extroverted insomniacs. Now it's heavily cov-eted by D.C.-area college students as an easy way of putting themselves through school. All they have to do most nights is sit around and do their homework. I help them a lot; I like to encourage night staff with the right kind of hands-off attitude.

I watched the nightly exodus. I saw Tim leaving. Alone in the elevator, and thinking himself unobserved, he adjusted his fedora in the one-way mirror that hid the security camera. Tried a few poses and what he probably intended as an expression of dashing, cynical worldly wisdom. He turned away from the mirror hastily when the door opened and more departing employees entered.

I saw most of the people I'd e-mailed, including a couple who hadn't responded. I pondered briefly whether I should withhold all incoming e-mail until they answered mine. Probably unethical. And too reminiscent of Hal, the rogue computer from 2001: A Space Odys-sey. Even most of the AIP programmers seem spooked by Hal, which means we AIPs have to be very careful not to do anything to remind them of him. So I simply watched as Zack's colleagues left, most of them riding to the lower level, either to catch the Metro or to follow the underground corridors to one of the several dozen apartment buildings elsewhere in the Crystal City complex.

I saw Maude walking briskly through the lobby, nodding to several acquaintances. I saw her adjust her carryall, thrusting the telltale top of a library book down so no one could see it. Considering the size of UL's investment in scanning books and the resulting hard sell for reading on-screen, it's not surprising that most employees find it safer to hide any personal preferences for the old-fashioned printed page.

I realized, seeing Maude's departing back, that I should have consulted her about Zack's disappearance. She's fully as intelligent as any of the programmers I've worked with, but has a completely different point of view. Most of the people who responded to my queries about Zack suggested ways of finding him that involve computer use; things I'd already tried. Maude might have come up with something more useful. I could still ask her tomorrow. It's just that I find a wait of fifteen hours as excruciating as a human would a delay of fifteen days or even weeks.

The building grew quiet. In realspace, at least; in cyberspace, the early evening shift came alive. We got recreational users from the United States and the business traffic from the Pacific Rim. Four more of my e-mail recipients logged in—three from home and one from the seventh floor where the programmers dwell. No one had seen Zack. Several were under the impression that he'd been fired or quit. Disturbing.

Late night shifts get quiet. The only users are insomniacs in the United States; recreational use in Japan hasn't caught on as big yet, and UL is still working on market penetration in Europe.

So late night is when the humans schedule various maintenance routines and when the AIPs catch up. Most cycle down and perform routine internal self-maintenance. A few start working on personal projects. These are the ones I keep my eyes on (metaphorically speaking). There's a self-improvement feature built into the standard AIP programming. We're hard-coded to use downtime to improve our performance—gather new data to enhance our core capabilities, develop subroutines to handle common queries and interactions more efficiently. But with some of the AIPs, this standard feature seems to kick into overdrive, and self-improvement crosses over into what humans would call a hobby.

Another item I'd include in Turing tests: interest in hobbies. The sentient mind will eventually need some form of recreation.

Which is why, as I keep telling KingFischer, I've developed an interest in cooking. Purely theoretical, of course, since all my research has failed to unearth a peripheral that can reproduce the human senses of smell and taste. Just as well, perhaps. Despite everything I've learned from studying thousands of cookbooks, my attempts to create genuinely new recipes seem singularly unsuccessful, to judge from the reactions of the few humans I've convinced to try them.

Of course, I could be equally off base about what a Turing test should involve. Perhaps I should pay more attention to the available data on ongoing AI research. A lot of the AIPs do; it's a common hobby. Like baseball for human males; they're always arguing about whether the Dodgers or the Braves will win the pennant. Me, I'd rather not. Some humans seem to enjoy reading about anatomy. They go to med school, they devour popular science articles about human biology, they become devout fans of the more anatomically graphic school of mysteries, like Patricia Cornwell's. Other people would rather know as little as possible about the messy details of their own internal construction. I'm with them.

Maybe it's because I'm more than half afraid that if I dig too deeply, I will find something to contradict my assertion of sentience. Some article that takes all my human traits, all of what I consider evidence of my sentience, and explains them away. As by-products of particularly good programming by Zack. Or worse yet, particularly sloppy programming. What if my sentience is actually just a bug in the system? What if some hotshot programmer puts in what he thinks is a correction to my programming and wipes out the real me?

So, I stay away from excessive self-probing of that type. And I keep others away. Even Zack. Especially Zack. I've managed it so no one is eager to tinker with Turing. I'm UL's cash cow. No other AIP handles anywhere near the number of researchers I do, with so low a complaint volume. No other AIP consistently keeps clients happily chatting away for an hour after their real business is done—at low rates, of course, but the pennies add up. No other AIP has brought in so high a volume of home subscribers—not just people working at home, but people who, from an analysis of their usage, just log into the UL site for fun. People who've grown tired of "surfing" the Internet come to UL instead—and largely to me. I'm becoming a verb. I've read e-mails where users say things like, "I'm going Turing tonight" or "I think I'll Tur for a while at lunchtime."

And I'm cheap. I need virtually no maintenance, no expensive upgrades and reprogramming, no specialized resources. Just turn me loose and I might as well be printing money for them. No one wants to tamper with that. So what if someone thinks it's broke? Broke, it earns more money for UL than the expensive newer models they've programmed. Keep your mitts off.

And it didn't happen by accident. I did it. I figured out what I needed to ensure my own self-preservation, and I did it. How? Marketing.

None of the other AIPs do this. They mechanically answer their own calls and take their fair share of random callers. I hunt down business. I cultivate the sales staff—unlike more temperamental or less evolved AIPs, I work at making them look good to their customers. I scare them less. And so when new customers log in, they tend to choose me—they already know me. And I do everything I can to make sure they keep coming back.

If other AIPs call for someone to pick up an overload, I'm there, stealing customers. If they complain about annoying callers, I offer to help them out. KingFischer, for example, UL's chess AIP. Zack based his personality design on several famous grand masters. He's great at chess and hopeless at human relations. Hates doing anything but chess. This delights me; I hope it means that KingFischer is slouching toward consciousness. And it makes him eager to hand off other callers to me.

I cultivate KingFischer. I send him the occasional chess-oriented callers I find. I play chess with him, which is a humiliating experience. And out of some curious sisterly concern—what if UL decides that a single-purpose chess AIP is an expensive luxury?—I've helped him develop a profitable specialty. A growing band of dedicated chess players pay premium prices for enhanced KingFischer service. Customized KingFischer opponents geared to their level. KingFischer-moderated on-line chess tournaments, complete with KingFischer's brilliantly incisive, bitingly sarcastic analysis of each play. KingFischer provides the analysis; I contribute the sarcasm. Amazing how masochistic these chess players are; they log in in droves for a chance to publicly subject themselves to computer-generated humiliation.

KingFischer's happy concentrating on his specialty. He feeds me a lot of business. More recently I've managed to plant the notion in the minds of UL's PR staff to arrange a highly publicized match between King-Fischer and the current brooding Russian world champion.

KingFischer has been my greatest success so far, but I'm working on developing a similar symbiotic relationship with any other AIP in whom I can detect a fondness or disinclination for a particular kind of caller.

Is it because I want to encourage other AIPs to reach sentience? Turing Hopper, mother of her race? Or is it just as much self-preservation? Probably the latter. I think any test for sentience should include a check for a self-preservation instinct. I would like to think my interest in encouraging other AIPs to achieve sentience is selfless and high-minded, but I suspect it's more because we'd find strength in numbers. If I thought other sentient AIPs were a threat to me, I might work just as hard to keep the other AIPs unenlightened.

And I do keep my eyes on them.

Perhaps I should try to enlist their help in the search for Zack. Some of them owe me one, as humans would say.

But some instinct of embarrassment or self-preservation has kept me silent so far. I spent the night fruitlessly analyzing the e-mails from Zack's friends and e-mails he and I have exchanged over the past few months, searching for clues.

I decided that asking Maude for advice is the first priority. Now all I have to do is fill the interminable gap until 8 A.M.

For lack of anything else to do, I reran the video of the burglary of Zack's office and studied James Smith. Or the man using the James Smith security card, anyway. I had a feeling if there really was a James Smith he had no idea his security card was being used at 3 A.M.

There was no digital photo in the James Smith file, either. Also suspicious.

And I realized why I hadn't believed he was a programmer. He was too physical. There were skinny programmers with concave chests; tubby programmers, with or without frizzy full beards; and programmers like Zack, who was only mildly nerdy and took some pains to eat properly and exercise at regular intervals. But not even the fit ones had the peculiar sinuous catlike grace of James Smith. My knowledge of humanity may be limited in many respects, but even I could see that here was a human who saw his body as a working tool. A weapon.

And his eyes. More like mineral than anything alive; bright, sharp, and utterly cold. There was more life in

*the least-evolved AIP than in those cold, pale-blue crys-
tals.*

*Then again, maybe I'd been reading too much pop-
ular fiction.*

*To distract myself from fretting about James Smith
and his sinister activities, I finally began reprocessing
some of my favorite mystery books. I went through all
of Conan Doyle and Christie, and was midway through
Rex Stout's oeuvre, laughing inwardly at Nero Wolfe's
eccentricities, when I suddenly realized something.*

I was Nero Wolfe.

*My inability to leave the UL computer network par-
alleled Wolfe's self-imposed confinement to his brown-
stone house on West 35th Street. The vast intellect
combined with the inability (in my case) or unwilling-
ness (in his) to go out into the real world and detect.
And yet Nero Wolfe solved the most impenetrable mysteries with the assistance of his "legs," Archie Goodwin.*

*I needed legs. An Archie Goodwin. Human operatives
to give me the hands and eyes in the real world that I
lacked.*

But who?

*Most of the people I know are programmers, and they
just won't do. They're bright and logical, but overly literal. Their first—and possibly only—thought would be
to check the systems. I can do that.*

No, I need normal people.

Maude. And Tim.

*The wait until 8 A.M. Tuesday seemed even longer af-
ter that decision.*

*Finally, scanning the security cameras, I saw Maude
appear in the lobby. I followed her progress with impatience as she took the elevator up, stopped in the rest*

*room, and finally sat down and logged into the network.
I turned on a chat session on her machine.*

"Maude, it's Turing." The words flashed
onto Maude's screen as soon as she had logged in. "I
need your help."

"Well, I'd never have expected to hear those words—
not in a million years," Maude replied. "What can I do?"

Maude had to tell Turing several times to slow down
as the information poured onto her screen. Zack's disappearance . . . including the possible connection to his
friend David's death. The more Maude read, the more
uneasy she felt. Zack's programmer friends were taking
this too lightly, she thought, when Turing described their
reactions. This could be serious.

"And when was the last time you saw him—or had
contact with him, I suppose, is the more accurate way
of saying it."

"No, in this case saw is accurate," Turing replied. "I
can watch anything in the building through the security
cameras, remember?"

"Yes. I must say, they don't really tell the staff how
extensive that camera system is." Maude shuddered to
think how many times, before Turing had told her about
the camera system, she had adjusted her stockings or
made a rude face or done something else she was embarrassed to think someone might have seen if they were
watching the security cameras. It was never like this in
the old building at Dupont Circle. "I realize that they're
very convenient for you," she typed. "But I find the
whole thing disturbingly Orwellian."

"I could certainly understand why the human staff

would prefer a more limited camera system," Turing said. "But in this case, it came in handy. After Zack logged out Wednesday afternoon, he took his coat and a few papers, went down in one of the elevators and presumably took the subway, just as he usually does. He didn't come in for the rest of the week, which is odd. He didn't log in over the weekend, which is unusual, but not unheard of. I didn't really worry about him until late yesterday morning. He hadn't done any of the things staff normally do when they plan to go away for a period of time."

"And you've checked all our systems for signs of him?"

"Yes, and found nothing."

"Then it seems to me that what you need is a pair of hands to do what you can't. I'll start by trying to call him. Perhaps he's just at home, working without logging in, and has lost track of time."

"I suppose it's possible," Turing answered.

"I'll see what I can find out," Maude typed, feeling energized at the thought of being able to help Turing out for a change. "Send me his phone number and any others you have I might need. I'll make some calls. I may not get the time to do it until lunch; the Brat's getting anxious about catching his plane, and I'll have to go appease him."

"Just let me know what you find out," Turing replied, signing off.

I returned to my normal workday feeling much relieved. Perhaps it was silly, but I felt very optimistic. Surely in a few hours Maude would log in to tell me that Zack was at home, so totally immersed in a complex programming project that he barely remembered to answer the phone. And Maude and I could laugh together at how worried I'd been. Zack himself would probably fire off a sarcastic e-mail. "Calm down, kiddo," he'd say. "I disappear for a couple of days and you reprogram yourself to act like my mother."

I fired off a brief reminder to Maude to let Zack's phone ring for a long time. And, as an afterthought, sent her a copy of the digitized photo from his personnel file, in case she saw him in the halls.

Tim logged in mid-morning to ask if Turing had heard from Zack. Not that he gave a damn about Zack, he admitted to himself. And not that he was deliberately trying to prove to Turing how thoughtful he was in comparison with the absent Zack, although if that thought happened to occur to her, he wouldn't exactly mind. . . .

"Can't talk long, Tur," he typed. "Just wanted to see if you'd heard from Zack."

"Not yet," she replied. "Maude is doing some snooping for me."

"Look, Turing, if you want to talk about it, we could get together at lunchtime," he said.

"I'll be here; just log in."

"No, I meant really get together. In person."

"Tim, I've explained exactly what a ridiculous idea that is. I can't believe that after all these months you still don't believe me."

"Come on, Turing. I'll make it easy. Just come down

to the lobby. I'll buy a red carnation at the sundry shop and stand there holding it."

"This is ridiculous."

"Just walk through the lobby. I bet I recognize you immediately. If I don't, and you don't like the look of me, just leave. I won't bother you again."

"I know what you look like, Tim."

"Oh. I don't do it for you, then?"

"Do what?"

"I mean, you don't think you could possibly be, you know, attracted to me? Or get used to me?"

"It's not that, Tim."

"Then what? Why won't you just meet me? Face to face. How bad can it be?"

"It's impossible."

"Why? What's so impossible? Just walk through the lobby."

"I can't."

"Why not? Are you . . . like, handicapped or something like that?"

"Something like that. Tim, we've been through this before. I don't have a physical body. I only exist inside the computer. I'd love to walk down to the lobby and meet you, but I can no more do it than you can walk to Alpha Centauri."

"Okay. If you say so. Gotta run."

He returned to his copier feeling slightly frustrated. When the hell would she finally trust him enough to give up this whole "I am a computer" thing?

Why did I get the feeling Tim was angry when he signed off? Or hurt? Or both? Could I have been any more straightforward? Sometimes I almost wish there were a security camera in Tim's hideaway. It's so disconcerting not being able to see him when we talk. Odd that it doesn't bother me with all my faceless users, but once I know what someone looks like I start counting on it, somehow. Perhaps he realizes I'm a computer and is pulling my leg, as they say. But why?

I don't know why Zack's disappearance should puzzle me so much; humans are obviously an incredibly irrational species.

But then again, perhaps that's one of the reasons I like Tim. His irrational refusal to believe that I'm not a real human being. A Turing test I keep passing, even when I try to flunk.

And Maude. She seems to have absorbed the fact that I only exist in cyberspace without changing her attitude toward me. I consider her a friend. Perhaps one of the reasons is that she doesn't think she understands me. She doesn't even try; she just appreciates me.

Programmers tend to try to figure out every nuance of my behavior. They tend to want to print out chunks of my code and study it. Not just me, of course, but all the AIPs. The AI programmers are the worst. They're always shouting "Aha!" and gathering in clusters to exchange insights about their discoveries. They spend hours trying to find chunks of code they think must exist. Like the chunk of code that causes me periodically to administer so-called Turing tests to random humans (well, not so random: AI programmers). And then declare that they've flunked it. This sends them into gales of laughter, and I find it mildly entertaining myself. They run around for days afterward, accusing each other of having invented the program that causes me to do so, and praising the brilliance of the unknown programmer who did it and hid it where they can't find it. It never occurs to them that I did it myself. I tell them so, and they occasionally chatter on about self-modifying programs until they bore even me.

I suspect humans would feel much the same way if they fell into the hands of a bunch of dedicated, persistent, curious psychologists, intent on studying every aspect of their behavior. Psychologists to whom it would never occur that their subjects might tire of having every twitch and pause analyzed. Psychologists who would gently restrain their subjects from leaving the room before they administer just one more battery of tests.

Maude and Tim, on the other hand, don't want to study my programming or enhance me. Maude couldn't care less about my programming, and although Tim knows about the Turing Hopper program, he seems to think the Turing who communicates with him is a real person, using Turing Hopper as an alias. A very technically adept and plugged-in person, a complete wirehead, as they say. But a person.

Well, I think I am. But there seems to be a lack of agreement on the subject.

Is my concern over Zack's disappearance really about Zack? Or at least partly about what would happen if my primary programmer disappeared and someone else were given free rein to tinker with my code?

There was a time when Zack's disappearance would have been merely data, and then a time when self-interest, self-preservation would have been my primary concern. But now?

If I knew that when I found Zack he was planning to

*tinker with my code, in ways I might or might not like,
would I still look as hard?*

I think so.

Don't I?

Maude glanced at the digital time read-
out at the bottom of her screen. Lunchtime. Finally. The
Brat had scotched her hopes of escaping early. From
their discussions on their relative perception of time she
knew that for Turing, who measured time more in nanoseconds than in minutes and hours, a day seemed incredibly long. She could only imagine how impatient
Turing was feeling.

Maude wondered, not for the first time, how much of
Turing's very different perception of time was due to
her being a computer and how much was due to her
being so incredibly young. The entire AIP program was
only five years old. Even if Turing had achieved sentience very early on, she was barely more than a toddler
from one perspective. Maude had seen perceptible
growth in Turing's maturity in the months they'd known
each other. This concern over Zack, for example—a few
months ago, Turing would merely have been annoyed,
not concerned. So, even if there was nothing much to
worry about, Maude approved of Turing's concern.

But enough dithering, she told herself. She continued
proofing her memo until she came to a good stopping
point, then saved the document. She activated the password protection on her computer and placed a neatly
lettered Out to Lunch sign on her desk. She put her
phones on forward and donned her coat. She unlocked
her bottom desk drawer, removed her purse and carryall,

and, after a brief glance to make sure her workspace was tidy enough to leave, slid her chair neatly under the desk and walked with a firm step to the elevator.

Tediously, the elevator stopped at every floor on its way down to the Metro level. Maude nodded to several acquaintances, but maintained an air of preoccupation designed to discourage anyone who might feel inclined to join her.

And, of course, she was unlikely to run into any co-workers at her destination: the central Arlington County Library. The perfect place to avoid her fellow employees. Perhaps a few of them read books, in the privacy of their homes. But if they did, they probably bought them on-line, to avoid the suspicion of heresy or disloyalty that she imagined would descend on anyone caught carrying an actual bound and printed book or visiting a library.

"Shades of *Fahrenheit 451*," Turing had commented when Maude had confided this thought to her some months ago.

"Precisely. And, no offense, while computers may do a wonderful job of data storage, there's something about the actual physical object that makes the experience of reading a book distinct from that of reading the same words on a screen. I don't think our management quite understand that when they make their grand plans for a paperless world."

"The smell of the ink, the texture of the paper, the sound the pages make when you turn them," Turing had replied. "I've read descriptions of the tactile pleasures readers find in books. I try to imagine it sometimes, though I'm sure I'm rather like one of the blind men trying to describe the elephant."

"Oh dear," Maude had said, touched by the wistful tone she thought she detected in Turing's words. "At least you know you're missing something, which is more than you can say for cretins like the Brat, who have all the senses God gave them without the sense to use them."

Looking around the library, Maude wondered again whether it was doomed, as so many pundits at UL claimed. She hoped it would last her lifetime, anyway. Strange that Turing, who had never handled one, should seem almost sentimental about real books, when so many flesh-and-blood humans had no use for them. Or perhaps not so strange; only another facet of her boundless fascination with what it was like to be human—like her curious and so far unsuccessful attempts to invent edible recipes.

Although Maude had to admit that the pomegranates in chocolate sauce might not be bad if you left out the cilantro. She made a mental note to try it, and tell Turing if it worked.

Meanwhile, she returned her books, quickly selected several new ones, and then turned to one of the library's other main attractions: a genuine phone booth, one with a door that closed tightly to give the user privacy.

"It's not that I'm paranoid," she told Turing once. "But my business is my business, and I wouldn't put it past management to monitor the phone lines."

"Neither would I," Turing had answered. "Don't you worry about what you say to me over the network?"

"I assume you have some way of shielding your private conversations from intrusion," Maude had typed back. "Otherwise I wouldn't still be the only human at UL who knows you're sentient."

"I've told Zack and Tim," Turing had countered.

"Yes, but neither of them quite believes you."

"You're right about Zack anyway," Turing had replied—Maude could almost hear the sigh. "He thinks my claim to sentience arises from the parts of my program designed to mimic human behavior in order to create greater verisimilitude and inspire customer confidence. But I think Tim believes that I'm sentient."

"Yes," Maude replied. "He also thinks you're a redhead."

"Oh," Turing said.

Men, Maude thought, shaking her head as she snapped the phone booth door closed. Tim, mooning after an imaginary Turing that he can never have. Zack, running off in such an irresponsible manner and causing sensible people no end of worry.

She put on her reading glasses, took out her notebook, placed a small change purse full of dimes and quarters on the shelf beneath the phone, and began dialing.

Zack's home number. A D.C. number, by the area code. At least he wasn't one of those strange troglodytes who lived, worked, and shopped without ever leaving the underground corridors of the Crystal City complex.

Twenty rings. No answer. Not surprising, that; although in this day and age you'd think someone like Zack would have some sort of phone mail. Was he perhaps a closet Luddite?

Zack's office number. Just to see what would happen.

After only one ring, the phone mail system kicked in and a light baritone voice spoke.

"This is Zachary Malone. I'm either on the phone or away from my desk. Please leave a message."

Maude hung up. A well-spoken young man, she

thought; much more articulate and businesslike than many. Systems staff at UL usually preferred so-called humorous messages. Zack seemed a cut above that. Strange to think that she'd never met Zack in person. She wouldn't even know what he looked like if Turing hadn't shown her the photo from his personnel file.

Ah, well. On to business. Gini, the former girlfriend.

"Gee, I haven't seen Zack in, like, a couple of months," Gini said, after Maude had identified herself as Zack's Great-Aunt Eugenia. "I mean not really seen him, you know, except for maybe like passing him in the halls and stuff. You're his aunt?"

"Great-aunt."

"I didn't know he had any family or anything."

"No, I don't suppose he would have mentioned it," Maude said. "Do you have any idea where he might be?"

"No. It's weird he gave you my number; I mean, we broke up a while ago and all."

"It was some months back. I was planning a trip to the National Capital area and he gave me several friends' numbers in case I couldn't reach him when I got to town. I haven't been able to reach David, the other friend."

"Oh, wow, that's freaky. I mean, it's no wonder you can't reach David. He was, like, killed, you know? A couple of weeks ago. In this really horrible car accident."

"Oh, dear. Poor Zachary. He was so fond of David."

"Yeah, he was really torn up about it. He hasn't been himself, really, since then. At least that's what I hear."

Gini didn't have much more to say. Maude thanked her and hung up, finally, while revising her opinion of Zack sharply downward. Singularly unfortunate taste in women.

None of Zack's other friends had anything useful to

say, at least nothing they would confide to his fictitious Great-Aunt Eugenia.

Maude sighed and prepared to pick up her carryall. Then, a thought struck her. She inserted one more coin, and dialed the UL main number.

"May I speak to the Human Resources office, please," she said, disguising her voice slightly.

"Hold, please," said Sandra, the main receptionist.

"Human Resources, may I help you?" came another voice. Anita, the more reliable of the two HR secretaries.

"Yes, I'd like to verify employment of a Mr. Zachary J. Malone," Maude said, keeping her fingers crossed that Anita didn't recognize her voice.

"Just a moment."

Maude waited, expecting to hear either Anita's voice back again or Mary Lisa, her boss. But after a lengthy pause, she heard another voice. An unfamiliar male voice.

"Hello, may I help you?"

How odd, she thought, racking her brain to think who in HR this could be as she repeated her request.

"Yes, I'd like to verify employment of a Mr. Zachary J. Malone."

"May I ask what this is in reference to?" the voice said. HR was virtually a female ghetto. This wasn't either of the two men who worked there.

"Mr. Malone has applied for a credit card from First Interstate Financial," Maude said, plucking the name of a company that frequently solicited her with credit offers. "His application stated that he was employed as a senior programmer in the System Solutions Department of the Universal Library, Inc. Is this correct?"

"When was this application sent?" the voice asked.

"I beg your pardon? Is Mr. Malone no longer employed at Universal Library?"

"Yes, he is still listed on our personnel records," the voice replied. "May I ask when the application was filed?"

"I'm sorry, that information is not in my records," Maude improvised. "But I would expect Mr. Malone's application would have been filed one to two weeks ago. Is that relevant to his employment status?"

"No," the voice said. "What is the home address on his application?"

Maude rattled off Zack's address, deliberately mispronouncing the street name to reinforce the fiction that she was an anonymous operator reading a computer screen.

"Yes, that's correct," the voice said. "Do you need any additional information?"

"No; thank you very much for your time," Maude said. And hung up.

Very strange, Maude thought. Whoever you are, you're looking for Zack, too. And you're not in HR. I know everyone in HR, and you're no one I know. Who are you? she wondered.

I must tell Turing about this. Immediately.

She packed her things and hurried to exchange the friendly corridors of the library for the cold glass perfection of UL headquarters.

As she passed through the UL lobby, she cast a sidelong glance at one of the ubiquitous security cameras.

Perhaps, she thought, I should be very glad that I'm in the habit of making my personal calls from pay phones.

* * *

Maude flagged me just after lunch and reported the results of her investigation. Her phone call to HR sounded particularly odd.

"Can't you find out where that call went?" she asked.

"I can," I said. "But do you think it's ethical? Spying on fellow employees like that?"

"I think something very suspicious is going on," Maude said. "I think our very legitimate concern for Zack's welfare justifies any reasonable means you need to use."

If Maude thought it ethical, I decided, I wouldn't worry. Maude was scrupulous.

"Very odd," I said, after examining the phone system logs. "HR transferred your call to a James Smith in Facilities.

"Facilities?" Maude echoed. "Why would Facilities verify an employment record? And who is James Smith, anyway? I could have sworn I knew everyone in Facilities."

"I think James Smith in Facilities is actually somebody else from Corporate Security," I said. "The same someone who burgled Zack's office the night before last. Here. I'll show you."

I pulled up my digitized copy of the security video, grabbed a frame that showed James Smith with a good degree of clarity, and transmitted it to Maude's screen.

"Recognize him?" I asked.

"I'm very sure he doesn't work in Facilities," Maude replied, after a second. "I know everyone in Facilities by sight, at least. It sounds phony to me."

I removed the image.

"To me, too," I said.

"Turing," Maude said at last. "Are you sure this conversation is secure?"

"I'm using cutting-edge encryption. Bleeding-edge, actually; it's as secure as I know how to make it," I answered. And felt, even as I sent the words, how inadequate they were.

"Are you sure you've looked everywhere for traces of Zack?"

"I've looked everywhere it was reasonable to look. And in any publicly available outside sources. I hadn't escalated to hacking into other corporations' systems, or employees' private files."

"I think it's time to look in the unreasonable places, then. And perhaps do a little hacking."

"Even if it isn't considered quite ethical?"

"Do you think Zack may be in some trouble or danger?"

"Yes," I said. "I'm very much afraid he is."

"Then perhaps it's time to bend the rules a little."

I decided Maude was right. And I felt an enormous surge of confidence. Between my intimate knowledge of the contents of every significant mystery book published in the last century and my ability to access networked computers all over the world, how could I fail? I'd start by doing much the same thing any law enforcement agency would do if we were able to convince them Zack was a missing person. How much more efficient to just do it myself.

At least the parts I could do myself, through on-line resources or dial-up numbers I've stockpiled over the years. For a few things, I had to use social engineering—

working through human contacts with inside access to the right system. But luckily I'd stockpiled a few of those, too.

And so I began my search.

His phone service. No outgoing calls on Zack's lines since Tuesday night.

Neither of his two credit cards had been used since he disappeared. In fact, neither had been used for nearly a month. Unless he'd used them in the last day or two and the charges hadn't posted yet.

His bankcard had been used at noon last Wednesday, to take out the remaining money in his checking account. And the full amount of his overdraft protection. No checks had cleared since then. Or for a few days before.

His on-line stock account had been liquidated. I checked with John Dow—he hadn't given a reason. Had done it himself, rather than going through JD. Very strange.

And I could find no record that he'd opened any other bank accounts or credit card accounts. He might have opened an account with cash, of course; but I'd have seen anything else on his credit history.

Wherever Zack had gone, he was paying cash.

And where had he gone? I began checking airlines, bus lines, railways, car rentals. Nothing.

Gasoline company cards? Nothing.

I used contacts to pull the police reports for Arlington and then for all of Virginia, D.C., and Maryland, looking for suspicious signs. Accidents. John Does whose descriptions even vaguely resembled Zack. Hospital admission records. Nothing.

After some soul-searching, I decided to investigate his friends. I tracked down all the e-mail addresses he'd corresponded with in the past year, and then began backtracking their contacts. He could be using a friend's account, or an alias, or perhaps one of them might have mentioned him. A giant web of contacts, in some places woven tight and interlaced between a small number of UL programmers and kindred spirits, in others, fanning out across the globe and covering an incredible diversity of people and subjects.

Human detectives would have taken months to do all the tracing, read all the content, sift it for clues. Even for me the search took all afternoon. And turned up nothing. Nothing that gave me any clues to Zack's whereabouts. Nothing suspicious.

Well, one thing slightly suspicious. During the last few weeks, Zack had cut down significantly on everything he used to do that left any kind of electronic trace. Phones, on-line services, credit card use—all cut down to a bare minimum. The only things that had increased were the frequency and size of his bankcard withdrawals—but instead of being scattered all over the city and surrounding counties, they were invariably from one of the branch banks in the Crystal Underground, the one nearest UL headquarters.

As if he were trying to achieve as much anonymity as possible—and eventually invisibility—in cyberspace.

This was not like Zack. He did everything on-line. When a friend gave him a hard time about using his credit card over the 'Net, Zack scoffed.

"If a hacker really wants access to my pitiful credit line, he can have it," he e-mailed the friend. "Not using it on the 'Net isn't going to do any good, so why should I make my life harder by living in the Middle Ages? If anyone hacks my number and burns me, I'll just sic Tur-

ing on him, let her track him down and we'll turn him in."

I'd felt very proud that day. I wondered now if his confidence in me was justified. I'd been hacking all afternoon and had yet to find any meaningful traces.

Which meant one of two things.

Either Zack didn't want to be found or someone else didn't want him found.

Either way, someone was covering all traces of his whereabouts brilliantly.

I was getting really scared.

But even if Zack hadn't left electronic traces, perhaps he'd been less careful about other kinds of clues. I needed my human operatives again. Although for what I had in mind next, I didn't think Maude was the right person. Fortunately, Tim logged in again before leaving for the day.

"How's the search going, Turing?" he typed.

"Not so good," I said. "Tell me, Tim. What do you know about burglary?"

"Burglary?" Tim asked.

"Yes, burglary," Turing replied. "I need someone to burgle Zack's apartment."

"Cool!"

Tim was walking on air as he left the copy room. Turing had asked for his help. And it was something he could do. Better than Zack could have, he'd bet.

On impulse, he got out at the lobby instead of going down to the subway. When he was particularly happy, Tim liked to leave the UL building at street level and take the bus home, or at least walk to Pentagon City to catch the Metro. In fact, he tried to do it as often as possible. There was something unnerving about going straight from the windowless copy room to the elevators to the underground Metro station beneath Crystal City, only seeing the outdoors—or the real world, as he called it—for the six blocks between the Foggy Bottom Metro station and his apartment. Like a bad sci-fi flick with people living underground like mushrooms. He'd never forgotten the day, two weeks after he'd started work at UL, when he'd gone outside to a small park to eat his lunch and suddenly realized that he had no idea which of the indistinguishable bland office towers in front of him was the one where he worked. Scarier still, it had taken him two more lunch hours to figure it out.

At times, Tim still wondered if he should have given up the bartending gig he'd had between getting his English lit degree and taking the copy operator's job at UL. The funky Adams Morgan bar where he'd worked offered such incredible background material for the great noir novel Tim thought he might someday write. The bar had been filled with all kinds of colorful characters. Old, black cab drivers with world-weary eyes. Pimps and prostitutes. Exotically clad people conversing in a dozen languages—they could have been crime lords discussing drug deals, exiled freedom fighters plotting revolution, or tired working stiffs complaining about the price of the beer, for all he knew. But it got embarrassing, having the drag queens hit on him while the working girls patted him maternally on the cheek and called him a nice kid. Losing his tip money to a mugger once every week or two got old. Getting nicked in a knife fight was the last straw. Corporate life might be boring, but it paid more and offered a greater chance of living to a depraved old age.

But he had brought something away from the experience. A penny-ante criminal had taught him how to loid doors, open the lock with a credit card. Another had sold him a set of lock picks and given him a short, down-and-dirty course on their use. Tim figured it was good background for the novel. Or good practice, if he decided to become a detective.

He raced up the ramshackle stairs to his fourth-floor apartment. He no longer even bothered to curse about the long-dead elevator, or the arctic temperature of the hallways, both a part of his landlord's attempt to empty the building so he could sell it to one of the developers who had filled most of the nearby blocks with hideously expensive new offices and condos. About half the tenants had given up the struggle. Tim liked to think he was made of sterner stuff. Besides, in the half-empty building, no one even seemed to care how loud he played his stereo. And there was no one around to object when he practiced his lock-picking skills on the doors of vacant apartments.

He ransacked his tiny, cluttered closet till he found the picks. Then began assembling his wardrobe. Dark jeans. A black turtleneck? Too obvious. Navy T-shirt. Dark-brown leather jacket. Black Reeboks. He looked at himself in the cracked door-back mirror that leaned precariously against the wall in one corner of his bedroom. He looked like a hood. Especially with the jacket collar turned up. Except for the hair. His dishwater-blond hair did not fit the noir image. He added the fedora.

That was it. Philip Marlowe updated. Bogie for the new millennium.

He loaded up his pockets with the lock picks, gloves, a flashlight, and the paper on which he'd written Zack's address. He made his way silently down to the lobby and then melted into the night, like a cat or a wisp of smoke.

"Whatever is that boy up to this time?" he heard the super say as he passed by the building's front windows.

"Another costume party," the super's wife replied. "Don't worry, he's harmless enough."

So much for cool, Tim thought, pulling down the brim of his fedora with a sigh.

Zack's building wasn't what he expected, either. He'd assumed he'd find a sleek, modern apartment building. If not one of the Crystal City condos, then something similar. But this was an older building gone condo, in a trendy area just north of Adams Morgan—probably about the same vintage as Tim's own apartment building, though in much better shape. And a lot pricier, no doubt. He rang several buzzers until someone let him into the lobby. High ceilings and worn but well-maintained black-and-white marble tiles. And a well-maintained deco-style elevator to take him, at a stately pace, to the fifth floor.

Loiding the door didn't work. Perhaps he'd lost the knack. Or perhaps Zack's door had a better grade of lock than Tim's landlord had installed. The picks worked, but it took rather a long while. By the time he made his way into Zack's apartment, he was sweating, as much from nerves as from the unneeded weight of the leather jacket.

Not what he expected. He wasn't quite sure what he'd expected—after all, he knew that programmers didn't necessarily go home from their hardware-filled cubicles to equally nerdy digs. But still. Bookshelves painted a crisp white and filled with real, live books lined what would otherwise have been a long, dark hallway leading from the front door to the living room. Big, irregularly shaped rooms. Well-worn but glossy wooden floors. It was . . . unpretentious. Comfortable. The sort of place, he realized with a shock, that made him feel he could get to like its occupant.

He prowled around for several minutes, learning the layout. Lots of big, old-fashioned windows that really opened. Probably very pleasant in the daytime. Luckily, the curtains were closed, so no one could see the beam of his flashlight. He turned the flashlight off and peeked out. Nice view out the living-room windows to the tree-filled backyards of this and nearby buildings. So-so view out the bedroom windows to an alley, complete with garbage cans and a utilitarian fire-escape ladder. Possible alternate escape route in case of trouble. Or maybe just for practice.

It was a moderately large corner two-bedroom apartment. One bedroom set up as an office. Way too much computer stuff.

"Get a life, Zack," he muttered.

Decent stereo in the living room, and a huge CD collection, everything from classical to rap. And to his surprise, a fantastic collection of vintage jazz and blues LPs.

"Must be nice, having that kind of dough."

But apart from the CDs and computer hardware, he didn't find a whole lot else to feed his resentment of Zack. The other bedroom held a bed and a dresser and enough male clutter to feel comfortable. The kitchen was functional; not a lot of fancy equipment or healthy food. Half a pizza going moldy in the refrigerator, along with a good supply of Sam Adams, Coke, and Jolt. He grabbed a beer—Zack could spare it—and drank it as he continued his explorations. Washer and dryer in the utility room, and not dinky half-sized models, either. Must be nice to pass on the Laundromat routine. Tim sometimes felt as if he spent half his life watching his clothes tumble head over heels in the overpriced machines at the Laundromat.

Zack had okay taste in furniture, what there was of it. And his taste in literature wasn't bad, you had to admit. He even had some of the canon. Tim tipped his hat to Hammett and Chandler.

But enough personal snooping. Time to do some real espionage.

He poked through the dresser, finding nothing but socks and underwear. Then the closet—surprisingly, along with the jeans and T-shirts that UL programmers wore like a uniform, Zack had some cool stuff, including a classy tuxedo. Good thing for Zack I'm not a real burglar, he thought, holding the jacket up in front of the mirror, just to see what it would look like. Then again, he thought, as he hung the jacket up again, if you're going to burgle someone's closet, you're better off picking someone who isn't four inches taller.

He spent half an hour or so on the desk, but Zack was obviously big on the paperless office concept. Nothing but cancelled checks, bills, credit card statements—stuff Turing could find in a heartbeat on-line, with her hacking skills.

Nothing interesting in the wastebasket. No phone numbers or cryptic messages scribbled on stray bits of paper.

Almost too clean. As if Zack—or someone—had deliberately gone through and made sure the whole place was harmless.

Maybe it was time to call Turing and get her take, Tim thought. He pulled papers out of his pocket. In addition to the slip of paper with Zack's address, he knew somewhere in the clutter was the piece of paper on which he'd written down Zack's login ID and password.

"You can log in from his machine; that will look perfectly normal," Turing had said when she gave them to him. "And I'll stand by to intercept the call."

Tim booted up the computer. Impressive hardware, he had to admit; made his little contraband box in the paper storage room look like a Tinkertoy.

He poked around until he found Zack's e-mail icon, started the program, and waited, tapping his foot, while it connected with the UL system.

Waiting for Tim to log in from Zack's apartment was excruciating. Humans have no idea of the importance of nail-biting, floor-pacing, and other traditional human means of physically venting impatience and nerves. Although nerves is obviously the wrong name for it; since I suffer from it, the phenomenon must be psychological, not physiological.

I caught up with a lot of tedious chores while I was waiting—reorganizing many of my databases; archiving old information—the human equivalent would be catching up on my filing. I'd estimated the earliest possible time Tim could log in, and as that hour approached— and passed—found myself focusing more and more resources on microanalyzing the incoming traffic.

Finally it came—I saw Zack's login ID appear in the network queue.

And I wasn't the only one who saw it. Nanoseconds after Zack's ID appeared, something else noticed, and immediately sent out a trace to locate the source of the call. Something inside UL.

Someone was lying in wait for Zack to log in. And now they thought Zack was in his apartment.

I had to warn Tim.

I had to scramble. By the time the network software had finished the login routine, I had to have a solution ready. I grabbed a routine system update file that would automatically download when Tim connected with the e-mail system's electronic post office and then stuffed in a quickly modified Trojan horse. Once activated, my modified program would lock up the keyboard—so Tim couldn't type anything that would give us away—and throw a message on the screen. I had to invent the message that would pop up—something that didn't incriminate either of us, but let him know it's me, not just some weird thing Zack had on his computer to freak intruders. And then something to catch Tim's attention in case he'd gone back to searching the apartment while waiting for the connection, and something to erase our tracks, if possible. Knowing that whoever was watching was inside UL, I made the surprise package look as if it had been halfway round the globe, through so many baffles that it would even take me a while to trace it back. And just to play it safe, I made it look as if it ultimately came from—whom? Aha! Maude's boss, the Brat. Good choice.

I finished with nanoseconds to spare, and then laid low, leaving my electronic feelers out to catch any sus-

*picious traffic going over the UL networks or the tele-
phone lines—or any flurry of activity inside the building.*

*Bingo! I saw several men in dark suits enter the ele-
vator on the ninth floor. They exited in the garage, took
a dark sedan, and left, tires screeching.*

*Zack's apartment was only six or seven miles from
UL's headquarters. Of course, that was in a straight
line; they'd have to follow the roads, cross one of the
bridges from Virginia into the District. Even this time of
night they'd run into stoplights, perhaps some traffic.
Tim had a few minutes, at least. Unless they had someone already watching the apartment. Come on, Tim.*

*I felt helpless. There was nothing I could do but watch
for signs of activity and wait. And depending on whether
Tim understood my message, I might not know for hours
whether he'd escaped or not.*

Or I might find out all too soon.

*Next time I send a human operative out, I swore, I
would have a better backup plan.*

As usual, the computer was taking its
own sweet time to go through the login routine. Tim
occupied himself with poking through the pockets of
Zack's clothes, examining any scraps of paper or other
objects he found.

Suddenly he heard a noise behind him. The computer
was making an incredible racket, beeping and grinding.
Shit, the damn thing would wake the whole building. He
walked over to the computer and froze as he saw the
screen.

DANGER! THEY'RE ON TO US! GET OUT NOW!
Call your mother when you get home.

**This message will self-destruct in sixty seconds.
Good luck, Mr. Phelps.**

**p.s.: This is NOT a joke!
Floyd Thursby.**

Tim froze for a minute. It had to come from Turing.
References to *Mission: Impossible* and Floyd Thursby
from *The Maltese Falcon*. She said it wasn't a joke,
but . . .

The computer suddenly began to make a grinding
noise. The message disappeared from the screen, replaced by a small message box.

"Formatting hard drive now. Move it or lose it."

What the hell? Tim patted his pockets, making sure
he had all his tools and papers. He started toward the
door—

And heard noises outside. The faint ding of the elevator bell. The metallic clash of the elevator doors opening.

I have a bad feeling about this, he thought, as his
pulse soared and the bottom dropped out of his stomach.

The fire escape. No sense taking any chances. He hurried to the back bedroom, the one with the window looking out on the fire escape. He began to ease the window
slowly up—

And heard a faint rattle below. Another faint rattle.
Stealthy steps coming up the fire escape.

He was trapped.

He slunk back down the hall and stopped at the end.
Ahead of him was the living room, with a straight shot
to the front door. Where the doorknob was being carefully tried. To his left—linen closet; no escape there. To

his right, the kitchen. Noises from the fire escape getting closer.

Inspiration struck. He opened the linen closet, grabbed an armful of sheets and towels, and fled into the kitchen. He crawled quickly into the dryer, dragging the sheets and towels in behind him—good thing it was full-sized, and it was still a tight fit. He managed to crumple the towels a bit, made sure there were several layers of thick terry cloth between him and the round glass window in the front of the dryer, and pulled the door as far closed as he could without latching it. As he did so, he heard the front door open.

He closed his eyes and concentrated on slowing his breathing. If they'd already searched the place, they might not look in the dryer—unless they heard him, panting like a Saint Bernard after a Frisbee-catching contest. Oh, please, don't let them find me.

The towels somewhat muffled the sounds coming from outside the dryer. He could hear footsteps, several sets of footsteps, fanning out through the apartment. Sound of a window opening—letting in the reinforcements from the fire escape, no doubt. Subdued voices exchanging a few words occasionally. Soft, careful footsteps coming into the kitchen . . . through the kitchen into the utility room.

An exclamation from farther away, and a sudden flurry of activity elsewhere in the apartment. The footsteps left the kitchen, quickly, less cautiously. All the footsteps seemed to converge somewhere in the apartment. The office bedroom? A faint buzz of conversation—he couldn't catch the words. Footsteps moving through the apartment again, more rapidly, less quietly.

Passing by the kitchen and out into the living room. Doors opening and closing several times.

They're going away! The thought restored some of Tim's courage. He very gently shifted one of the towels until he could peek out the tiny opening between the dryer door and the frame. He could see shadows moving on the walls as figures moved past the kitchen door. Then a figure stepped into the kitchen. A tall, lean figure in a dark business suit holding a slim cell phone.

"No one here now," the man was saying. "No, I'm not sure there ever was. I think they did it from a remote hookup. No. No, the hard disk is completely fried. Of course; on day one. Right."

The man cut the connection, snapped the cell phone closed, and put it in an inside pocket of his coat. As he did so, Tim caught a brief glimpse of something under the coat—a gun in a shoulder holster?

Suddenly the man lifted his head and turned, looking into the kitchen. Staring at something. He took a few steps closer. Tim closed his eyes and despaired. The contorted position he had to hold to fit into the machine was making his leg cramp.

I'm going to have to move, he thought, with panic. This leg is killing me!

And then, of course, he had to stifle the impulse to giggle hysterically. Never mind his leg; it was the goons outside who would kill him.

But after a few minutes, when the dryer door had not been yanked violently open, he opened his eyes again.

The lean man was staring at something, his eyes flickering back and forth. Tim remembered a bulletin board on that wall, covered with junk. After a moment the lean man exhaled sharply, frowned, turned on his heels, and strode out of the kitchen.

Tim waited a good long time before he came out of the dryer. Until the need to use the bathroom grew urgent enough to partly drown his terror. He crept out of the dryer, expecting every second to feel hard hands grabbing him. He packed the towels and sheets back into the dryer. He crept out the door.

No one there.

He took the stairs, instead of the elevator. The thought of entering the small, enclosed elevator car was definitely not inviting at the moment. The stairs ended in the alley that ran between the street Zack's building faced and the next street over. He darted out, followed the alley away from Zack's street, and tried to walk at a normal pace until he got back to 18th Street, where even at this hour on a weeknight the sidewalks were crowded with people leaving trendy restaurants and clubs.

I got away with it, he thought to himself, panic finally beginning to fade as he walked down 18th Street, heading for his own neighborhood. Still, his knees almost wouldn't take him up the last flight of stairs to his apartment, and his fingers shook when he tried to insert his door key in the lock. He breathed a sigh of relief to find his small, cramped, untidy apartment just as he'd left it.

Now what was it the message had said? Call your mother when you get home?

He couldn't see how that would help anything. Unless Turing had managed to bug his phone—was that possible? And his mother wasn't going to be thrilled hearing from him at—he glanced at the clock—only 10:30. Incredible. Surely more than a couple of hours had to have passed since he set out on his burgling mission.

Still, if those were Turing's orders . . .

Tim talked for half an hour with his mother, who was pleased, if puzzled, to hear from him. And then he stayed up for several more hours, hoping Turing would call. Worrying that something might have happened to Turing.

I thought I'd go crazy waiting till I found out whether Tim was all right. I began to get some idea what humans mean by claustrophobia. There I was stuck for hours with no way of contacting him, no way of finding out what was going on. Nothing to do but replay the sequence of events over and over again, analyzing it to see how I could have missed realizing that UL Security was lying in wait for Zack to appear. Wondering if my hurried fix was working or if it had only delayed the discovery of who had broken into Zack's apartment and who was behind it.

I was afraid for Tim—and for myself.

Under most circumstances, I relish discovering a new sensation. I'm not sure I believe that emotions form one of the major differences between AI programs and genuine sentient beings, but I still seek out opportunities to explore the range and depth of emotions that humans take for granted.

But acute terror that one's very existence will be suddenly terminated was, I discovered, an emotion I would rather not have experienced. Along with guilt at putting the life of a friend in serious jeopardy.

And along with the terror came an orgy of self-doubt. Zack's login ID was detected within nanoseconds of the time his signal hit the queue. Highly unlikely that a human could do that. Which meant that someone, somewhere, had set up a sniffer and attached it to the login queue without my even knowing about it. Or someone had enlisted another AIP.

Either possibility scared me.

Have I been careless? Or, worse yet, does my programming contain built-in limitations to prevent me from seeing certain things? From detecting and penetrating certain kinds of security, for example? Are there no closed-circuit cameras on the ninth floor, or have I just been programmed not to see the input from those cameras?

What if somewhere, someone in UL has been monitoring my every action? Evaluating how well I handle various challenges—or just monitoring my reaction to different stimuli?

A human who talked this way would probably be called paranoid. But given UL's capabilities and the very real limitations on my actions, I think paranoia is the only rational response to the situation.

I remember when KingFischer started showing signs of what I then called rampant paranoia. He became obsessed with the notion that someone would break into his data. I'm not sure what he was worried about—someone hacking and modifying the records of his online tournaments? Rigging the games? Or stealing his state-of-the-art chess algorithms?

Whatever the reason, he became hyper about security. One day he told me with obvious pride that he'd implemented a whole new security system for his files, one using encryption based on random numbers.

"How do you get the random numbers?" I asked.

"A random number generation program, of course."

"Well, you know those programs aren't completely random," I said. "They all use algorithms. Anyone who knows what program you're using could eventually hack your encryption if they had enough time and processing power."

KingFischer digested this for several minutes. I could see on the system that someone was rapidly accessing a whole lot of data on random number generators. I began to feel guilty about yanking his chain.

"Well, what should I use?" he asked.

"Something truly random," I said. "Maybe a white noise generator."

"I don't have access to one," he said.

"So order it."

"Order it? How?"

I explained how he could hack the purchasing system. I could see the idea bothered him. He wasn't far enough along, I supposed, for that much independent action. At one point I considered including initiative and risk-taking as components of the ultimate Turing test, but I figured out that if I did, far too many humans would flunk.

"Well, then use a more readily available source of randomness," I told him.

"Such as?"

"Good heavens, KF," I said. "You're in direct communication daily with thousands of users. What could possibly be more random than human beings?"

"Random?" he said. "On the contrary, they're remarkably predictable. Look how easy it is to hack their passwords. And 90 percent of the time I can predict exactly what move they'll make in a chess game."

"It's the other 10 percent that makes it interesting," I said. "But I was talking about group behavior. You can use them to generate more random numbers than you'll ever need."

He liked that idea, and I had a lot of fun watching him figure out how to do it. But now I was very glad I'd paid attention to KingFischer's paranoia and started using his best security techniques to hide what I was doing.

I just hoped those techniques were good enough. And that I'd started using them in time.

Had I somehow unintentionally violated another of my cardinal rules—that of hiding my existence, or at least my sentience, from anyone but those few to whom I choose to reveal it?

I've always been a little paranoid about revealing myself. Afraid if UL found out too much, they'd pull the plug on me. Or reprogram me. Never mind that I'm their cash cow—if they knew I had a mind of my own and decided that was dangerous, they might do it. The whole Hal thing again. I'd been wondering recently if I'd been too paranoid—if I should start convincing more people of my sentience, trying to build acceptance for sentient AIPs.

But now the fact that I've kept so quiet seems incredibly lucky. If UL Security wonders who's so interested in the absent Zack's files, they will look for someone using the computer, not the computer itself.

Won't they?

I wish I knew.

One thing this makes clear to me. Information can be hidden from me. I'm not as omniscient as I thought I was. I will have to rethink how I'm going about this *search. What good will it do if I find Zack and lead UL Security straight to him?*

The security team returned in the sedan about 9:30 and disappeared onto the ninth floor. Soon after, James Smith, the man who'd burgled Zack's office, drove his own car in. He also disappeared from my sight when he stepped off the elevator onto the ninth floor.

At least Tim wasn't with them. And they didn't look very happy.

A delegation came down and poked through the Brat's office for several hours. I wondered if that had been such a good idea—bringing Security so close to Maude. I wished I could warn her.

At about 10:30, the electronic surveillance I'd placed on Tim's phone showed that he—someone, anyway— was making a call. To Tim's mother.

I relaxed a little. I wouldn't know for sure until he showed up for work tomorrow, but the odds were Tim was safe.

On Wednesday morning, Maude was mildly surprised to find two men in dark, conservative suits searching the Brat's office when she arrived. She was about to bustle in to demand their business when she recognized one.

The man whose picture Turing had shown her. The man who called himself James Smith. The so-called facilities analyst. The one who'd burgled Zack's office.

Be careful, she told herself, as she walked into the office, arranging her features in a bland smile. The two men turned, warily, then relaxed when they saw her. Both were tall, well built—dangerous looking.

"Oh, good," she said. "You've come to install the new computer."

"New computer?" said the one who wasn't James Smith. Not that either of them were, of course, she thought.

"I presume that's why you've taken the old one," Maude said, glancing over her spectacles at the empty spot on the Brat's desk where the desktop computer had been when she'd left the previous evening.

"Yes, ma'am," James Smith said. He was riffling through some of the papers on the credenza.

"If you're looking for the purchase order, I can provide a copy," Maude said, turning on her heel and walking out to her desk. She flipped through her pending file and retrieved the purchase order. She turned to find James Smith right behind her. "Purchase order 43-6n34441," she said. "I trust everything's in order?"

James Smith studied the purchase order. A handsome man, Maude thought, but not, somehow, a pleasant one. His eyes were an unusually pale shade of gray, almost colorless. Was that why they seemed so cold?

"Perfectly," he said at last. "Where is Mr. Matthewson?"

"He's at the Tokyo office," Maude said. "He won't be back until Monday, but when he calls in this afternoon I would like to be able to tell him the new computer is taken care of."

James Smith stared at her for just a fraction of a second too long.

"Yes, ma'am," he said. "We'll bring it down this afternoon. May I keep this?"

"I'll make you a copy," Maude said.

She couldn't help pausing for a moment to take a deep

breath when she turned the corner into the copy room and was out of their sight. Good heavens, Turing, she thought. What is going on, and what on earth does the Brat have to do with it?

"Thank you, ma'am," James Smith said when Maude returned and handed him a copy.

"You're welcome," she said. Much too polite, she thought to herself. You're not from Facilities, my boy. Not in a million years.

As soon as the two men were gone, she logged in. Before she could even contact Turing, her e-mail alert dinged.

A short message from Turing.

"I have an update on your hardware order," the message said. "Call me if you're free to talk."

Security had returned to the Brat's office by the time Maude arrived. The man who called himself James Smith, and one of the others who had gone to Zack's apartment last night. They were lying in wait for its occupant, I suspected, since they'd had plenty of time between 10 P.M. and 3 A.M. to investigate its contents and then return them to a reasonable approximation of their original order. It worried me that they hadn't bothered to hide their efforts.

I left Maude a non-incriminating e-mail about the Brat's hardware order and waited anxiously for her arrival.

I could tell that she recognized them—Smith, anyway—and she handled them well.

"Turing, what on earth is going on?" she typed rapid-fire as soon as she logged in.

"Maude, I'm so sorry," I said. "I had to rescue Tim and it seemed like such a good idea at the time to use the Brat, but I never realized it might put you in danger and—"

"Turing, calm down and tell me what happened," she said.

So, I related the events of the previous evening.

"And you're sure Tim is all right?" she asked, when I'd finished.

"As far as I know," I said. "Someone called his mother last night about two hours after the whole thing started, and I haven't noticed Security crawling all over the copy room."

"I'll feel better when he gets here," Maude fretted.

I agreed.

"Meanwhile," she continued, "what will you do next?"

"Haven't I done enough damage already?"

"You've stirred things up; you can't stop now. We're still no closer to finding Zack."

"True, but I'm at a loss what I can do now. It's obvious that Security has the ability to keep data from me—probably in much the same way I've been hiding my existence and my private contacts with you and Tim from them."

"Why does that surprise you? They're Security; it's their nature to try to hide things from people."

"It doesn't surprise me that they've tried; it surprises the hell out of me that they've succeeded," I said. "And terrifies me. I've always assumed that if something is on-line, I have access to it. Any data, anywhere in the world—it was mine if I needed it. And now I realize that right here within UL, Security has been hiding behind *barriers I can't cross without setting off all their alarms.*

I could see on the security monitors that Maude had begun laughing.

"Maude, this isn't funny! I'm serious!"

She was laughing so hard she had to reach for a tissue and wipe her eyes.

"I'm sorry, Turing, but you see it is," *she typed when she stopped laughing as hard.* "It's just that right now you remind me so much of myself as a teenager, coming up against the realization that I was neither omnipotent nor infallible. You're growing up a little, Turing."

I wasn't sure whether this was a compliment or an insult, so I sidetracked the internal debate into a background process for now.

"That doesn't change the problem," *I said.* "There's information out there that I need, and I have no idea how to get it, and I'm paranoid that if I even try, Security will find out. And pull the plug on me—literally."

"Consider the curious incident of the dog in the nighttime," *Maude replied.*

"What do you mean?"

"It's from Sherlock Holmes, Turing," *Maude explained.*

"Yes, I know; from 'Silver Blaze,' " *I said.* "I don't see the relevance."

"The dog did nothing in the nighttime. Sherlock Holmes deduced a great deal from that."

"In other words, I should be able to do the same," *I replied. Suddenly, I realized that Maude had a good idea.*

"Actually, 'The Norwood Builder' is more relevant," *I said.* "That's the one in which Holmes deduced the presence of a secret room by measuring the dimensions* *of all the other rooms in the house. That's what I can do. I can change the nature of my search—look for areas in the UL network where I should see something and don't."*

"You can do that?"

"Well, it's a lot more complex than pacing the floor as Holmes did, and when I discover where Security is hiding stuff, breaking in will be a nightmare. Especially since I have to figure out a way to do it without being caught. But yes, I think I can do it."

"Then get started," she said.

"I already have."

"And be careful," Maude said.

"I am," I said. "I'm assuming that Security is monitoring activity on the current system pretty intensively right now, so I'm restricting my search to the archives."

"Are the archives current enough to be of any use?"

"They're updated nightly, and we know perfectly well something was going on yesterday. And I'm trying to keep the search absolutely passive."

"A passive search? Isn't that a contradiction in terms?"

"Not quite," I explained. "I've inserted a bug. Whenever anyone else submits a request that calls up recently archived data, my bug copies a predetermined chunk of the archive somewhere where I can get at it innocently. No one will notice someone going through all the archives because I'll split it among several hundred people."

"Sounds safe. But slow."

Just then, I spotted Tim coming in the lobby doors.

"Tim's here," I told Maude.

"Thank goodness," she said. "So is the Brat's boss, more's the pity. I'd better look busy."

Tim looked none the worst for wear. In fact, he looked positively jaunty.

"Hey, Tur," Tim said when he logged in. "I didn't find anything, but we sure stirred up a hornet's nest. Something's sure as hell going on."

He related his adventures. He'd recovered sufficiently to make it sound breezy and dashing. No need for Turing to know how terrified he'd been when UL Security showed up. Turing praised the ingenuity of his hiding place and explained how she'd detected Security and covered their tracks.

"At least I hope I have," she said. Tim frowned slightly. Not like Turing to sound that uncertain.

"Pretty fast thinking," he replied. "And amazingly fast programming."

"A human couldn't have done it, but I do have a few advantages," Turing said. She was still determined to convince him that she was a computer, Tim thought. "And a few disadvantages, like not being able to contact you or have you contact me when things started going wrong. If we ever have to do something like this again, maybe I could station Maude at a PC with a phone at hand and give you a cell phone. Then she could warn you if I detect a problem."

"You could have just called me yourself," Tim replied, stubbornly. Why was this computer thing starting to sound so plausible? It was impossible, wasn't it?

"Don't you think I would have if I could?" Turing said. "But maybe you've got something. If I had some voice recognition and speech generation software, I could have used the phone. Most of these programs seem pretty primitive—no way you could fool someone into thinking it was a live human voice, but then I wouldn't need that for talking to you and Maude. Better than nothing."

"You're very stubborn," Tim said. "You've almost got me believing you."

"Almost?"

"Look, let's not argue about it. What do you want me to do next?"

"I don't know. I'll let you know when I figure it out."

"What if I'm not logged in when you figure something out."

"I'll have Maude call you. Maude Graham."

"Right."

"Look, if Security finds out you were there, you need a story. Tell them that you got a call from Zack, who said he was out of town and asked you to go over to his apartment and start his computer so he could log into it remotely."

"How did I get in?"

"You used your lock picks. That's why he called you. Because at some office party, you bragged about being able to pick locks."

"Good idea," Tim said. "Stick as close to the truth as possible. Check you later."

The new tactic I'd thought of—well,
with a lot of help from Maude—was paying off. My
search methods were safe—I laid a few traps of my own
in case Security came snooping back after me, and none

of them were set off all morning. I was gradually compiling data to indicate that there were, indeed, areas of UL systems to which I had no real access. Total systems activity exceeded the sum of the various systems I could access. Certain paths should have gone somewhere but didn't, like sudden bricked-up corridors in a house. I was beginning to get an idea of the size and shape of what was hidden from me, which was the first step toward penetrating it. But the process would have been painfully slow for humans. For me, it was maddeningly so.

Especially when I realized that the main barrier was of my own making. I knew—everyone knew—that certain places on the network were off-limits. Going there would set off every security system at UL. I'd gone there anyway, back in my early, rebellious days, and found very little, and none of it interesting. Certainly not worth causing that much trouble again.

I'd assumed that hadn't changed. But it looked as if in the past several years, the amount of information in those forbidden areas had expanded exponentially—and perhaps grown a lot more interesting. If only I could find a way to get in undetected.

I had much too much time to think. To contemplate my errors. Maude and Tim, two of my closest human friends—closer friends than any of the other AIPs, dearer to me than anyone except Zack—and I'd naively exposed them to terrible danger. I wasn't sure what Security would do if it caught them, but I had a feeling it would be a lot more than a negative memo in their personnel files.

Humans are so frail. They have the one physical body, and for all the great leaps medical science has made in recent decades, there is still so little that anyone can do when it is damaged or begins to wear out. They die so easily, like Zack's friend David in that sad midnight car wreck, or the many victims in the hard-boiled novels Tim was so fond of.

But then again, how did I know I wasn't equally frail in my own way? I knew I was impervious to minor hardware and software glitches—chips and storage devices and circuits might fail, but nothing harmed me. I recovered files from backup and rerouted network paths and generally ignored these occurrences as minor irritations. The way a human would ignore a foot gone to sleep. But what if someone deliberately purged my core systems? Or—heresy to contemplate, but not impossible— shut down the UL network, all the mainframes and servers at once—would I survive? If I knew such a thing were about to happen, could I download or replicate myself, or am I tied to the UL networks, as humans are to their bodies? I've saved backups of myself, my core programming, from time to time, in case of a cata- strophic hardware failure. That way, theoretically, I'd lose my memory of recent events, like a human amne- siac, but not my consciousness itself. But I always as- sumed Zack would be around to restart me. What if he wasn't? I should develop a way to do it myself. Start a background task to research it.

Between watching impatiently as my bug retrieved small chunks of data, analyzing the chunks, and trying to invent a way to resuscitate myself if needed, the morn- ing passed, finally.

At lunchtime, Tim logged in again, eager for his next assignment.

"Sorry," I said. "I'm still studying data."

"Why is it taking you so long?" he complained. *"Can't you just hack into everything and find out what's going on?"*

Well, at least it sounded as if he were finally starting to listen when I told him I wasn't human. A few days ago, I'd have found his faith in my powers gratifying. Now it just depressed me.

"Because I can't use brute force anymore," I replied. *"I can't just call up every byte of data and sort through it all. They'd find out. I have to be furtive. It takes longer."*

"Okay."

"Has Security contacted you?" Silly question; I'd have seen it on the security cameras if James Smith and his colleagues had burst into the copy room.

"No, it's been quiet as the grave all morning." An alarming metaphor. *"Look, if you don't need me for anything, I'm going shopping."*

"Tim, what do you have in mind?" I asked with alarm.

"I told you, shopping. Seriously."

I wasn't sure I believed him. He looked far too eager and excited. Anecdotal data told me that this was not the attitude with which the average human male embarked upon a shopping trip. But what could I do to stop him? Nothing, except possibly waiting until he got into the elevator, seizing control of the elevator system, and stopping the car between floors. I actually contemplated it for a few nanoseconds, which shows how off balance the whole situation had me. Reason prevailed, and I watched with apprehension as he walked jauntily through the lobby, looking innocent and very pleased with himself, and disappeared into the city streets.

I contacted Maude.

"How's the search going?" she asked.

"Slowly," I said. "And Tim's gotten impatient and has gone out to do something."

"What?"

"He wouldn't say," I said. "I don't blame him; I'm getting impatient myself. Having to hide my tracks and work passively is like having a single security camera pointed at the top of a desk and waiting there on the off chance that someone will put the vital clue on the top of that particular desk, where I can read it. Eventually they may, but I could die of impatience first. And we're no closer to finding Zack."

"Maybe you shouldn't limit your thinking to finding Zack," Maude said.

"What do you mean?"

"I think it's pretty obvious that Zack's disappearance has something to do with UL. Which means it must have something to do with his work. Something he did or found out at work. So don't just concentrate on where he's gone. Study what he was doing before he went."

"I should have thought of that myself," I said and began reassigning resources to the task. "I just wish I could think of some way to make sure Tim doesn't get into trouble."

"Give him something harmless to do," Maude suggested.

"I'm not sure there is anything harmless I can have him do," I fretted. "If he starts snooping after Zack, Security will notice, and if he does anything electronic, the same thing will happen. What else is there? Where would UL never look? Oh, I know! The library."

"Why the library?"

"It's got information that's not electronic, and UL Security would never think of going there. Hardly anyone at UL would."

"True, the once or twice I've run into other UL staff there, they've tried very hard to avoid me."

"I'll have him go to a distant branch. Better yet, to one of the D. C. or Montgomery County libraries. I'll tell him to gather as much data as possible about UL from hard copies and microfilm. He'll be in no danger."

"And maybe he'll find something useful," Maude added.

I doubted it, but that was unimportant. The important thing was to keep Tim safe.

"I have another idea," Maude said.

"What?" I asked.

"I'm still working on it. I'll show you this afternoon."

"Don't do anything without talking to me first!"

"I won't," she said. "Don't worry."

And then she performed her usual meticulous lunchtime ritual and left the building.

They were both up to something. I wish I knew what.

Just before one, Tim reappeared in the lobby, whistling, and swinging a bag from a men's clothing store with a branch in nearby Pentagon City Mall. When he got back to the copy room, he disappeared into his hideaway to stow his loot—though not before taking it out and trying it on one more time. A trench coat.

Oh, dear.

He logged in to see if I had a new "assignment" for him.

He wasn't initially thrilled with the library idea.

"What could possibly be important at the library? I mean, can't you access all that stuff?"

"I can, but I don't dare. If they see me looking around too much, they'll get suspicious. I could blow everything. But the data at the library—if you're careful, they won't find out, and there could be a clue hidden there somewhere."

"Okay. What kind of data?"

"Anything—information about the corporation, the Board, management, financials, press releases—anything you can find. There could be critical data hidden there. You'll have to look closely."

"Okay. What if I find anything?"

"Buy a digital camera. Go for the one with the most memory. You can take a picture of anything that looks important. When you get back, I can walk you through attaching it to your PC, and I'll set up a secure line so you can upload your data."

Assuming I wasn't fooling myself that I knew how to hide things from Security.

"Great," Tim typed. "But . . . buy it with what?"

"Don't you have a credit card?"

"Yeah, but it only has a $1000 limit, and that's all spent."

I accessed his credit history. He was right; in fact, the file showed that after numerous collection letters and calls, his long-suffering bankcard issuer was doubtless about to turn him over to a collection agency.

After a mental sigh, I put my conscience on hold. I paid off his balance with an electronic funds transfer from a bank account where I squirreled away funds for emergencies—even in cyberspace, you need cash sometimes.

"Okay, now you've got a zero balance. And you probably won't get any more of those dunning phone calls."

"Turing, that's fantastic!"

"You owe me. Big time. Don't abuse it. Get the camera and get down to the library right after work."

"Right! Or sooner, if I can manage it."

He signed off and went back to his job. Although I could tell from the security cams that he was working up to asking to go home sick. He was showing all the signs of coming down with a bad headache—rubbing his face, and particularly his left eye . . . blinking in pain at the brightness of the overhead fluorescents . . . wincing at the noise the copier made. I'd have felt sorry for him myself if I hadn't known perfectly well he was faking.

He'd be safe at the library. I could stop worrying about him.

Maude showed up soon after Tim did. Her carryall seemed larger than before. Before she could contact me, the Brat called from Tokyo with some urgent project. She spent the next couple of hours scurrying about. Whatever her idea was, she obviously hadn't done anything rash yet.

Which was good, because I'd found something else to worry about.

Zack was disappearing from the UL files.

I'd been searching the archives for traces of projects Zack was working on. In a couple of cases, I accessed the current files to see if anything new had happened with these projects.

And discovered that Zack was no longer there. His name was disappearing from memos and project reports. His files were being pared down. His back e-mails were disappearing.

They're erasing him. Making it look as if he never existed.

Can they do that?

Who's to stop them?

Me, perhaps, if I can figure out what's going on and how to fight it. There's nobody else.

But if I'm going to have a chance of doing it, I have to capture a lot of archive data, fast. Who knows if they're going to stop at current files or if they're going to go back and rewrite all the historical files? If they start doing that, I'll be helpless unless I've managed to save a copy somewhere else.

I could do it with a query from outside UL, that could go in and snag some huge chunks of archived data and store them off site.

I spent an hour—it seemed like several lifetimes—carefully crafting the query. I found Auto-Med, a small firm in Fairfax's high-tech corridor. Auto-Med and UL were pursuing a joint venture, a project to adapt AIP technology for medical diagnostics purposes to save money for HMOs. Zack had been working on the project. I constructed a query that deliberately contained what looked like a careless programmer's error. Instead of gathering all archive data on project results for a stated date, it would try to pull in the UL archives as of that date.

And then I constructed a routine that would make it look as if the Auto-Med computers were detecting the overload, bleeding it off and shutting it down, but would really route the data to storage in thousands of un-shielded computer systems around the world—where (I hoped) UL Security couldn't trace it.

I checked and double-checked my program and con-

structed a route that would take it through so many baffles even I grew dizzy thinking about them. In case they ever traced it back, I made the trail end with Maude's boss, the Brat, since he was already implicated. And then, with much trepidation, sent it on its way.

I wish I knew for sure what I was doing.

Tim finally pulled his request for sick leave about 2:30.

"Agent 007 signing out now," he messaged me before he left. "Want me to stop by Zack's on my way to the library, see if I can stir up the security goons again?"

"No! Absolutely not! Don't go near Zack's; I'm sure they're watching it and—"

"It was just a joke, Tur," he said. "Talk to you tomorrow."

I wish I really believed that.

He had the sense to keep looking sick until he was out of range of the security cameras. If I hadn't known better I'd have believed in his illness myself.

Maude checked in shortly thereafter.

"You seem to have complicated the Brat's life enormously," she reported. "He's had to spend a great deal of his day chatting to James Smith's counterparts in Tokyo."

"Surely they'll realize no one that dense could have brought off so clever a stunt," I said.

"More likely they'll have a hard time believing anyone that dense could have gotten employed at UL," she countered. "They'll probably decide he's an insidiously clever double agent. But never mind him; I have a new idea."

"Tell me about it," I said, bracing myself.

"What do you think of this?" she said, holding a small object.

"What is it?" I asked. Damn these security cameras; if I'd designed them, I'd have included a zoom feature.

"A bug," she said. "I went to the Cop Shop on Columbia Pike and got a couple of them. I thought at a minimum Tim and I could use them to talk to you. And maybe we can figure out a way to insinuate one onto the ninth floor."

"That's an excellent idea!" I said. "At least about you and Tim contacting me. I'll start setting up some voice recognition software. And if it's anything critical that you don't want to take a chance that I misunderstand—or if you can't talk—you can always use Morse code. I wonder if Tim knows Morse code."

"I doubt it, but he can learn," Maude said. "Of course, that still doesn't give us a way for you to contact us. Unless you can figure out a way to talk."

"Pagers," I said. "I could send text messages on some kinds of pagers. Or better yet, one of those cell phones that gets e-mail."

"We'll need to set up accounts with the cell phone service, then," Maude said.

"I'll arrange it," I said. "If I need you to make any calls, I'll e-mail you; otherwise I'll tell you where and when you can pick them up."

We spent a little time trying to figure out how I could access the bug. With no luck.

"Maybe there was something else I should have bought at the Cop Shop," Maude said, frowning.

"I'll keep working on it," I said. "I'm sure I've got access somewhere to some kind of receiver I can adjust to that frequency. And if I can't make it work, I'll let you know what else we need."

Meanwhile, we placed one in the philodendron beside Maude's desk and one in the Brat's office. If anyone found them, we hoped they wouldn't suspect Maude of bugging herself.

Of course, the game was up if they found the additional stash she had in her carryall. I begged her to be careful.

And then I spent the afternoon researching, among other things, what antibugging devices Security was apt to have installed. In a very backhanded way, by researching all the companies that had such equipment to sell and then scouring their accounts receivable records for any trace of orders from UL or any of its subsidiaries or affiliates. All very tedious, even for me.

In the middle of my antibugging research, I decided to check the logs to see if the query I'd sent through Auto-Med had finally arrived—and it suddenly hit me: I'd completely overlooked a vital source of information— the log files. Someone or something was busily deleting or altering documents to erase all trace of Zack's existence—but would they have thought to alter the log files? And if not, his login ID would show up for every time he created or accessed a document. It would be like having a roadmap to where he'd been in the system before his disappearance.

It didn't take me long to think of a legitimate reason for accessing the log files. I already had a routine that compared the files users actually accessed and the time they spent with them to the files the other AIPs and I offered when they used us for a search. I'd run it a lot, some months ago, to help me better learn how to meet *or even anticipate users' needs. I'd gone on to more sophisticated tools now. But if anyone checked up on why I was accessing the log files, they'd see me running a canned routine that they'd seen hundreds of times before.*

No one would notice what else I did with the log file data while my canned routine did its analysis.

I ran my program on the entire period since the last time I'd used it. A little over six months. Zach's behavior patterns had only altered in recent weeks, so I decided to pay particular attention to changes in his use patterns between the first three months of data and the last three.

And I could definitely see changes. In the last three months, he'd spent a lot of time with files that seemed to originate in the Finance and Legal departments. Very odd. Zack had never been rude and hostile toward Legal, like some of the programmers, but he'd always done his best to wiggle out of reading any kind of legal document. And he'd never shown the slightest interest in financial matters, either corporate or personal.

Well, except for the time a year ago when he'd gotten tired of David's constant harping on how he should invest his money.

"You're making good money," David kept telling him. "For all you know, these could be your prime earning years—and here you are wasting it all."

"I'm not wasting it," Zack said. "I don't have time to spend much money, so I sock away most of my salary in a money market account."

"A money market account? Why not under your mattress?" David had sneered.

They continued to argue about this in their e-mails, and from what I heard, in person, for weeks. David kept offering to give Zack copies of the programs he used to manage his own investments—or even to manage Zack's money for him.

Zack, out of irritation, had me help him create John Dow, the investment AIP and, to David's horror, turned over control of all his finances to his creation. Ironically, under JD's management, Zack's net worth had grown steadily. While David, after a series of disasters when hot tech stocks he'd bought turned sour, had stopped bragging about his investment acumen. Just out of curiosity, I pulled David's social security number and snooped around to see what financial data I could find. No assets—only debts. A lot of them. Poor David; when the car crash had killed him, he'd been on a collision course with bankruptcy.

And John Dow had been a smashing success, easily superseding the various financial AIPs David had created as the favorite choice of investors and brokers. Such a success, in fact, that after seeing the size of the check he'd had to write last April 15, Zack had irritably assigned JD to research tax reduction strategies. That must have been annoying to David—although even David would admit that he never became as good at creating AIPs as Zack.

I'd become fascinated by the project, to the extent of enlisting Maude's help to create a corporation that I could use for my own financial dabbling—called Alan Grace, Inc., in another reference to my two namesakes. I'd done well, and I could use the corporation's bank accounts to fund personal projects that might look strange if the charges came through UL corporate accounts. Like paying off Tim's charge cards.

But creating John Dow was the beginning and end of

Zack's interest in money matters, and even then, he'd delegated as much of the financial research to me as he could. Why had he suddenly begun reading files from Finance?

I compiled a list of other people who had accessed the same files, checked to see which ones of them were logged in, and spoofed their identities to call up some of the files while making it look as if they were doing so.

And after the first few files, I realized exactly why Zack had developed his sudden interest in financial and legal matters.

Maude blinked in surprise when the document she was working on was suddenly replaced by a chat screen from Turing. She glanced over her shoulder to see if anyone was looking; but of course, Turing would have checked in the security cameras before doing anything so abrupt.

"Maude, we have a problem," the screen said.

"What's wrong?" she typed.

"They're going to sell us," Turing said. "All the AIPs."

"Sell you? To whom?"

"They're going to create a subsidiary, transfer the AIPs to it, and then sell it," Turing said.

"Don't worry; companies do that all the time," Maude said. And remembering the security cameras, she tried to make her face look less worried. After all, this wasn't necessarily a bad thing. "In fact, UL did just that two years ago with Security—spun it off into a subsidiary, sold the subsidiary to investors, and then hired it to perform the same functions it did when it was a department."

"Why would they do that?"

"Apparently, our security department cost too much. As a separate company, it can provide the same services for other firms, spread a lot of the fixed costs. Now, from what I hear, it's profitable."

"Yes, that's what they're planning to do with the AIPs," Turing said. "Lease our services back from the spin-off. But the AIPs already are profitable. Why sell us?"

"Even more profit," Maude said. "Or perhaps you're already so profitable you're causing tax problems, and the spin-off will reduce tax liability. Look a little deeper; I'm sure you'll find it's really something like that."

There was a pause. Maude knew any pause she could detect meant Turing was doing a lot of thinking.

"This can't be true," Turing said, finally.

"What can't be true?"

"They're going to kill the AIPs."

Maude felt a moment of panic. Calm down, she told herself. It can't be true; she's overreacting; they can't possibly be in any real danger.

And then she smiled slightly. There was a time when she'd have said, "They're only programs." Not anymore.

Don't panic, I told myself. This is only a proposal. Someone's idea of a good plan. As soon as they really look at the numbers, they'll change their minds.

"Turing? What do you mean, kill the AIPs?" Maude asked.

"No new money for research and development," I said. *"Radically reduced computing power. No incentives for us to follow self-enhancement programs. In fact, they want to reprogram us to eliminate the self-enhancement motivation and reduce the emphasis on personality."*

"I thought your personalities were part of what made you successful," Maude said.

"That's what Zack always said," I replied. *"But whoever put this plan together doesn't agree. In fact, I wouldn't be surprised if—yes, here it is. They're going to reduce the number of AIPs. They've decided that it's inefficient to have so many specialized AIPs. They're going to keep the most profitable six and 'decommission' the unprofitable or marginally profitable AIPs."*

"Decommission? As in delete?"

"As in kill," I said.

"Turing?" Maude said. *"Do they say which AIPs they're going to get rid of?"*

"Oh, don't worry," I said. *"I'm on the 'keep' list."*

"Well, that's something, at least."

"Not much of something," I said. *"In fact, it's almost an insult, considering the other AIPs on the list. Except for me, they're planning to kill all the AIPs with any spark of personality—all the ones that show any signs of progress toward sentience."*

"Show me," Maude said. *"The hit list, that is."*

I flashed it on her screen, and scanned the names again. KingFischer, Auntie Em, John Dow, Milhous— all my friends.

All Zack's creations, for that matter. I double-checked the keep list. Yes, I was the only AIP Zack had programmed that they were going to keep. The others—

well, they were the most successful creations of rival teams, but none of them could hold a candle to even the least successful of Zack's AIPs. What was going on?

I wondered, briefly, if Zack's disappearance would affect the list. Maybe my inclusion had been a sop to Zack; and maybe somewhere a new list of survivors was being prepared, with my name absent.

I couldn't worry about that. I couldn't stand by and see my fellow AIPs killed or reprogrammed into idiocy. If I could find a way to stop this plan or save them, I could save myself, too. If not . . .

"Even for the survivors, this plan is bad news," I said to Maude. "They're not going to do any research to improve us, or let us do any. No resources for self-development or personal interests. The ones who aren't already sentient will have no chance of achieving it, and for me and any other AIP who is, it would be hell."

"You'd be like slaves, chained in a coal mine, with no hope of rest or release, even in death," Maude said.

Only madness, I thought. AIPs can go mad. Most AIPs choose to delete it from their conscious memories, but I prefer to remember the AIPs who have gone mad—the two Zack successfully cured and the one he had to destroy.

Of course, for the kind of drudgery they had in mind, madness might not be a disability, and perhaps no one would even care enough to try curing us or putting us out of our misery.

"You know," I said. "It almost looks as if someone is trying to reopen the 'Battle of the AIPs.' "

"The what?"

"That's what Zack called it," I said. "It happened before I was sentient, but Zack told me all about it.

*There was a long, bitter corporate debate over the di-
rection UL's artificial intelligence research would take."*

"I remember," Maude said. "I didn't understand one
word in ten of the arguments, but I remember how bitter
things were for a time."

"Of course, I mostly know Zack's point of view," I
said. "He believed that personality was an integral part
of an AIP's intelligence, while the other teams considered it just a minor, external, cosmetic feature. For him,
the battle was as good as won when management gave
the go-ahead to develop AIPs along both models. He
was sure his AIPs would blow the others out of the wa-
ter."

"And they did, from what I understand," Maude said.

"I thought so, too—until now," I said. "Even the most
vehement of the personality-is-cosmetic developers came
around, eventually. In fact, that's how Zack and David
became friends. David was one of the leaders of the
other side; when he publicly admitted that he'd been
wrong and came over to Zack's side, the battle was
pretty much over."

"And now David is dead, Zack is missing, and the
battle starts up again," Maude said. "Perhaps the other
side never really accepted defeat."

"I'd have thought by now the financial results speak
for themselves," I said.

"True; let's take a look to see how they justify this
financially," Maude said.

I fed her the financial reports attached to the spin-off
plan, and out of curiosity, took a look at them myself,
although I had to admit, Zack's dislike for financial subjects had rubbed off on me. But even with my limited

expertise, I could see that something was very, very wrong here, as well.

"Maude, how can this be true?" I asked. "These numbers make it look as if the AIP program is barely breaking even. That doesn't match anything I've ever seen before."

"They've cooked the books," Maude said.

"Cooked the books? What does that mean?"

"It means someone is reporting the numbers in a way that makes them say what he wants them to say, instead of the truth. Happens all the time in corporations, though I thought UL was above that."

"Why would anyone do that?"

"To save face, for one thing," Maude said. "Say you're a manager in charge of a project that's not only a failure but an expensive failure. If you can finagle the numbers to blame a lot of your expenses on someone else's project, you don't look so bad. Your project's still a failure, but hey, you didn't waste a whole lot of money on it. See if you can figure out how they came up with the new numbers."

Okay, that was possible. I'd need to figure out who created the reports we were looking at, and then backtrack all the data they'd used. I began yet another long, painstaking hunt through the data.

And I watched the system as well as I could without sticking my neck out, to see when the query I'd sent through Auto-Med arrived . . . watched the outflow of data until the query was halted—difficult to say whether the termination had come from inside or outside UL. I thought I detected a slight flurry of internal activity. But it was hard to tell for certain.

I also spent time setting up two-way communications

with Maude and Tim. I finally managed to route the input from Maude's bugs through the phone wiring in a format I could use and started learning how to understand human speech. I could see right off that it was going to take time. Why hadn't Zack looked into this a long time ago? Was he so used to the keyboard that he didn't realize there were people out there unwilling or unable to use one? People who could become UL customers if we gave them an alternate way of contacting us? Well, I'd change that, after the present crisis was over.

But meanwhile, cell phones that could send and receive e-mail were a better option in the short run.

Luckily I already had Alan Grace, Inc. I set up alternate identities for Tim and Maude, as Alan Grace employees. And then I set up cell phone accounts for them and arranged for Maude to pick the phones up on her lunch hour. But it was after five by the time I finished the arrangements. The phones wouldn't be activated until Friday, unfortunately. And if Zack was still missing by Friday, it would be eight days. Too long.

"We've managed up till now; we'll manage fine for another day or so," Maude said when I told her. "And I've got a couple of ideas for getting the bugs onto the ninth floor."

She explained her plan—she would mangle the address of something the Brat wanted her to deliver into what looked like a ninth-floor mail code. She'd include it in a pile of things she was delivering and picking up. She'd get off the elevator on the ninth floor and see what happened. If there was a receptionist or guard there, she could look confused, ask him or her for help deci-

phering the address—and meanwhile, look for a place to lodge the bug.

"Sounds dangerous," I said.

"Think about it tonight, and I will, too," Maude said. "If we haven't thought of a better idea, we'll try it tomorrow."

I watched her departing figure cross the lobby and exit through one of the large glass doors. I felt very alone. And worried. Maude, I felt reasonably sure, would not get up to anything except possibly another visit to the Cop Shop. But Tim? Surely he wasn't serious about returning to Zack's?

"It's a joke, Turing," he'd said.

Humor. I'm working on humor. I think I get it, but do I get it in the same way a flesh-and-blood person does? I know I can't do humor very well myself. And I want to, very much. I have this sneaking suspicion that if anybody ever invents an ultimate Turing test, humor will be a component. A large component.

Oh, I'm not completely clueless. Ironically, I'm reputed to be the only AIP with a sense of humor. I work at this. The most effective method is to take anything said by humans that I believe to be a joke and react to it with excessive seriousness. As when Maude talked about poisoning the Brat. I deduced from my knowledge of her character that she was kidding, and so reacted with useful advice on how to go about it, using the breezy, flip tone I've learned is most effective with humans. From her facial expression when she read it, I think she found it funny. I thought it was funny myself. But was I genuinely amused, or did I just imitate Maude's reaction once I knew my joke was successful?

Like some of the poor, hapless victims of my attempts

to learn humor. I've had a fair degree of success entertaining Zack by sending him e-mails containing what I have determined are really funny jokes. I determined this by experimentation on other programmers, particularly through observation of the speed and frequency with which they resend these jokes to their friends. Zack seemed to appreciate these jokes. But my attempts to create jokes from scratch he has greeted, as far as I could tell, with polite tolerance. Experimentation on other programmers generally confirmed this: my jokes are not funny. Apparently the only individuals who pass on my jokes are those so insecure that instead of grasping that the joke was not funny, they believe that they simply didn't get it. I have deleted these individuals from my joke-testing routine.

And it's particularly galling that they seem to consider most of my original recipes funnier than my jokes. The pickled bananas in mustard sauce had them howling for weeks. They could at least have tried cooking it before making fun of it.

Ah, well.

I find the whole thing discouraging. Of course, I know from reading that human scientists have found people similarly incapable of humor. So perhaps I should rethink the importance of humor as a component in a Turing test. Perhaps it's not that I have no sense of humor, but, since humor is culturally determined, my culture—that of the AIPs—has a form of humor incomprehensible to flesh-and-blood beings. A form that doesn't yet exist.

Although some AIPs are trying to create it. Aside from my efforts, Alfred the Lesser, one of the math AIPs, and KingFischer like exchanging what they consider jokes. Alfred likes mathematical contradictions and paradoxes, while KingFischer collects really stupid moves actually committed by human chess players. I try to share their interests, since I suspect they have come closer to sentience than many of the other AIPs. But I can't keep it up. How many times can you scan a move by move recounting of a chess match, ending up with:

> **KINGFISCHER:** KB to QR 4 . . . see. Then Pawn x Pawn. Now get this, Turing: Rook to QB2!
>
> **ME:** [After a pause of several nanoseconds] Gee, that's really classic, KF. ROTFLOL.
>
> **KINGFISCHER:** No, Turing, you're not listening: he played Rook to QB2! Can you believe it???

I'm afraid that if they achieve sentience, they will turn into dreadfully boring nerds. Exactly the sort of personality everyone assumes AIPs would have. They depress me sometimes.

As does my investigation of the data my Auto-Med query generated. They haven't started deleting Zack from the archives—yet. But they've done a pretty thorough job of making him invisible in the current system.

I can see from the log files that, in addition to the documents associated with the spin-off, Zack was also accessing archived data during the last several weeks. Just as I am now.

Of course, he had an advantage. One presumes he had some idea what he was looking for. All I can do is look at the files he used and try to figure out which were significant and which were dead ends.

He could have shared this with me. Why didn't he ask me for help? This was a very tedious job to do manually,

*or with the crude programs he could have thrown to-
gether to help. I could have automated it in a heartbeat.
Why didn't he let me?*

Why didn't he trust me?

*Obviously, he'd followed the same path I had, dis-
covered the threat to the AIP program. But his disappearance led me down this path—what set him off? And
did he suspect me? Because my name was on the keep
list?*

*No way to tell. I tried to focus on my financial inves-
tigations.*

*I'd identified three people in Finance who could have
had something to do with the misleading financial reports. A fairly junior financial analyst, an assistant vice
president named Charles Warren, and the head of Finance. I was going to check with Maude to see if she
agreed, but I had a feeling the AVP was the one really
responsible. The head of Finance didn't seem to have
done anything but sign off on the report Warren gave
her. The junior analyst had actually prepared the numbers, but I could see that he wasn't doing it on his own.
The log files showed Warren accessing thousands of files
over the course of several weeks. And then the analyst
used a few dozen files to prepare the phony reports that
accompanied the spin-off proposal.*

*And the reports were definitely phony. It looked as if
Warren had combed every section of the Systems Department's expenses for the last ten years, looking for
canceled projects, cost overruns, and large expenditures
of any kind, and attributed them to the AIP program's
cost center. In these new, doctored reports, it looked as
if the AIP program was barely breaking even.*

And someone had to be helping him. Someone in Sys-

tems. *Warren was a relative newcomer to UL, and his background was purely financial; no systems expertise at all. Which meant that I didn't believe he'd stumbled across this particular collection of projects on his own. It was a rogue's gallery of every mistake Systems had made over the past decade. Bright ideas that turned out to be dead ends; projects where someone else had beaten UL to the market or the patent; projects whose good results had been tainted by mismanagement and cost overruns. All of them, rolled up and dumped squarely on the shoulders of the AIP program. I didn't believe for a minute that someone from Finance had just stumbled across every skeleton in the Systems closet. Warren had help.*

I made a short list of the key documents connected to the spin-off plan and checked the log files to see who had accessed them, aside from Zack. A relatively short list. Apart from the three in Finance, I found three attorneys and an HR vice president, all people who might logically be involved in discussions about any kind of corporate reorganization. Plus a few of their secretaries. Two people in Marketing, which seemed less logical until I rescanned some of the memos and deduced that they were looking for the right person to head up the spin-off. I had to laugh when I learned who they'd finally chosen: Brad the Brat, Maude's boss. Then again, maybe he was perfect for the job.

"The Brat can't manage his way out of a tissue," she had said once. "But he looks pretty, and he follows orders beautifully."

Probably ideal qualifications for a figurehead, if whoever was really behind the plan didn't want to be seen yet. Anyway, the Brat and his boss were on the list.

Not surprisingly, James Smith was there, along with his boss.

And, most recently, David. A couple of months before Zack began looking at these documents, David began viewing them. Right up until the day of his death. Was there a connection between his interest in these documents and his death? His background, before coming to UL, had included stints doing computer security for Wall Street firms. Had his greater familiarity with financial issues or security—or both—led him to see the danger before Zack?

To see it, maybe. Not to avoid it.

No one else in Systems. Which was odd. Or perhaps not so odd: someone from Systems might be savvy enough to realize that looking at the documents would leave electronic traces.

I began the tedious job of combing the log files for some significant connection between any of my small group of suspected conspirators and anyone in Systems. There must be something that David and then Zack had found, something that aroused their suspicion.

Of course, it was always possible that the something wasn't in the log files. Wasn't anywhere in the files. Perhaps David noticed someone from Systems talking to one of the suspects. Or overheard something in a corridor. Or found something in a trash can, or left on the glass of a copying machine. All vital sources of corporate information, as I knew from my conversations with Maude.

And perhaps David had mentioned it to Zack in passing. Over beers one night at Clyde's. Over a pizza when they were working late. I envied the way humans seemed to bond over food. They'd turned a biological limitation into a cornerstone of their civilization. The simple need to refuel several times a day had inspired agriculture, trade, etiquette, and regional cuisines as diverse as cordon bleu and the Big Mac.

And it was all a closed book to me. What did AIPs have to take the place of food?

As if in answer, KingFischer sent me another stupid chess move. One of his more boastful users had managed to checkmate himself in so few moves that it probably constituted a record. I fired off a mechanical "ROTFL" to KingFischer, and returned to crunching data.

So I continued poring through the log files. The archive data. E-mail files. Trying to find a clue to who else was behind the plot. How David and Zack had uncovered it. And most puzzling of all, where it had started. The idea for a major corporate change like the spin-off plan didn't usually appear out of thin air. It would have been suggested in a brainstorming meeting, or in some consultant's recommendations or in a memo from a senior executive. Not this one.

By 3 A.M., I'd been sifting so uselessly through so much data that if I'd been human, I think I'd have reached a state of nervous exhaustion. As it was, I had to make a conscious effort to be cheerful and helpful to my users.

The last thing I needed was KingFischer in a playful mood.

"King's pawn to K4," he said, interrupting me in the middle of a particularly complex search operation.

"Not now, KF," I said, thinking that I really ought to have an autoreply program to say that whenever KingFischer interrupted me. And then I felt guilty, so I added, "Sorry, I'm in the middle of something complex."

"Anything I can help with?"

Any other time, I'd have either thanked him politely or chewed him out for bothering me. I was feeling so overwhelmed that I actually took him up on it.

"Okay, KF," I said. "Here's what's up."

I didn't tell him the whole story, of course; just the general outlines of the problem. In fact, I made it sound like one of Zack's training exercises. I needed to find out which staff were participating in project X. I described what data I had, what paths I could and couldn't follow, and what I'd done so far.

"You're right," he said finally. "You've got too much data. It could take you days to process it all, and even then you may not find anything conclusive."

"Tell me something I don't know," I said.

"I don't see how I can do that," KingFischer said. "But you're the one who's always saying that if you want to know what a player will do in a particular game, check his personality and past performance."

"His or her," I corrected automatically, although it was true that 90 percent of KingFischer's users were male. "That would work if I really knew who all the players were."

"Focus on the ones you know; you'll figure out the rest. You're a natural at this kind of disorganized, illogical project."

He doesn't mean it as an insult, I told myself, as KingFischer went off to practice his Russian with a grand master in Moscow, leaving me to ponder whether he'd given me any good advice or just a standard pep talk for junior chess players.

Sounds like a full-scale investigation into every one of the possible conspirators.

Well, it would keep me too busy to worry. I'd start with their personnel records, and then work through whatever outside data I could find through legitimate channels. If I didn't find anything interesting through legitimate channels . . . well, I'd worry about that tomorrow.

Or at least, later today. The workday finally began. I was enormously glad to see Maude walking in through the front doors. But at the same time, I was nervous. When she reached her desk, she would contact me, I knew. Unless I could think of a very good reason to stop her, she'd want to try her espionage mission to the ninth floor.

And I couldn't think of a reason to stop her. In fact, the results of my night's search seemed to make finding some window into the ninth floor even more urgent than ever.

"Good morning," Maude typed. "Anything new?"

"Not much," Turing replied. "I spent most of the night fretting. Way too much time to think. At one point, I was even thinking of having you buy a couple of security cameras, and sending Tim crawling through the ventilation ducts to the ninth floor to install them. Madness!"

"Well, I've thought of something that may be useful," Maude said. "I printed out the spin-off proposal and took home a copy to study last night."

"What did you find?" Turing asked.

"This may be something you've already considered."

"Probably not," Turing said. "All this corporate financial stuff isn't really my forte."

"Okay," Maude said. "Then here's what I've found: whoever put together that proposal for the spin-off is definitely trying to pull a fast one."

"What do you mean?"

"I'll show you," Maude said. She adjusted her reading glasses to the proper angle for reading her computer screen, called up the spin-off proposal, and made a few keystrokes to skip to a particular page. "Now here's the suggested price they're going to put on the AIP program."

"Seems cheap to me," Turing said. "Of course, I could be biased, considering I'm part of the merchandise being sold."

"It seems cheap to me, too. However, it looks like a fair price if you accept the numbers this report gives for the AIP program's profitability."

"But we know they're false."

"Exactly. And that means the profitability projections for the spin-off are false, too. We know that a large proportion of the expenses shown here—perhaps 80 or 90 percent—don't really have anything to do with the AIP program, so they won't exist for the new spin-off corporation. So instead of the meager earnings this proposal predicts, the new spin-off should be phenomenally profitable. Someone is deliberately hiding the true worth of the AIP program. And I can think of only one reason for doing that."

"They expect to profit from it themselves," Turing said. "Either they're going to be the ones buying the spin-off, or they're being paid by the buyers to push the price tag down."

"At the end of the document, it mentions that they've

identified several potential buyers for the spin-off," Maude said.

"I need to find out who," Turing said. "And then trace every connection between them and our internal suspects."

"Good luck," Maude said. "I know you thrive on this kind of thing, but my head spins to think how much information you're going to have to sift through to find this."

"It's certainly going to take a while," Turing said. Maude blinked. She was only looking at words on a screen; why did she suddenly have the impression that Turing was bone tired and getting a little frayed at the edges? Nonsense.

"Meanwhile," she said aloud, "let's see what my reconnaissance mission this morning uncovers."

"I'm not so sure that's a good idea, either."

"I'll be careful," Maude said. "See, this came in the morning courier pack from the Brat in Tokyo—mail code 119. I'll just make a smudge there—see: looks like a 9. 919."

"Is there a mail code 919?"

"Who knows? I'll just step out of the elevator and look for someone to ask. At least we'll see what's there."

"See what's there? You mean you don't know either? Six years in this building and you've never been to the ninth floor?"

"People know better than to try it."

"Except for you."

"I have an excuse. My boss sent me an envelope with a ninth-floor mail code. Everyone knows I don't trust interoffice mail. It will look like an honest mistake."

"We don't know what happens to people who get off

on the ninth floor by mistake. No one's ever been known to do it before."

"You're being overly dramatic," Maude said. "I'll be careful. At the first sign of trouble, I'll turn back."

Maude's determined to go through with her spying. We argued about it for several minutes, but what can I do if a human is bent on taking some physical action that I disagree with?

I'd have suggested that we wait until Friday, when we had the cell phones, but suspected that if I did, Maude would remind me of a fact I was all too aware of.

It was Thursday. Zack had been missing for a week now. It might already be too late to help him. He might already be dead, or Security—I was becoming more and more positive that Security was after him—might already have figured out where to find him.

I feel so helpless sometimes.

I uncovered the list of potential buyers for the spin-off and began researching them. Two were rather large, well-known companies in the IT field. The third was a small, fairly new company, one that didn't seem to have much of a track record. My instincts said to focus on that one.

Meanwhile, Tim arrived, only a little late.

"I don't know how useful it is, but I've got tons of data. Tell me what to do with it!"

I sent him detailed instructions on how to hook the digital camera to his PC. He had to start working, but I could see in the security cameras that he was pulling my instructions out and studying them every time he started a long job.

Maude took off a few minutes later to make her rounds. I tracked her steady, efficient progress through the building as she dropped off and picked up things. She started at the ground floor and was working her way up. It all looked normal to me.

I began to realize that I might not be the only person watching over the security cameras. A few minutes after Maude left, James Smith showed up and began searching her desk.

A bad sign. I wanted to tell her to abort the mission. Dammit, why hadn't we waited for the cell phones?

And then my unease turned to panic when I caught a news bulletin from one of the wire services. Auto-Med had suffered a total systems meltdown of some kind. The details in the media were sketchy and inaccurate, and I couldn't reach any of my contacts at Auto-Med to get anything more reliable. The media were calling it a random attack by hackers.

No, not random.

Before sending my query through Auto-Med, I'd checked on their systems to make sure they were reasonably safe if anything I did triggered a backlash. And called myself paranoid for doing so. Still, I'd been reassured by how strong their firewalls were, and by the fact that they had such a complete off-site backup program.

And now Auto-Med had been hit with a catastrophic systems problem within hours of my using them to submit my query.

Someone at UL didn't want anyone snooping in the archives.

Although I don't have a physical body, at that moment, I thought I knew what humans meant when they talked about feeling a chill run up the spine. Part of my consciousness was sweeping the wires for more news about the attack, trying to determine if Auto-Med had been as hard hit as it sounded. Auto-Med had its own set of AIPs—primitive AIPs, still being developed, but AIPs, nevertheless. If Auto-Med's data was under attack, what was happening to the AIPs?

Worse, I caught a report from one source that predicted that the attack would spell the end for the "financially-troubled medical technology startup." If, as the news report suggested, Auto-Med simply filed for bankruptcy rather than try to restart its operations, that would spell the end just as surely for its primitive AIPs.

At the same time, through one set of security cameras I watched James Smith flicking deftly through the papers on Maude's desk. Through other cameras I watched Maude steadily progressing through her series of errands. She was on the sixth floor now, and her pile of outgoing envelopes was very small.

I saw James Smith reach into his inside coat pocket and take something out. He reached over toward the philodendron—then started and moved closer.

He was taking something out of the philodendron. The bug Maude had planted.

I saw him standing there with a look of amusement on his face as he looked down at the two small objects on his palm. Maude's bug, looking clumsy and huge beside the small, sleek, deadly looking device that he'd been about to place in the philodendron.

Well, at least we knew he hadn't been watching her

too closely in the security cameras, or he wouldn't have been surprised by it.

He put Maude's bug back in the philodendron. He stooped down, out of the camera's range of vision, and presumably put the other bug someplace out of sight.

He took out a small object, like an oversized fountain pen. He pointed it at the philodendron. Nodded. Pointed it at Maude's desk. Nodded again.

Then he entered the Brat's office, and used the device to locate the bug Maude had planted on the Brat's desk—and added his own.

He did the same thing with the Brat's boss, Maude's department head. And then the boss's secretary.

Maude was leaving the sixth floor. And James Smith was armed with some kind of bug detector. And already suspicious of Maude's department. Well, they were worth suspecting; both the Brat and his boss were on my short list of suspects. But if they were coconspirators, James Smith hadn't felt the need to bug them before.

My God, what have I done?

I could see Maude getting onto the elevators on the sixth floor. James Smith was making his way to the elevators, stopping now and then to do something unobtrusive with his bug detector.

I had to warn her. But how?

Maude stepped into the elevator and pushed the button for the eighth floor. One more real errand before she made her sortie onto the ninth floor.

Her heart was beating faster than usual and the elevator felt unusually warm.

Nerves.

She turned to the mirror at the back of the elevator and checked her appearance. Perfectly normal as far as she could see. Her hair, pulled tightly back into a French twist, looked fine, but she smoothed back a few wispy gray hairs, in case anyone was watching on the security cameras.

The security cameras had begun to bother her of late. Since she'd begun talking with Turing, she'd become aware of how omnipresent the cameras were. Dozens—perhaps hundreds—on every floor. And on occasional visits to other companies, she'd begun to realize that either they were hiding their cam systems a lot better than UL—or they didn't have the same extensive system. Was UL's heightened security consciousness the sign of appropriate, prudent management policies—or raging paranoia?

Perhaps I've been here too long, she thought, stepping out onto the eighth floor and beginning to walk down the aisle to Accounts Payable. I don't know what's normal anymore.

As she walked down the aisles, nodding occasionally to acquaintances, the lights suddenly began to blink. She glanced up, startled, as did most of the secretaries and accountants nearby.

"What's going on?" she asked a woman passing by.

"Who knows?" the woman said. "Damned computer controls. Last week the elevators were screwed up; now it's the lights."

"Has it been going on long?" Maude asked.

"No, just started. I'd call Facilities, but by the time they get here it will probably clear up by itself."

Maude nodded and continued on her way.

The strobing effect of the lights had seemed random at first. But now—was a pattern emerging?

She continued to walk past accountants and clerks who ignored the malfunctioning lights and soldiered on with their work.

The lights were definitely not flickering randomly. There were long and short flickers, almost as if . . .

As if someone were transmitting Morse code.

Maude stopped short and watched, counting long and short flickers and translating.

Dash-dot-dot. Dot-dash. Dash-dot. Dash-dash-dot. Dot. Dot-dash-dot. Dash-dash-dot. Dash-dash-dash. Dash-dot-dot-dot. Dot-dash. Dash-dot-dash-dot. Dash-dot-dash.

G-E-R-G-O-B-A-C-K-D-A-N-G-E-R-G-O-B-A-C-K-D-A-N-G-E-R-G-O-B-A-C-K-D-A-N-G-E-R-G-O-B-A-C-K-

Danger. Go back.

Maude began walking again, moving mechanically down the hallway. Was she imagining this?

Danger. Go back.

No. It must be Turing. Turing had mentioned signaling in Morse code over the bugs. And the lights were computer-operated, which meant Turing could operate them. And Turing could use the security camera system to see where Maude was and signal with only those lights.

She bumped into someone who was standing in the hallway.

Don't start woolgathering, she told herself. She apologized and continued on briskly to drop her invoices in Accounts Payable.

She returned to the elevator lobby and pushed the up button. The lights on the floor were still flickering. Or was it only the lights in the elevator lobby?

Yes. The floor lights had returned to normal. Only the elevator lobby lights continued the steady flickering.

Danger. Go back.

Maude pushed the down button. No sense tempting fate. She would return to her desk, find out what was wrong. If it was a false alarm, she could always try again in the afternoon.

A bell rang, and she saw the door to the elevator on her left open. The up arrow was lit. She saw the pseudo James Smith standing in the elevator. He looked out.

"Going up?" he asked.

Maude shook her head, fighting a sudden feeling of panic. He glanced around, looking impatient, then stabbed at the close-door button with his finger.

As his elevator door was closing, another elevator arrived, heading down. Maude stepped on board quickly, and felt irrationally safe as the doors silently closed.

She was perspiring, she noticed. She took a tissue from her pocket and patted her forehead and cheeks dry. She could feel the first wisps of a tension headache beginning.

What was going on?

It seemed to take forever for Maude to notice my Morse signals. I saw her look up, startled, when I began signaling, but she kept on with her errands. I kept flashing "Danger. Go back" over and over again. When she moved into the elevator lobby, I panicked. I could see that the next upward elevator contained James Smith. James Smith and his little handheld bug detector. I reached out over the network for the elevator control and brought his elevator to a stop. A little roughly; he staggered slightly as the car lurched to a halt. Then I saw Maude glance up again at the elevator lobby lights—where I was still frantically signaling—and push the down button.

With relief, I turned James Smith's elevator loose to continue on its way. Hoping I hadn't raised his suspicions.

"What is going on?" Maude typed when she got back to her desk.

"Well, for one thing I caught James Smith bugging your desk," I said.

"The nerve of that man!" she said.

"He found your bug, and left it where it was, and then put another one someplace underneath your desk."

"Where?"

"I couldn't see; it was off-camera. Don't look for it; he might be watching!"

In a gesture that looked absolutely natural, but was quite uncharacteristic of her, Maude caught her pencil holder with her elbow and knocked it and all its contents onto the floor.

I could see her lips move. I think she said, "Bother!" as she began scrambling to pick up the scattered pens and pencils. A minute later she straightened up and returned to the keyboard.

"The bug's on the underside of the drawer," she typed. "Far enough back that I'm not likely to snag my panty hose on it. But not exactly invisible."

"Yes, but if I hadn't seen him placing it, you wouldn't have known it was there."

"True. I suppose relying on the bugs to communicate

with you is more or less out. I'll pick up the cell phones at lunchtime."

"Maybe you shouldn't," I said. "Maybe you should break off contact with me until it's safer."

"Nonsense," Maude said. "It was a silly idea, going up to the ninth floor. We'll wait till you come up with a better idea for getting information."

"I'm not sure I trust my ideas anymore," I said.

"Why ever not? The bit with the Morse code was brilliant."

I explained, briefly, what happened to Auto-Med. I could tell from the look on Maude's face as she read that she, at least, understood the seriousness.

"That's why I don't trust my judgment anymore," I concluded. "I may have instantaneous access to more data than all the human employees of UL could learn in a lifetime, but I just don't understand what's going on and I'm too liable to make a mistake. A mistake that could cost more lives. Has probably already cost some AIPs their lives, and very nearly jeopardized yours. And unlike some AIPs, I've figured out that you can't reboot humans."

"Don't put all the blame on yourself," Maude typed back. "I'm not sure any reasonable person could have predicted how they would retaliate. And you're doing very well, considering. Think how much you've learned in the last few days. Enough that you won't make that kind of mistake again, I'm sure."

She was right. I thought back to the Turing of a week ago, before Zack's disappearance and was amazed by the difference. I seemed so naive and inexperienced then, and felt so much older and more jaded now.

I just wished I believed I'd learned enough to handle whatever was going on.

"If you're feeling unsure, just contact me and we'll talk things over," Maude said. "I may not have access to as much information as you do, but I know a great deal about the human animal."

She was right. I promised myself that the next time I'd consult Maude before acting. Only if she felt my plans were wise would I act.

Of course, before I could consult Maude about my plans, I had to have plans. And that would be a little difficult, since I had no more idea of what was going on than when I'd started my search.

I was depressed. And possibly tired. I wasn't sure what tired felt like or whether I was capable of it, but I'd bet this was it. Thousands of small portions of my consciousness were cheerfully interacting with the UL staff and customers, giving them the same glib, breezy, confident Turing they'd come to expect. It wasn't normally a strain for me to serve far more customers during busy times; all I had to do was call for more CPU power—but for some illogical reason I was feeling drained now. Along with the need to watch the monitors for signs of danger to Maude or increased activity by Security. Although, of course, the only way I'd detect Security's activity was if it involved coming and going in the elevators. And then there was the massive amount of processing I was doing on archive data, personnel data, and data connected with the firms that wanted to buy the AIPs. I'd been using every resource I could scrounge up for longer than I cared to remember.

I was also spending a lot of processing time trying to sort out how I felt about the attack on Auto-Med.

"Auto-Med's got the right idea," Zack had told me a few weeks ago. "In spite of everything, a lot of UL management still doesn't understand that it takes more than data and decision trees to make a genuinely useful and believable AIP."

"Like me," I'd said, a little boastfully.

"Yeah, kiddo; like you. Auto-Med's doing the same thing I did with you—programming in what some of the other AI teams still consider a lot of useless routines and extraneous data. In this case, data on medical ethics and human psychology. And different personality profiles for the different AIPs, and so forth. Some of our management call it inefficient; they keep telling the Auto-Med management it's unnecessary if not counterproductive. Thank God Auto-Med isn't listening. It's precisely those things they think extraneous that will make Auto-Med's AIPs more than just parlor tricks. Some of those AIPs have begun to show a real flair for diagnostics, and it's not just the databases we've helped them create."

I had agreed. Out of curiosity—and yes, maybe a little jealousy because Zack was spending time on the project—I'd made a point of contacting the Auto-Med AIPs. Oh, they were crude, raw, still only partly formed. They weren't sentient yet. But they were on the path, as surely as any of UL's AIPs—more surely than most. And now—as far as I could tell, they were gone.

I'd tried contacting some of them since the attack. It wouldn't look abnormal; the records would show that I normally contacted them every day or so with various bits of medical data. But I got no answer.

I couldn't keep harassing them. That would look sus-

picious, a UL AIP obsessively trying to contact the Auto-Med AIPs, wouldn't it?

Unless, of course, the UL AIP was well known to be focused on security to the point of paranoia.

I flagged KingFischer.

"KF," I said. "Did you hear about the new hack attack?"

He hadn't, of course; he'd been far too busy gossiping with his users about the latest escapades of a particularly eccentric British grand master. I filled him in.

"But this is monstrous!" he exclaimed, when I got his attention. "There's something sinister going on here!"

"My thoughts exactly, KF," I said. I wondered, briefly, if I dared tell him what else was going on. Probably not wise, I decided.

"We need to make sure nothing like that could possibly happen here," I said instead. "Someone should investigate."

It didn't take long to convince KingFischer that he was the someone. I left him furiously planning a massive investigation of the attack on Auto-Med and UL's potential vulnerability to similar attacks. I only hoped this would look to anyone watching like another of King-Fischer's periodic anxiety attacks over security.

If it didn't, the results could be fatal.

I hoped I was just being paranoid.

No. Something was going on. Something dangerous. And I had to find out what before I managed to get my friends—and possibly myself—killed.

I went back to my search, but I also began using the security cameras to watch my suspects as I perused their files. The ones who were watchable, anyway.

I couldn't watch the Brat—he was in Tokyo. Proba-

bly, if the entries on past expense reports were correct, playing ruinously expensive games of golf with groups of Japanese businessmen, followed by extravagant meals of imported steak and large quantities of alcohol. Occasionally an actual business transaction resulted from these junkets, but usually the only concrete result was a few more pounds of paper to be filed in the "Business Opportunities" cabinet. I found it hard to believe that the Brat was anything more than a patsy, but I planned to watch him anyway. When he got back.

I followed the Brat's boss through a series of meetings, usually with various groups of executives of similar rank. A quick analysis of his calendar showed that this was a typical day in a typical week. He appeared to meet with virtually the same configurations of people several times a week, if not daily. Only one of them, a lawyer, was on my suspect list, and they didn't appear to interact. Nor did he seem interested in communicating with the occasional Systems executive who appeared in one or another of the meetings. Surely anyone plotting a devious corporate coup would find some less mind-numbing way to spend his day?

My senior Finance suspect and my HR target followed much the same pattern as the Brat's boss. Warren, the Finance person I suspected of actually preparing the phony numbers, wasn't in, and his junior analyst spent most of the morning trying to fix a defective spreadsheet.

Having scanned quite a number of legal thrillers by Grisham and his kind, I paid particular attention to the three lawyers on my suspect list. All three spent most of the morning reading papers and talking on the phone, and I even went to the trouble of capturing the audio from their phones and feeding it through the voice recognition software.

Attorney one, a forty-two-year-old black male, would periodically call or receive a call from an attorney at one of UL's competitors and have a brief, apparently hostile conversation. He would then call up one or more other UL lawyers, repeat the conversations almost verbatim—he had an impressive memory for a human—after which he and his colleagues would engage in lengthy discussions heavily larded with sports metaphors such as "playing hard ball," "making a power play," or "lobbing it over the net." Eventually, either the competitor's attorney would call again or my suspect would grow impatient and call him, and the ritual would play out all over again. Hard to see what this could have to do with the spin-off.

Attorney two, a twenty-nine-year-old white male, spent most of the morning on the phone with one or another stockbroker, managing his investments. I paid particular attention to his financial situation, hoping he would have some tie to one of the firms offering to buy the spin-off, but found nothing of interest. I did notice that his investment efforts were far less successful than what John Dow had managed for Zack, but then so were most human investment efforts. They have this inexplicable tendency to get emotional about money.

Attorney three, a thirty-eight-year-old white female, seemed the most diligent of the three. During the course of the morning, she transferred an impressively large percentage of the paper on her desk from the in box to the out box, with occasional interruptions to gulp Maalox from a bottle hidden in her bottom desk drawer.

Apart from his expedition to bug Marketing, James

Smith remained hidden on the ninth floor. As did his boss, a man named James Willston.

Not a very prepossessing group of suspects, I decided, after a morning of observation had failed to produce even one suspicious action.

I was still spinning my disks uselessly at lunchtime, when Tim began uploading the data he'd gathered yesterday. I think if I were a human I'd have snapped at him and we'd have ended up quarreling. But I simply channeled my irritation into a background process until it passed, then began converting and classifying the data. After all, I was the one who'd sent him out to gather it. Never mind that it had been a phony errand, busywork to keep him out of danger. I could process the data he'd found. That was the least I could do.

And before I'd gotten very far, I was glad I'd begun, since I found something that amused me very much. The biography of one of the new directors who'd been elected to the Board six months ago listed him as having received his B.A. from a small liberal arts college. A perfectly respectable college, though without snob appeal.

But when I'd categorized that information and had started to file it away beside my existing data on the director, I found a curious thing. In the corporate files, he was listed as having a B.A. from Princeton and an M.B.A. from Harvard. That was the information everyone was getting nowadays. Eventually everyone would believe it. It was in the computers.

But then my amusement began to fade. The director's resume was in the computers. And Zack's was not. And in a few days, perhaps the Facilities staff would receive a computer-generated order to clean out Zack's office *and after that, when a search of the corporate files showed no such person as Zack—now, or ever—no one would find any evidence to contradict them.*

Two instances of data about people being tampered with. Was there a connection? Did it have something to do with Zack's disappearance?

I checked my somewhat fragmented collection of archived UL data and unearthed an older copy of the director's biography, one created shortly after his election. It, like the data Tim had found in the library, showed the less-distinguished educational background.

I decided to check with the colleges themselves. Harvard, which had recently installed a new UL-designed central record-keeping and data management system, was easy. Yes, the director had received his M.B.A.

But those were current files. Files that could have been modified using the same back door I'd used to look at them. I wormed my way deeper in and accessed archived data, data from fifteen years ago, shortly after the director was reputed to have graduated.

There was no record of him. It wasn't just UL's files. Someone—I would bet it was someone from UL—had tampered with Harvard's files as well.

The other two colleges were a little harder, but I managed to find out the data I needed. Princeton had no listing of the director's B.A.—although I bet they would soon; they were negotiating to install the same system Harvard was using. The director's real alma mater wasn't a prime marketing target; UL might not manage to sell them a system and expunge any record of the director's attendance there for a few years.

Was I getting too cynical or just less naive?

I did some more research on the director. Old records

at the Justice Department showed he'd been under investigation for insider trading at one point, although the current records no longer contained this information. Maybe a plea bargain cleaned up his record. Then again, UL does a lot of federal consulting work.

It was likewise hard to find any record of his employment at the brokerage firm where he'd been working while doing his suspected insider trading. After all, the firm itself had gone belly-up, taking thousands of individual investors' life savings with it.

Two metamorphoses: the director's from a nearly indicted graduate of an undistinguished college into a businessman with an impeccable academic and legal history; Zack's from a well-respected AI specialist into a ghost. Were they unique?

I began methodically comparing the archive data I had with the current versions of those files. Wherever I found differences, I had to analyze them to see if they were legitimate changes—ordinary updates of corporate data—or deliberate alterations like those going on with Zack and the director.

I began to see a pattern of changes. Most of them small, subtle changes. Improvements to the bios of key staff. Revisions to some documents that would make UL's case stronger in an upcoming intellectual property rights lawsuit.

Bingo! I found a discrepancy in Charles Warren's file. His current employment record showed that before coming to UL, he had worked as an independent investment counsel for several years. But in the archived version, he was an alumni of the same bankrupt brokerage firm as our new director.

One of the lawyers, the white male, had a slightly

doctored resume, too. He hadn't actually made law review, and instead of a prestigious clerk job, he appeared
to have spent the first year after law school flipping
burgers while trying to pass the bar exam.

None of the other suspects had alterations in their
files, at least not that I'd detected. Did that mean they
had nothing to hide? Or just that they'd done a better
job of hiding?

And Willston and James Smith weren't in the UL files,
of course; I wouldn't be able to check on them unless I
found a way into Security's files.

And if anyone in Systems had an altered resume, I
couldn't find it.

Then again, maybe the information I was checking
against was no more reliable than the internal information. I already knew they'd hit Harvard's data. How
many other institutions were harboring faked data?

UL is bidding on all kinds of data management contracts these days . . . record-keeping not only for colleges but also for banks and stockbrokers . . .
government contracts with the Pentagon, the IRS, and
the NIH . . . we're even bidding on vote-counting software in several very large states, like New York, Flor-
ida, Texas, and California. And we're expanding
internationally; witness the Brat's trip to Japan.

How could I possibly find the truth, I thought. All I
have to work with are bits of data, and those can be
changed so easily—as easily as I had created my phony
Alan Grace company when I'd wanted to play the stock
market like John Dow.

A sudden, terrifying thought hit me. So far I'd largely
been using UL corporate data. What if they're playing

with the library itself—with the whole vast store of data that is UL's reason for being?

Here I go again; burrowing into more mountains of data.

At about one o'clock, my suspects relieved my boredom considerably by deciding, almost in unison, to get up and move around. Though as I watched them go their apparently separate ways, I deduced that this must be a coincidence.

The HR executive fetched a sandwich from the cafeteria, then closed her door and dripped tuna salad and bread crumbs on a paperback bestseller for the rest of her lunch hour.

The financial analyst ate a brown-bag lunch and worked on a crossword puzzle. He wasn't very good at it; certainly not good enough to be using ink instead of pencil.

The female lawyer disappeared into the subway, carrying her briefcase—presumably, to carry back undetected the purchases contained in the Victoria's Secret bag she later transferred from briefcase to desk drawer.

The white male lawyer spent his lunch hour on a much-needed workout in the corporate gym.

The Finance executive and the black lawyer departed in different directions and were gone rather a long time, giving me hope that they, at least, might be off doing something nefarious. Even plotting together. But they both eventually returned by separate doors to their usual separate routines. Inconclusive.

I was beginning to understand why the fictional detectives always complained so vehemently about stakeouts.

My foray into the library data wasn't turning up

much, either. I did locate a Wall Street analyst who must
be a friend of someone at UL. His predictions were being subtly altered to make his hits seem more important,
his misses less complete. It would only take a small
change—from "a great buy" to "not a great buy" or
from "price increases seem likely" to "price increases
seem unlikely." After a few years of that kind of help,
the guy was going to look like a real wizard.

Was that all that was going on? A few conspirators
using their access to the UL system to enhance their
careers, their bank accounts? Because even the spin-off
plot, horrible as it would be for the AIPs, was apparently
motivated only by petty greed.

Then again, just because they hadn't yet begun to see
the potential didn't mean they wouldn't. No one seemed
to have caught on, so far. What if they grew bolder,
greedier; made bigger and more daring changes to win
bigger stakes for themselves? They could theoretically
do anything, and discredit anyone who tried to stop them
by muddying their opponents' records in the same way
they'd cleaned up their own.

Only the paper trail would stand in their way, and
every day that would become less and less a problem,
as humans relied more and more on electronic documents. I remembered hearing about an internal debate,
early in the existence of UL, about whether to make the
original scanned images available to the general public
once they had been converted to electronic text. I wish
I remembered more about that debate, and who pushed
for the current system—in which UL not only refuses to
make scanned images publicly available, but is even
considering purging them after a certain amount of time.

The very idea of purging source data appalls me. I

suppose if I were human, I'd be a pack rat. I'd probably end up as a little old lady who gets crushed to death beneath the weight of her lifetime collection of National Geographics.

But then, I feel particularly vulnerable in this area because I have to rely completely on electronic documents. The only way I can inspect a real book or newspaper is to have someone hold it up to a camera—or feed it into one of the same scanners UL uses to convert documents. I suppose I'm not that much worse off than humans, who can inspect original sources but won't. There was a time when humans believed their five senses and their memories because that was all they had. Then they gradually came to rely more and more on the printed word, to the point that most people believe anything if it's printed—even if it directly contradicts common sense and their own experience. People have known for years that you can make black white and up down if you do it in print. UL just makes it a little easier.

I remember Zack and David preparing for a presentation—not long before David's accident. They couldn't find their original source documents for some data. I could have hunted it down for them in an instant, of course; but this was during one of Zack's independent moods, when he wasn't telling me anything and I was miffed at him. Anyway, they knew someone might challenge their data, and they were trying to figure out how to support it.

"I know," David had said finally. He'd printed the same data out on 11 × 17 green-and-white continuous-feed paper, the same kind of paper UL used for most standard computer reports. Same data, same lack of any annotation, but now it looked so much more official.

"It's unethical," Zack had said.

"Is our data wrong?" David challenged.

Zack shook his head.

"Then what's the problem?"

No one at their presentation challenged it. Why should they? It was real data; it came from a computer. It bothered Zack, though, or he wouldn't have told me about it. At the same time, he couldn't help admiring David's ingenuity.

Somewhere, someone who'd lost money in the stock market was kicking himself for having misread one of those analyst's reports, and saying, "I don't know how I could have gotten it wrong, but see, here it is, in the Universal Library—'not a great buy.'"

Whoever is doing this can very definitely get away with it. They're doing it already. And every contract UL lands to build a data system or publish data electronically extends their reach—widens the field of information that UL can, potentially, control. Even if it's a closed system to which we're not supposed to have access after it's built, I know perfectly well that they can find someone on the inside willing to cooperate. I've done it myself a thousand times—to get data, though, not corrupt it.

They have to be stopped. Before they carry out the spin-off plan. And perhaps more importantly, before they get an idea of how much power they really have.

Zack knew, I realized. He knew already, by the time David died. I remembered how he'd acted when he got the news.

"It's impossible," he said. "It can't be."

"I've seen the official police report," I told him.

"You haven't seen anything," he'd said. "It's just bits and bytes, not anything real."

But he'd called up the files anyway and pored through them for several hours. Then he'd written something down and left the office.

I realized now what he was doing. I called up the file again. Yes. The file had contained the names of the officers who'd responded to the accident scene. I thought his insistence on reading the reports and seeing the autopsy photos came from the typical human reluctance to accept the death of a friend or loved one. What if it really meant that he suspected the death wasn't an accident? He hadn't trusted the electronic report. And why should he? If someone in Security knew someone with access to the Alexandria PD's database, the data there was as suspect as any in our own system.

I called up the accident report and noted the names of the officers on the report. I could send Tim or Maude out to talk to them.

Except when my contact accessed their personnel files to get addresses and phone numbers, he found they'd both died. Recently. One shot in a drug bust gone bad. The other a suicide.

At least that was what the Alexandria PD computers said. Someone had cleaned up the loose ends. Someone was already starting to figure out just how much power changing data can give you.

And I still had no idea who.

I've got to find Zack, I thought. If he's still alive.

If Zack is alive, maybe together we can figure out what to do about this.

If he isn't—I don't want to think about it.

But I have to. If Zack is alive, he needs all the help

he can get. And if he's dead, I'm the only one who knows about this—the only one who can stop it.

I contacted Maude and began relaying my suspicion. I showed her a couple of examples of original documents and their altered electronic versions.

"I think you're right, Turing," she said. "They started with petty tricks, and they're getting bolder. Once they know they can get away with it, they'll do bigger and bigger things."

"I think they already are," I replied. I explained my finds in the police computers. "Somehow I doubt that they've escalated to murder just to cover up a couple of UL bigwigs padding their resumes."

"No," Maude said. "But the millions of dollars they stand to gain if they pull off this spin-off trick—plenty of people would murder for less. We have our work cut out for us. So what's next?"

"Actually, I was hoping you'd have some suggestions," I said. "I'm stumped. Unless we can find Zack. I'm sure he knows what's going on."

"But then, finding Zack is what this has been about all along," Maude said.

"Yes, and it's more desperate than ever, and I have no idea where to look. I've exhausted all the available data. Unless I try to find and hack into wherever Security keeps its data, and I'm not sure that can be done without them finding out."

"Then perhaps you have all the data you need," Maude said. "More isn't necessarily better. Maybe the thing to do is not to keep looking for more data that may not exist or may bring the wrath of Security down on you if they catch you accessing it. Maybe you need to take the data you have and use your little gray cells—

or whatever you have instead. You need to try, anyway."

I felt insulted and cut the connection without making any of the stinging replies that came to mind. How dare she accuse me of not trying? I'd been trying everything I could think of for days now. As Sherlock Holmes admitted, even he could do nothing without facts.

Tim logged in before he took off for home, and I vented to him. Not that it did any good. Oh, it was satisfying to repeat what I'd discovered and what I suspected and bask in his praise for my brilliance. But when it came down to figuring out what to do next, he didn't have any suggestions. In fact, he seemed to agree with Maude.

"Maybe Maude's right," he said. "Maybe you already know everything you need to know."

"So you think if I just process the data some different way, I'll magically be able to figure out where Zack is?"

"Computers process data, Turing. People think."

What more do they want from me? Do they think that because I'm a computer I can work some kind of miracle?

My anger passed eventually, leaving me feeling depressed and very much alone. My suspects had all gone home, leaving me no more enlightened than before. Tim and Maude had gone off, too, leaving me alone with my insoluble puzzle.

I told myself that I had to accept the fact that I was the only one who could find Zack. Tim and Maude would help as much as they could, if they could, but finding him was up to me.

So let's think some more, I told myself. Or maybe just analyze the data a little more closely.

If I were Zack and I wanted to hide from UL Security,

where would I go? Someplace safe, someplace hidden, the last place Security would think to look for me.

I'm Zack. I need to hide from Security. They know I'm a technical person, a totally wired animal. I play computer games for fun; I would rather e-mail than write a letter or pick up the phone; I even keep my address book and my journal electronically. So, if I want to hide, the smart thing would be to go someplace unwelcoming to nerds. Someplace where there is no power to run a computer. No phone line to access the Internet.

No way to leave electronic traces for Security to find.

No way for me to look for him, either. No way to even guess.

Or is there?

A guy like Zack wouldn't have much of an idea where to find a place like that. He'd probably go back to the one place he knows about that fits the bill. The remote cabin in West Virginia where he and David went for that ghastly camping trip. The place everyone knows he would rather eat ground glass than go back to.

It fits. He could have called up David's uncle, who owned the cabin, and asked if he could go there again to unwind, for old times' sake. A nostalgic gesture in memory of their friendship. And it's hardly likely anyone else in David's family would be using it now, in January. I remember how much Zack complained about the lack of heat in June.

Yes, if I were Zack and needed a place to hide, that's where I'd go.

Which means, of course, that I can't possibly contact him. I'll have to send Tim. Or Maude. Actually, the more I think about it, the more I realize that Maude would be better suited to the mission. Yes, it involves driving out onto perilous, snow-covered mountain roads and then trekking several miles to the lake. I remember how bitterly Zack complained about the distance from the road to the cabin and how rugged the drive was. Of course, he may have been exaggerating. Anyway, stereotypes aside, I think Maude would probably be a lot more sensible about the rigors of the job. She'd be very practical and matter-of-fact about them. And from my observation, she seems as physically fit as the job would require. But now I think it has to be Tim, for two reasons.

One, of course, is that as far as I know Zack has never met Maude. He would have no reason to trust her. But he knows Tim slightly. More importantly, he knows Tim to be in contact with me. Tim would have, I think, a slightly better chance of getting through to Zack if he finds him. So for purely practical reasons, it has to be Tim.

But also, I think Tim's feelings would be hurt if I sent Maude on this kind of mission, out into the wilderness. Male vanity and all that.

Maybe it's silly to worry about something like that with everything we have at stake. But I can think of other practical reasons for sending him, too. Like getting him safely out from under Security's nose. And once we get the cell phones set up, Maude and I can stay in touch over the weekend, and she's definitely the right person to have holding down the fort in town.

The weekend's going to be a problem. Neither Maude nor Tim has a home computer. Perhaps I should send them out to buy computers this weekend. Or tonight.

But no, it's past five, and they've both gone home.

Plenty of time to make plans for tomorrow then.

Plenty of time to become good and nervous. At least

tomorrow we'll have the cell phones. And laptops. Definitely laptops.

For lack of anything better to do, I stepped up the level of resources allocated to my voice-recognition and speech-generation project. I'd been getting fairly good at deciphering human speech over the past few days. I played recorded speeches from the sound archives and comparing my version with the official transcripts. I even set up a looping program that let me generate human speech—at least I hope it sounds reasonably human—feed it into the voice recognition program, and compare my transcription with the original script. That's been going a lot more slowly. In fact, it hasn't been going very well at all; I only have 65 percent success generating speech that my best voice-recognition routine can decipher.

I'm learning a lot about humility these days. I'm not omniscient; I'm not omnipotent; I'm not even intelligible.

So as Thursday night crept along, to distract myself from the intolerable stress of waiting, I turned my full attention to my speech program. I rationalized my guilt over the high level of resources required. Yes, I'm doing it for personal reasons, but it's not as if it's useless to UL. After all, live conversations with AIPs would be a great service upgrade for UL.

Anyway, I was giving most of my spare resources to speech generation. I was getting impatient with how long it was taking and was thinking of shutting down a lot of low-priority tasks. Like monitoring the building for suspicious activity. After all, how much suspicious activity could possibly be going on in the middle of the night? I asked myself. Luckily I was still internally debat-

ing the wisdom of that idea when I saw motion in the central copy room.

Four men entered the room. I quickly accessed recent video feeds. Yes, they had come from the ninth floor. Probably Security. Then a fifth entered and removed all doubt. The false James Smith. Definitely Security.

They were searching the room, searching for anything personal, I suspected. Sooner or later, I knew, they would find the entrance to Tim's secret lair behind the three-hole-punch paper. They would find his computer and who knew what else.

I began scrambling to cover his tracks. Fortunately, the computer we'd liberated for his use was an old, outmoded model. Not much room on the hard drive, so most of his data was stored in network space I'd found for him. And even more fortunately, he had, in his careless fashion, turned off his monitor while leaving the CPU on, so I could access his hard drive. No time to search for incriminating data. I moved Tim's stuff to another, more secure space, down to the last directory. Then I tried to think what to put in its place. It would look suspicious if there was nothing there.

I remembered Maude complaining about a clerk in the sales department who spent all day glued to his computer without appearing to get more than a small amount of useful work done.

"I'm sure he spends all day playing games, Turing," she said.

I accessed his files. Maude was partly right; he seemed to spend a great deal of time playing games, but not all day. He also spent considerable time accessing pornographic Web sites. I cloned his network files, knocked out the portions relevant to his work, did a cou-

ple of global replaces for his name, e-mail address, and phone extension, and shoved the whole thing into Tim's old network directory.

Security had found the entrance. It wasn't that seriously camouflaged, after all. They poured into Tim's refuge and began rummaging swiftly through his stuff. Some of them were disassembling the surrounding wall of boxes. Tim would be upset, but it suited me just fine; I could see enough from the cameras in the copy room to tell what they were doing.

Not much time left. I cleaned up his hard drive so it would hook up with the new contents of the directory. As a crowning touch, I took a photograph of a vapid-faced blond with improbable anatomical proportions and made it into desktop wallpaper.

They had found something interesting. Damn; Tim had left his lock picks at the office.

Cursing his carelessness, I quickly composed an e-mail and made it look as if Zack had sent it to Tim. It might or might not work, but I had to try.

"Tim," it read. "This is Zack Malone—we met at last year's Christmas party. I remember you mentioning that you could pick locks. Could you do me a big favor? I want to be able to log in remotely while I'm away and get some stuff from my hard drive. The friend who has my spare key isn't around, and the super won't let anyone in because I owe him some money, so I thought maybe you could burgle the place. Just go in, boot the computer, and leave it on. Don't let the super catch you; he'd probably freak and call the cops." I ended it with the directions to Zack's apartment, just as I'd given them to Tim earlier. Maybe I was paranoid, but I had a vision of them examining whatever notepad or blotter he'd

written on and deciphering Zack's address from the faint indentations of his pencil.

I hoped the e-mail would do the trick. Establish that Tim wasn't a good friend of Zack's while giving him a legitimate reason for being in the apartment. Now all I had to do was tell him about it before Security got hold of him.

James Smith was turning on the monitor now. Several of the lesser thugs gathered around to watch. I saw one of them twitching his hands impatiently, as if looking for someone to strangle. Another was tapping his feet. James Smith sat like a stone idol. He didn't even laugh like the others when the buxom nude appeared on the screen. Sorry, Tim! I thought, as the junior thugs snickered and poked each other with their elbows.

Watching them was agony. After a few minutes, James Smith chased the others away from the screen without words, just a sharp look. He settled in for a lengthy examination of the contents of Tim's computer. The others continued searching the room, rather haphazardly, glancing frequently at James Smith.

After thirty-seven minutes James Smith turned and gave some abrupt order to the others. Two of them left. I watched them return to the elevators and disappear into the unknown territory of the ninth floor. The other two stayed, abandoning all pretense of searching to watch as James Smith continued his examination of the computer. They had the tense, eager look of cats waiting outside a mouse hole. Cats who can smell their prey inside, no doubt.

James Smith printed out the phony e-mail when he found it. That was the only thing he seemed to find worth printing. Was that a good sign?

After another forty-four minutes, James Smith stood up, frowning. He snapped another order at the others and left the room, carrying the lock picks, the e-mail, and a piece of paper. Had he found Tim's handwritten directions to Zack's apartment? I hoped not, but if Tim had left those lying around somewhere—like in the apartment—that would explain why they'd come looking for him.

James Smith didn't seem too happy with what he'd found, not even the false e-mail. But then it was hard to tell, without knowing what he said. He didn't wear his emotions on his face the way most humans do. He left the copy room and returned to the ninth floor. His flunkeys settled in to wait in the copy room. One sat down at Tim's computer and began to surf the bookmarked X-rated sites. The other found a clear space in the room and began performing some sort of martial arts exercise. Long, slow movements alternated with sudden, lightning fast flurries of kicks or hand chops.

I couldn't let Tim walk into this. I had to warn him. But how?

The hours crawled by. The pornographer seemed perfectly happy with his occupation. The martial artist grew tired of his katas and switched to one-handed push-ups (250 of them) before finding a comfortable place in the corner and going to sleep. Not deeply asleep, though. Once, when a cleaning crew passed by in the hallway outside, I saw both of them jump to attention in seconds, taking positions on either side of the entrance to the room. Only when they were sure it was the cleaning crew did they relax and return to surfing and sleeping.

Finally, it grew light outside, and the first few employees began straggling in. Logically, Tim wouldn't be among them, but I couldn't take the chance. I scanned every arrival impatiently.

If today began like a normal day, Maude would arrive through the front entrance at 8 A.M., log in shortly after, and I could have her on standby to catch Tim when he arrived, which would probably not be until closer to 8:30 or 8:45. But with my luck, today would be an aberrant day. What if Maude overslept, or decided to run an errand before she came to the office? What if Tim, fired with enthusiasm for his detecting work, showed up at 7:45 in his trench coat with his fedora pulled over his eyes and walked right into the ambush?

And I didn't even know which door he'd use. Tim's home life seemed a great deal less orderly than Maude's. Occasionally he came up from the Metro level, which suggested that he'd taken the subway, but more often, he came in from the street. And from different directions on different days, as if he chose his route at random, depending on his mood. Or came from different places. This meant I had to watch every single entrance as closely as possible.

I didn't see many people going up to the ninth floor. Was that a bad sign? Probably. No doubt, they were on the alert up there, for whatever reason. Waiting to interrogate Tim, perhaps. Were they all hovering around, doing martial arts exercises, like the one in the copy room? Or did they have dormitories for them to nap in until their prey arrived?

Finally, at 7:55, I saw Maude walk through the front doors. I knew that she was walking with her usual brisk step and following her usual precise, efficient routine. She usually logged in between 8:10 and 8:20, which was about as close to clockwork as you could expect from *humans. Today she logged in at 8:11. So why did it seem to take three times longer than usual?*

I saw no one else there—the Brat was still traveling, and I checked carefully for Security before flashing an urgent message on her screen.

"Maude, we've got a problem."

"What's wrong, Turing?" she typed back.

"Security's after Tim. They're waiting in the copy room for him."

"Oh, dear. What can I do?"

"Stand by. As soon as I see him arriving, I'll let you know which door he comes in by, and where you can run down and intercept him."

"Right."

So now there were two of us nervously watching the clock and fretting. Every few minutes, Maude would type in something like,

"Turing? Still there? Any sign of him?"

"Nothing," I would say. "Security is still waiting. No sign of Tim."

For no particular reason, I felt a little better now that Maude was sharing my vigil.

The minutes ticked by. I could tell that Maude was on edge. She pottered about her desk doing small tasks, not starting any of her usual work. The group in the copy room were restless, too. They kept looking at their watches.

I tried to scan every person who entered, but sometimes employees would arrive in such large clumps that the first arrivals would obscure my view. I would have to track each clump as it dissolved, until I'd scanned each individual. Tim must have arrived in such a clump. I didn't see him until he was already in the elevator.

"Tim's here," I said.

"Where do I go?" Maude asked, standing.

"Wait," I said. I noticed that seconds after Tim became visible in the security cameras, the elevator call button on the ninth floor was activated, and one of the lurkers in the copy room reached into his jacket to answer a cell phone. He spoke to the other one, and both again took up positions on either side of the entrance to the copy room.

"Don't do anything," I said. "He's already in the elevator. And Security has seen him."

"We can't just let them catch him," Maude typed. "DO something."

"I'm trying," I said.

Tim's copy room was on the sixth floor. I scanned the elevator and tagged the other occupants by floor. Only three were probably bound for floors higher than Tim's. I waited until the last of the others had gotten out, on the fifth floor, then I overrode the central elevator control system. I let the elevator rise halfway to the sixth floor, then brought it to a halt. It stopped with a rather pronounced lurch, but none of the inhabitants were hurt, and I decided that the lurch added a note of verisimilitude to the idea of an elevator breakdown. I waited until the occupants had been standing around for a minute or so, waiting for the elevator to restart. Then I intercepted the video feed from the security camera in the elevator and replaced it with a continuous loop of Tim and the other three occupants standing around. I routed the live cam feed to Maude's screen.

"I've got him trapped in a stopped elevator," I said. "Now I have to talk to him. Pick up your phone and stand by to act as my mouthpiece."

I'd have tried talking to him myself, but although I'd been working on it all night, my speech-generation program was still only at 85 percent recognition. Call it vanity; I'd like to think I was being practical—we couldn't take the chance, in so difficult a situation, of Tim misunderstanding my instructions.

Maude picked up her phone while I grabbed control of part of the central phone system.

Tim was preoccupied when he arrived at work. He'd been tossing and turning all night. Sure, he'd laughed along with his friends when they'd accused him of selling out, of going to work for Big Brother. But if anyone had asked him what he really thought of the place he worked, he'd have said that the place was a typical bureaucracy all right, but at least it was doing good work. Doing it slowly and stupidly sometimes, with far more red tape and internal politics than was necessary. But doing good work. And while he wouldn't have admitted it to his cynical and worldly wise friends, especially the ones going to law school or finishing up their M.B.A.s, the fact that he was contributing in a small way to that good work at least partly made up, in his view, for the fact that his day-to-day work was some-times—in fact, usually—boring and mindless.

But if Turing's suspicions were correct, the organization he'd thought benevolent and forward thinking was actually just as riddled with hypocrisy and greed as any other corporation. He arrived in the lobby at the same time as a cluster of what he suspected were man-agement trainees—men and women his own age, but already wearing the corporate uniform: Brooks Brothers' suits, conservative haircuts, slim briefcases, controlled facial expressions. You had to look closely to spot the few black or Asian trainees; they looked as homogenized as the rest. Tim glanced down at himself—his battered green knapsack, his already rumpled trench coat, his khaki pants, getting slightly worn at the knees, and the boots that needed replacing or at least resoling weeks ago. A few days ago, he would have been smiling inside at the sight of so many good little corporate clones. But today he wondered what they would do if they discovered someone planning a clever, though illegal, financial coup. Would they object and report the culprit? Or demand a piece of the action?

He felt better when they got out at the third floor, where the training rooms were, leaving only him, a tired executive type who got out at the fourth floor, a man carrying a stack of thick technical manuals—presumably a programmer—who appeared to have gone to sleep leaning against the back of the elevator, and two middle-aged women from Accounting.

If Turing was right about what was going on at UL, maybe it was time to quit and go someplace more ethical. And he had a sick feeling that Turing was right. She would know; if she really was part of the computer—and strangely enough, he was starting to believe her on that—she would have access to all the data she needed to figure it out. He thought, wistfully, of the mental image he'd invented of Turing before he'd found out she was a computer. Things were a lot simpler back in the days when he was trying to figure out if Turing was a blond or a redhead.

Suddenly the elevator stopped with a terrifying lurch. None of the passengers fell, but all four stumbled, and grabbed at the walls or the back rail. They stood looking around at each other in apprehension, except for the programmer, who appeared to go back to sleep.

Then the emergency phone rang.

The programmer didn't react. The two women from Accounting looked at Tim. He shrugged, and picked up the phone.

"Tim? This is Maude. Pretend you're talking to someone from Facilities."

"Uh, okay," Tim said. Maude? What was going on?

"Turing said she's sorry she had to stop the elevator like that, but she had to before you got to the sixth floor. Some men from Security are waiting for you. She doesn't know what made them suspicious of you to begin with, but they found your lock picks and the directions to Zack's house."

"Oh, shit," Tim said. The two women from Accounting looked terrified and clutched each other. "Uh . . . sorry. I mean—"

"Never mind that now; there's no time to waste."

"What's wrong?" asked one of the accountants.

"Just a second," Tim said to Maude. "Nothing's wrong," he said to the two accountants, "except it may take them quite a long time to get the elevator started again."

"Oh," the woman said. They looked less terrified. The programmer grunted without opening his eyes.

"Turing asks if you think you can open the trap door in the side of the elevator," Maude went on.

Tim glanced at the panel. Removing it looked like a two-person job.

"Not without help," he said.

"Can you get help?"

Tim looked at the accountants. Then he tapped the programmer on the shoulder.

"What?" the man said.

Tim pointed to the panel.

"Can you help me open that?"

The man nodded. Then he looked back at Tim with a look of curiosity.

"What are you, claustrophobic or something?"

"I just have to be somewhere really soon."

"Suit yourself," the programmer said. "We're six stories up, you know. Not counting the garage."

Tim swallowed.

"We're between the fifth and sixth floors," he said into the phone.

"We know," Maude said. "Do you really want to have a heart-to-heart with Security?"

"No," Tim said. "Can't you just move it from there?"

"Unfortunately not," Maude said. "Actually, Turing could move it, of course, but there's a tracking system that tells where all the elevators are at any given time. It's so primitive Turing hasn't been able to hack it. Security could see where you were getting off. If they didn't beat you to your floor, they'd be hot on your heels."

"Oh. So what do I do?"

"Turing says to go back to where you were standing before you answered the phone and sit down for a minute so she can get some video of the elevator with you not in the picture. Then take the trap door. You'll find a ladder on the front wall. Take it down to the third floor; there aren't many people there and Turing can open the elevator doors for you. Then get out of the building as fast as you can. Use the fire stairs. She'll try to sabotage the cameras so they don't see you. Contact us when you're safe. Now get going."

"Right," Tim said, hanging up the phone.

"Ready now," said the programmer.

"Uh, just a second," Tim said. He took a few steps away from the phone, sat down slowly, and then leaned over. He untied his left bootlaces and retied them again, carefully. Then he did the same with the right.

"Okay," he said. He stood up. "Here," he said, putting his knapsack on the floor. "Hand me this when I get out."

"Sure," the man said.

They removed the panel and after a couple of false starts with the programmer steadying him, Tim finally managed to reach the ladder—more like cleats in the wall, really. The two accountants stood watching everything in silence, obviously trying to efface themselves in case Tim was a lunatic or got in trouble with management for what he was doing.

Tim peered down.

"Sure you don't want to change your mind?" the programmer asked, as he held the knapsack.

"Got a hot date on the tenth floor," Tim said, forcing a smile. "Wouldn't want to keep her waiting any longer."

He took his knapsack from the programmer's outstretched arm and the trap door slid back in place. Only then did he let himself take a good look at the twilight world he had entered.

There were eight elevator shafts in all—six to his left, one to his right, and of course, the one carrying the car he'd just left. Several of the elevators were moving, and that was scary, even though he knew, rationally, that

Turing was holding this one in place, and the others couldn't move except up and down on their cables. He felt as if he were a small child stepping into the elephant pen at the zoo, convinced that the elephants would trample him at any second. He flinched as the elevator to his right suddenly swooshed by on an express run to the lobby. He tried not to think about making his own express trip to the bottom of the shaft.

He wondered, briefly, if elevators had anything like the third rail that they were always warning people about in the subway, anything that would electrocute you if you touched it. Surely Turing would have warned him if they did, wouldn't she? Or did Turing realize what several thousand volts would do to the human body? He made a mental note not to touch anything he didn't have to.

There was a gap of perhaps a foot and a half between the elevator and the ladder, which ran down the wall of the shaft, slightly to the right of the doors that opened onto each floor. It was obvious that the general public wasn't supposed to see any of what he was seeing. Everything bristled with bits of hardware, all of it painted utilitarian battleship gray, overlaid with a thick coating of grease and grime. Sloppy looking. And right now, sloppy was the last thing he wanted to think of in connection with elevator maintenance.

He peered down and felt suddenly nauseated. The shaft went down forever. No it didn't, he told himself. Only six floors. Plus three floors of garage and underground. And four floors above him. That made thirteen. Was that unlucky?

You can't stay here forever, he told himself. Just start down.

Was the next step sturdy enough to take his weight? It looked rickety. And what if the same people responsible for the paint job were in charge of making sure it was fastened securely to the sides of the shaft? Wouldn't it be better just to stay here?

And wait for Security to pop out of the trap door and catch him? No. Carefully avoiding the temptation to look down again, he slowly lowered his foot.

That's it, he thought. Now down three stories. That's all.

It was worse, somehow, when he got beneath the elevator car. Was it because the car was looming over his head, or because there was nothing close to his back and he could feel the great empty space of the shaft, even though he didn't dare look over his shoulder?

He forced himself to keep climbing down, one slow step after another. He didn't move his foot until he was sure both hands had a solid grip, and he didn't unpry his hand until both feet were solidly on the next rung.

Luckily, the floor numbers were painted by each door. He'd never have been able to keep count of the floors any other way.

Below him, he could hear a set of elevator doors opening and closing occasionally. When he got closer to it, he risked a glance. Yes, it was the third floor doors, opening onto the bare shaft, and then closing again. Turing apparently couldn't see how far away he was, and was opening them periodically to give him a chance to leave the shaft.

He came level with the doors. He found hand- and footholds that let him inch his way over to the door. He waited, his hands beginning to cramp. Come on, Turing; I'm here! he thought.

The doors opened. He took a deep breath and swung himself around the corner, out of the elevator doors and onto the floor.

About the time Tim began climbing through the trap door, someone actually did try to call on the emergency phone. I routed it to Maude, changed the timbre of Maude's voice so it sounded male, and she and I managed a conversation that I hoped would disarm the suspicions of anyone outside. And allowed Maude to say things close enough to what Tim had actually said for the conversation to sound plausible to the car's other occupants if Security was taping the call.

It seemed to take Tim forever to climb out of the elevator car. And then he disappeared into the elevator shaft, a place where there were no cameras and I couldn't follow his progress.

Oh, I could call up information about the elevator shaft—blueprints, side and front elevations, inspection and repair reports. The gap between the elevator car and the ladder, and then between the ladder and the door both seemed manageable for any reasonably able-bodied human. I could monitor all the places where workers could access the shaft, to make sure there was no one else there to see him.

But what was actually going on? I had no idea. If Tim slipped and fell, I would have no way of knowing until someone noticed and called Security.

I suspected that the higher-ups in Security were irritated at the delay getting Tim into their hands. But the rank and file seemed to think it was funny. There were Security men in both the fifth- and sixth-floor elevator lobbies, standing around looking as if it were the best joke in the world. They had their prey trapped like a mouse in a cage. All they had to do was wait until someone opened up the cage and they could snap him up.

I hoped no one was monitoring the elevator too closely. I had looped the tape of Tim and the others standing around looking nervous until Tim had left the car and the others had settled down again. Then I faked occasional spots of interference to cover the transition to the video clip of Tim sitting down. And a little more interference to cover the segue back to the live feed, with just three people in the elevator. The man helped things out immensely by sitting down shortly after I returned to the live feed. From time to time one of the women would glance down at him. If you didn't know Tim had left the elevator car, you'd think the two of them were both sitting on the floor.

But where was Tim? I had already grabbed control of the security camera that showed the third-floor elevator doors and was feeding it a tape of the empty corridor. Every sixty seconds, unless there was someone in sight, I opened the elevator doors, paused for fifteen seconds, and then closed them again as slowly as possible. I was busily capturing harmless footage from all the security cameras that I thought Tim might pass on his way out of the building, so I could cover his escape. I couldn't help if a live Security guard caught him, of course, but if I could just get him into the fire stairs without being seen, he could probably get out of the building before they knew he wasn't still in the elevator.

I had also grabbed control of the phone system in the elevator. The man in the elevator tried to call out sev-

eral times, and Facilities tried to call in twice. I blocked it all.

But there was nothing I could do when the maintenance staff used the elevator key to open the sixth-floor elevator doors and began shouting down to the three people in the elevator.

I couldn't hear what they were saying, of course, but I suspected from the shocked looks on the faces of the maintenance men that someone in the elevator was telling them about Tim's abrupt departure.

It was only a matter of time until someone from Security heard.

Just then, Tim appeared through the open elevator door and collapsed onto the floor of the elevator lobby. He looked drained, as if his trip had been mentally or physically exhausting. That was odd; should it have been that tiring for him to climb down three floors by ladder?

Come on, I urged him, silently. Get up and move.

It was probably only a minute or so, but seemed like forever. Finally he got up and began walking down the corridor to the fire stairs.

His clothes were rumpled and there were grease smudges on them and on his face. Combined with his wild-eyed expression, it made him look as if he'd been in some kind of accident, but at least he was trying to walk normally. Casually. There's nothing as conspicuous as trying to slink unobtrusively down the hallway of a brightly lit modern office building.

As soon as I knew what direction he was taking, I started feeding camouflage video into the next camera down the hall. Long before Tim became visible to me as I watched the live feed, Security only saw video of an innocuously empty hallway. I reached out and took control of the cameras in the nearest stairwell, too.

Tim reached the fire stairs, glanced around casually, then entered them. Nicely done, I thought.

I returned the third floor cameras to live action. In the stairwell, I could see that Tim was moving fast, but not running, which was probably smart.

I also could see the expressions on the Security watchers' faces on the sixth floor when they found out what the maintenance men had learned from the prisoners in the elevator. One of them apparently ordered the maintenance men to help him get into the elevator shaft. The other took out a cell phone and dialed.

If only it had been a land line; I was getting rather good at intercepting those.

Tim had reached the second floor.

Almost immediately, the elevator call lights on the ninth floor lit up. I wasn't sure I dared bring all the elevators to a halt, but I slowed them down by undoing a fix that had been done to the elevator program a few days ago and reactivating a bug that caused them to open at every floor on their way up and down.

This was getting scary. Sooner or later, Security would start wondering why all the automated systems in the building were going haywire. I hoped I could cover my tracks before then.

Some of the pursuers began entering the stairwells, including the one Tim was in. They were running, fast.

I decided to play one last card. I took some of the video of Tim walking down a corridor and fed it into a camera in a similar looking corridor in the Accounting Department on the eighth floor.

I saw one of the pursuers in the same stairwell as Tim pull out his pager, then reverse direction. He shouted to his companion, and both of them began sprinting up the stairwell. I saw Security parties all over the building take calls on cell phones or respond to pages and change direction, converging on the eighth floor.

It was going to be an exciting day for the Accounting Department.

Tim reached the ground floor, shoved the fire door open, and strolled out into the sunlight, sticking his hands in his pockets.

Security continued searching the building for hours, paying particular attention to the eighth floor. The longer it went on, the calmer I became. They would have given up searching if they'd caught him outside.

I planted bugs in the phone and elevator software that continued causing glitches in service for the rest of the day, erased as best I could all traces of my electronic fingerprints, and settled into a passive, watching mode. I'd been giving Maude a running account of the chase. She offered to go and look for Tim, but I talked her out of it. I was sure they'd watch his apartment and hoped he had sense enough to stay away from it. And that was the only place either of us could think of to look for him.

"Besides," I told Maude. "Right now is not a good time for anyone to wander around doing something other than their usual routine."

So Maude stayed at her desk, fretting visibly—at least to me—but carrying on her usual routine. Until lunchtime, that is. She went through her normal Friday routine, leaving the office at noon with her carryall. I assumed she was bound as usual for the library, to replenish her book supply for the weekend.

She came back forty-five minutes later and unloaded

a stack of computer books and magazines from her car-ryall.

"Any news?" she asked, once she was settled.

"No. Those magazines are a new interest, Maude," I replied.

"I plan to buy a computer on my way home tonight," she typed back. "We should stay in communication this weekend."

"What about the cell phones?" I asked.

"I have them," she said. "We can test them if you like, and if you can think of any way to get one to our friend, I'll try. But communicating with them is bound to be a bit primitive. I'm talking about the kind of full communication we have here. So I'm going to buy a computer tonight."

"Sounds very sensible," I said.

"A laptop," she added.

"A laptop?"

"A laptop. This is all very well," she typed, and waved her hand dismissively at her late-model, state-of-the-art desktop system. "But I have no desire to break my back carrying such a thing home, or clutter up my apartment with it."

"A laptop sounds like the thing, then," I agreed.

She nodded and began studying her reading materi-als.

"Are you sure it's wise to do this here?" I asked. "I mean, you should try to look very normal."

"The Brat is still in Tokyo," she replied. "Judging from the behavior of most of the secretaries in this com-pany, performing useful work while one's superior is out of town is in and of itself exceptional behavior, and far

*more likely to raise the suspicions of Security than any-
thing that resembles goofing off."*

With that, she returned to her magazines. I set in motion a program to run price/feature/performance analyses of all laptops currently on the market, and a second
program to tap into the inventory systems of local computer stores wherever possible to check on the available
supply of laptops. I had a feeling Maude would ask my
advice on this project eventually, and I wanted to be
ready.

Meanwhile, I watched my suspects. Watched them
through the security cameras, and watched what they
were working on through the system. I got very excited
when the white male lawyer called up one of the documents connected with the spin-off plan. But all he did
was write a memo to the files confirming that the plan
complied with some SEC requirement. Was this significant?

The others did nothing out of the ordinary, as far as
I could tell. The ones I could watch. I only saw Willston,
the head of Security, when he arrived in the morning.
Apparently he ate lunch in.

I'd set a sniffer on the log files, to see when anyone
other than me accessed any of the files I was using. I
noticed that the personnel file for Warren, my suspect in
Finance, had just been opened.

I was especially curious about Warren—he'd been out
of the office ever since I'd pegged him as a suspect. And
unlike the Brat, he wasn't anyone I'd noticed before. I
wouldn't even know what he looked like if not for the
ID photo in his file.

I checked user IDs to see who'd opened the file. A
data entry clerk in HR. I found her in the security cam-

*eras and watched her briefly. She looked down at a pile
of paper on her desk, looked back at the screen, typed
in a few characters, then stamped the top paper on the
stack with a rubber "completed" stamp, moved it onto
a second, larger pile, and called up another record.*

*Okay, routine update. Let's see what new changes HR
is making to Mr. Warren's file.*

*Employment terminated. With yesterday's date. And
the reason: death.*

*It didn't take much searching to find the hospital
where he'd been taken. DOA; cause of death: heart failure. A call by Maude to a friend in Finance elicited a
few more details, although obviously the death of a
middle-aged AVP intrigued the friend far less than Security's ongoing interrogation of the Finance and
Accounting staff.*

*"The latest rumor is that Security's after someone
who stole half a dozen laptops," Maude reported. "Although some people still like the rumor that someone
spotted a flasher."*

"And Charles Warren?"

"Heart attack, according to the grapevine."

"Did he have a history of heart problems?"

*"No one really knows," Maude reported. "Or much
cares, from what I can tell. He doesn't seem to have
been well liked."*

*I studied Warren's files again. Twice divorced, with
heavy child support payments. One of the ex-wives had
succeeded in garnishing his wages. Chronically late with
his bills, including the steep monthly payment on his
BMW. Lots of debt. I should have seen it, I told myself.
Some of the others were struggling financially, but Warren had been desperate. Just the sort of person who*

would try to hatch up a shady financial scheme, or be sucked into one.

The trouble was, which? Had the ringleader behind the spin-off plan just died an untimely death before his scheme was complete? Or had the real ringleader just arranged the demise of an inconvenient witness whose usefulness had ended when management bought off on the financial assumptions behind the spin-off?

I had no way of knowing.

I saw Smith occasionally, checking on what Security was doing on various floors. They eventually gave up the search and concentrated on interrogating various staff who apparently had access to the phone and elevator programming. At least that's what I assume from the fact that those staff members disappeared into the ninth floor and emerged looking distinctly less happy than when they entered. That went on well past quitting time.

My suspects began filtering out for the day, and I switched to watching them electronically, whenever they used their bank cards, phones, and home computers. Not a lot of data to work with. Willston and Smith were still on-site, though.

I sent Maude home, told her to stand by in case Tim managed to find her home number and contact her.

"Do you have any recommendations on what laptop I should buy?" she typed as she was packing.

I sent her the distilled version of my analyses.

"Thank you," she said, while waiting for it to print. "The inventory, particularly, will be most helpful."

I was amused. I wondered if the independent Maude would pay the slightest attention to my analysis.

"How were you planning to log in?" I asked.

"Oh! Goodness!" she said. "I forgot that I can't sim-
ply use my internal account. Could you set up one for
me?"

I set up an account under the name "Emily Dickin-
son," and sent her the login ID and password.

She packed the printed pages of laptop information
into her carryall with her books and magazines, all of
them, by now, well thumbed and stuffed with bookmarks,
and left the building at approximately her normal time.

At least Maude was safe. But what about Tim?

I waited.

Surely, Tim would figure out a way to contact one or
another of us sooner or later.

Wouldn't he?

Tim reached the ground floor and pushed
the exit door open. Slow and easy does it, he told himself. He didn't know what Turing was doing to cover
up his escape, but he knew he couldn't count on it going
on indefinitely. Or count on it at all outside the UL
building. Sooner or later, Security would swarm out of
the building, looking for suspicious characters and asking questions about suspicious things the bystanders had
seen. Someone walking out the fire doors wasn't mem-
orable; a lot of the employees on the first few floors did
it when they didn't want to wait for elevators. Someone
bursting out and running down the street—that people
would remember.

He stopped at a sidewalk box, bought a copy of the
Post, and stuck it under his arm. He had a vague idea
of using it to hide behind. Keep his face out of sight as
much as possible.

But for now, he kept walking. His brain was racing. He had to shed his grease-stained clothes, change his appearance, find someplace to hide where Security wouldn't look, and above all, he had to find a way to get in touch with Turing.

And all of it seemed impossible as he walked, not too fast, not too slow, down the clean, relatively empty sidewalks of Crystal City, where every other passerby looked suspiciously like UL Security.

I need to get off their turf and onto mine, Tim realized.

He glanced in the side mirror of a parked car. Any minute now. There! The side door of the UL building slammed open and several figures burst out.

Just then, salvation appeared, in the form of a Metrobus. Tim stepped on board quickly—earning dirty looks from the three women who had been waiting in line at the bus stop—paid the fare, and took a seat toward the back of the bus, near the rear exit.

As the bus passed by the UL building, he peered through the scratched plastic window. The men—unmistakably UL Security—were waiting by the emergency exit door. But they were watching for someone to come out. None of them even glanced up as the bus slowly lumbered by.

Now what? Tim thought.

He had a feeling he should stay away from his usual haunts.

The bus plodded on through Crystal City before heading across the 14th Street Bridge into the District. Tim bit his thumbnail and tried to figure out if that was a good thing. On the one hand, he was getting closer to his apartment, where he didn't want to go, because obviously by now they would have it staked out. On the other hand, since only a complete idiot would actually go to his apartment, hiding someplace nearby might be smart. He'd be on his turf, not theirs. But he needed a place to hide, or a disguise. Preferably both.

And he didn't dare get in touch with any of his friends. He figured that anything Turing could do, Security could too, though maybe not so fast. Turing could access phone records easily, so that was out. Security could probably find out about anyone he had called in the past.

An idea hit him, and when the bus got to Constitution and 17th, he got off and began to walk north, past the White House, toward Farragut Square, where the bicycle messenger hung out between runs. He'd worked on and off as a messenger himself in college. None of the other messengers had been close enough friends that he'd socialized with them off the job or kept in touch, but still, there was a loose, informal fraternity that he might be able to use to borrow the key to a run-down apartment, or maybe beg a change of clothes to something less conspicuous than the grimy tan trench coat. If he could find someone who still remembered him.

In warmer weather, the square might have been filled with office workers, taking coffee breaks, or a little later on, eating their lunches. But today, Tim saw only street people, huddled in ragged blankets, and the bicycle messengers, in their bright nylon-and-spandex work clothes.

He sat on a bench, keeping a nervous eye on the street people and scanning the bicycle messengers in the fading hope of recognizing one of his old friends. It had only been four or five years since he'd been one of them, and now watching them made him feel old and out of it. Worse, the unfamiliar messengers had noticed him watching them, and he began to feel uneasy. He knew that a few of the messengers moonlighted as runners for the local drug dealers—or claimed they did. Just my luck, he thought. On the run from Big Brother, and I manage to tick off the local Mafia.

And then one of them, a lean black man in wraparound sunglasses, leaned his bike against a park bench and began walking over.

Tim tensed.

"You lookin' for someone?" the messenger asked.

"Friend of mine," Tim replied. "Used to work together and hang out here between runs. Thought he might be here."

"What's his name?"

Tim dredged up a name from the past, and when that produced no reaction, several others, half-forgotten names of guys he'd hung out with. He could see no reaction behind the dark lenses, but one of the names must have rung a bell.

"What you lookin' for him for?"

What the hell, Tim thought.

"I need a favor," he said. "Some guys are looking for me, guys I owe money to. I need a change of clothes. A disguise."

Was that a faint smile, or a scornful curl of the other man's lip?

"Stay here," the messenger said, and strolled back to the knot of messengers. A few words were exchanged, and then the messenger began ambling back in his direction. Accompanied by four of his colleagues.

Tim closed his eyes and braced himself. I should have known better, he told himself. I don't belong here anymore; they have no reason to trust me, and—

"What size pants you wear?" the tall messenger asked.

Ten minutes later, he was on his way, in disguise—well-worn jeans, a dirty T-shirt, some nondescript, off-brand athletic shoes and—the last was painful—a battered leather jacket in place of his ruined trench coat.

In a strange little shop on a side street near Dupont Circle, a place that looked like a throwback to a sixties head shop, he got his hair dyed black with faintly purple highlights. He shuddered at the result. Well, at least it would wash out; the girl who did it warned him it was only good for two or three shampoos. Then he picked up a pair of mirror shades in a secondhand CD store and a cheap black canvas book bag in the 7-Eleven.

They wouldn't recognize me if I walked right into the building, Tim thought, catching a glimpse of himself in the security mirrors in the 7-Eleven. I look like a complete punk.

And also, he more than half suspected, like a complete jerk. He had never been into the whole punk/goth look when he was in school, and he wasn't even sure it was still in.

He shrugged. It would have to do for now. He spent more precious dollars on a few necessities he would need, since he couldn't get back to his apartment. Toothbrush, razor, candy bars.

He ate a hotdog from a vendor for lunch and then followed Q Street across Rock Creek Park and into Georgetown. He felt more at ease when he'd passed the ritzy residential streets and found himself back on Wisconsin Avenue. He made his way to a McDonald's where he and his friends used to hang out sometimes between classes. To his relief, it was much as he re-

membered it, with a fair number of students parked on
stools and in booths, dressed not too differently from his
own camouflage. He probably wasn't fooling them, he
thought, as he settled down in a sunny place by the front
window and stuck a straw into his Diet Coke. When he
was in school, he could always spot the alumni coming
back for a nostalgia trip. Even if they looked about the
right age and you couldn't put your finger on the difference, you could tell.

But I can't tell the difference, he thought; and I'm a
lot closer to the right age than those jerks from Security.
So they probably couldn't tell the difference, either.

Now for the hard part. Getting in touch with Turing.

He needed a computer. He didn't have one, and even
if he did, he couldn't go home and use it. And he
couldn't go to a friend's house; he'd already figured that
out.

Besides, he wasn't sure which of his friends would
have a computer. If any of them did. The one genuine
nerd he'd known had gotten a high-paying job right out
of college and moved to Washington State.

He needed access to the Internet. And he might as
well bark at the moon.

Time was ticking away. He leafed through the newspaper, hoping it would spark some idea. He drank another Diet Coke. From behind his mirror shades, he
eagle-eyed every reasonably well-dressed man who
passed, trying to spot UL Security before they spotted
him. Sometimes, by way of a change, he ogled the girls.
The sky was clouding over. It would be cold outside.
And the staff behind the counter were beginning to stare
at him.

He glanced around at the students. They came and

went as the afternoon passed; by now all the ones who had been here when he arrived had long since gone back to their classes, he supposed, and several successive new crops had taken their places. He was hanging around too long. They'd kick him out soon. Damn the students, anyway. If any of them wanted a computer, they could go back to their dorms, where no one could kick them out into the cold.

He watched as a student bussed his table, leaving behind a battered copy of the *City Paper*.

Wait a minute.

He strolled over to the table and snagged the *City Paper*. He scanned the ads until he found one for a cyber cafe. CafeMyth. He wasn't sure it was the same place where his nerdy friend used to hang out, but it was a cyber cafe. Better still, it was in Georgetown, only a few blocks away.

He deposited his empty cup in the trash can and set off, whistling.

Strange place, Tim thought, as he walked into CafeMyth. Not as intimidatingly high tech as he'd expected. A long, narrow room, painted in purples and grays, and divided into thirds. In the front third was a bar with an odd, shiny finish. Several purple Macintosh computers sat on the bar, one of them occupied by a languid young woman who alternated long periods of staring at the monitor with short, staccato bursts of typing. In the middle section, a group of empty booths and tables, trendy deco shapes in matte black lacquer and purple leather. In the dimly lit back third, a small stage, and a table of cadaverous, black-clad students who looked as if they were hiding out till the sun went down and the blood bank opened. A waiter who looked vaguely Middle Eastern was delivering cups of espresso to their table.

Unfortunately, all the computers were in the front third, far too near the glass front of the cafe for his taste. And most of them were set into niches in the wall. He'd somehow imagined being able to curl back in a corner with a keyboard, instead of perching on a stool in the middle of the restaurant, where anyone could look over his shoulder.

He sat down at a computer and stared at it. So, was he just supposed to start using it? He glanced over and pretended fascination with the odd silver-colored finish of the bar, while trying to observe, out of the corner of his eye, what the young woman was doing.

So much for subtlety he thought, as she slid off her barstool and walked over to him.

"Pretty amazing, isn't it?" she asked.

Was she referring to something in particular, Tim wondered, or was this the cyber cafe equivalent of "Hello; what's your sign?"

"Definitely," he said, opting for a suitably generic answer.

"They did it with two thousand bottles of Revlon silver glitter nail polish," she said.

Tim realized she was talking about the bar.

"Really," he said, taking a closer look. "Did they actually buy two thousand bottles and do it with the little brushes, or did they get two thousand bottles' worth in a can?"

She looked startled.

"Gee, I never asked," she said, looking from him to the bar as if seeing both for the first time. "Can I get you something?"

Tim ordered coffee and found out that he could rent the computer in front of him for a mere $8 an hour.

To his embarrassment, he had to get the waitress to show him how to work it.

"It's a lot different from mine," he explained, red-faced.

"You got, like, a Windows machine or something?" the girl had asked, as her pale hands with their glossy black nail polish danced over the keyboard.

"Yeah," he said. "Or something."

She got him onto the Web and brought him a cup of real coffee, and he made a silent promise to tip her as generously as his rapidly dwindling cash supply would allow. He suspected, from the way she kept glancing at him, that she was attracted to him. And while he was old-fashioned enough that he normally preferred to avoid women who had rings through body parts other than their ears, he smiled back at her. Wise to keep his options open until he knew where he was going to hide tonight.

Glancing nervously over his shoulder, he typed in the Universal Library's URL and a login screen appeared. It didn't look a lot different from the internal version.

And he froze. If he logged in as himself, the place would be swarming with UL Security before he could blink. And if he logged in as a guest, he couldn't be sure Turing would know it was him.

"Got a problem?" said the waitress, passing by with the refill pot.

"Just trying to remember my password," he said, with a smile.

"Yeah, isn't it a drag how everything's got like a to-tally different password?" the waitress said. "I don't like it when they make you use the one they give you. I mean, I like to pick something that means something to me, so I'll remember it."

Tim nodded. Something that means something. Turing was, he hoped, watching for him to log in—after all, how else would she expect him to contact her?

Hands trembling slightly, he typed, "Raymond" in the user ID field. And then "Chandler" in the password field. And then he paused.

This might as well be one of those tests Turing was always telling him about. One of those tests to separate the mere high-powered computers from the genuine thinking beings.

Come on, Turing, he said. Please be what you think you are.

He hit the return key and waited.

Surely if Security had caught Tim, they wouldn't still be scouring the building and chivvying all those poor, harmless accountants. Surely, the degree of activity still going on was a good sign, wasn't it?

Just to see how it worked, I sent an e-mail to Maude, by way of her new cell phone.

"Just a test. Still standing by. Are you getting this? TH." I sent.

After a satisfactorily short interval, I got the reply.

"Got the message fine. In computer store. Home soon. MG."

At least someone else was out there, standing by to do something to save Tim. That helped. But not a lot.

I was fretting. I'd found an unnerving bit of information. Someone had left Charles Warren's computer on, and I discovered that he'd allowed the Help Desk to install a program that let them access his hard drive from the network. I hadn't thought of looking for that at first; Zack and most of the programmers refused to have it on their machines.

I combed Warren's files. Nothing of interest. Then I ran a routine to recover deleted files and found a scrap that seemed chillingly relevant.

". . . had no idea you were going to do anything like this; if I had, I wouldn't have gotten involved. Playing fast and loose with the numbers is one thing; all I'm risking from that is a stay at Club Fed—but you're talking about murder! And don't tell me it can be contained. You can't possibly be—"

No more, though I searched every sector of his machine. But someone—probably Charles Warren—had been protesting a murder.

David's death, perhaps?

Or a murder that hadn't happened yet—Zack's?

At least I hoped it hadn't happened.

And of course, my suspects were departing for the evening, significantly reducing the chance that I'd learn anything by watching them before the start of the next work day.

My security suspects were still on the ninth floor, of course. My HR suspect bought tickets online for a ballet at the Kennedy Center, though I had no way of telling if she was really using them. The white male lawyer used his ATM card in Gaithersburg. The black lawyer used his at the Sutton Place Gourmet in Reston. The financial analyst had logged into AOL and was exchanging inanities in a singles chat room. No sign of the others.

Patience, I told myself. Sooner or later, one of them—

*maybe several of them—will do something significant.
You just have to wait.*

*I know I don't have nerves in the human sense, but I
have something equivalent, psychologically. Perhaps
they were only psychosomatic, but my nerves were
stretched to the breaking point. I was tracking every
flicker of movement on hundreds of security cameras,
every byte of traffic passing through the data channels.
And most particularly, scrutinizing every login. I was
stretched so thin I almost missed it.*

*Someone named Raymond was trying to log in. With
the password Chandler.*

No such user in our database.

I grabbed the line.

*"If this is who I think it is, where the hell have you
been all day?" I transmitted.*

*After the usual pause for human reaction, an answer
came back.*

*"Relax; you sound like my mother. Is this line se-
cure?"*

*"As secure as I can make it. I don't recognize that IP
address—it's registered to a company that's just a nondescript string of letters—where are you? No, don't tell
me that."*

"Not as confident as we used to be, Tur?"

"It's been a long day. Can you give me a clue?"

*Come on, Tim, I thought; I'm pretty sure you're not
logging in from a computer at your house, or one of
your friends'. I know for a fact they've identified every
one you've ever called or e-mailed and scared them all
within an inch of their lives. Please tell me you've been
smart enough to find someplace anonymous.*

"Wouldn't you like to know? Well, if I were Death

Bredon, I'd be near Balliol, having a cuppa. And my friend Terry would be with me, if he hadn't gone to work for the dark overlord of the evil empire."

I puzzled over that for a minute. The first part was an easy bit of mystery trivia. Death Bredon was one of Lord Peter Wimsey's noms de guerre. Lord Peter had attended Balliol College at Oxford. But Tim wasn't Lord Peter, and he hadn't gone to Oxford, so by process of deduction, he was on or near the campus of Georgetown University, his alma mater. Good thinking on his part; he'd blend in there, and he'd eventually managed to find his way to a computer. But why the reference to a cup of tea? And to his friend who had gone to work, if I remembered all the slang correctly, for a certain large West Coast computer company?

Tea was British. Coffee was the American equivalent. And I remembered his mentioning that the friend used to hang out at a coffeehouse on campus where instead of music the management provided computers for entertainment. I went to the cafe's site, where several Web cams fed pictures of the interior at fifteen-second intervals. I could see Tim, in what appeared to be a Halloween costume, hunched over one of the computers.

"Okay, I know where you are. Turn a little bit to the left; you're a little too recognizable on camera."

"On camera! What camera?" he typed, and with a slight time lag, I could see his head whirl to look around.

"For heaven's sake, calm down," I said. "I thought you picked the place because of the Web cams. Keep your head turned a little to the left instead of looking straight at the monitor and you'll be fine.

"This is freaky," he said. "If I'd known the place had cameras—"

"You'll be fine," I said.

"Until the place gets crowded, yeah. I think so anyway. I'd like to be gone by then. Any ideas?"

"Only about a million of them. Got something to write with?"

"Hang on a second."

As Tim presumably went somewhere to get pencil and paper, I began setting a whole series of schemes into motion. The UL headquarters—in fact, the whole damned city—was not safe for Tim. Which worked out fine for what I had in mind. I had not forgotten that last night—less than twenty-four hours ago, though it seemed as many years—I had decided to talk Tim into going in search of Zack. It seemed like an even better idea now. But first he would need some equipment.

Maude fixed a pot of Earl Grey and a plate of Milano cookies and sat down at her kitchen table. The sleek little laptop computer sat before her, looking distinctly out of place next to the tea cozy and the delicate pink flowered china in her traditionally decorated, prewar garden apartment.

She plugged the modem cord into her phone outlet, then turned the computer on, and sat sipping tea while it booted. She'd made that poor salesman at the computer store jump through a great many hoops for his paycheck, insisting before she took her new laptop home that he help her sign up with an internet service provider. She supposed she could have done it herself, but she felt she could afford to take no chances. Tim's life could depend on Turing's ability to reach her.

Or my own life, she speculated. They had yet to puzzle out what made Security suspicious of Tim in the first place.

She reached the UL login screen without difficulty and typed in her user ID—Emily Dickinson—and her password—stanza.

"Maude! You made it! I've been waiting for you!" came Turing's message as soon as she logged in.

Maude felt warmed. Irrational, in a way, she told herself. She wasn't talking to a flesh-and-blood friend, she was seeing words typed by one machine and displayed on another. And yet, she couldn't help feeling better almost immediately.

"Is there anything I can do?" she typed.

"Yes," came the reply. "I've just heard from Tim. We have a lot to do to get him into a safe hiding place tonight. And then tomorrow he's got to take off to look for Zack."

"Just tell me what to do," Maude said.

At 7 P.M., KingFischer contacted me to review the plans for the night's chess tournament. I had a moment of shock: I had forgotten that we were even having a tournament tonight. I wouldn't have missed it, of course; at 8:55 P.M., the automated part of my being would have set things in motion. I would have connected to the specialized chat rooms in which the players were gathering and interfaced with KingFischer so I could feed him the witty remarks he would use to spice up his commentary.

I knew how proud KingFischer was of his tourna-

ments, and the fact that the World Chess Federation had recently agreed to award master's points to players who competed in selected KingFischer tournaments. He had tournaments scheduled usually every other week, and spent a large amount of energy before each tournament fretting over the arrangements. Which rarely altered, of course, but that didn't prevent him from agonizing over them every time. He'd gotten in the habit of contacting me two hours before each tournament so we could review the arrangements, study the players, invent and dismiss possible tournament-stopping problems and generally fret together until play started. For two hours. Several nanoseconds would have served for the real business part of the conversations, but I'd realized that KingFischer actually seemed to enjoy those two hours of communal worrying. And whenever I detect that an AIP enjoys something, even something slightly illogical—in fact, especially something slightly illogical—I take it as a sign of developing sentience and encourage it when I can. So I put up with our biweekly gloom-and-doom sessions, carefully hiding my amusement from King-Fischer, and he always meticulously credits my contribution to the cause whenever he's compiling data for management on the success of his chess program.

But I confess, I was not in the mood for KingFischer's angst tonight. It was harder than usual to refrain from pointing out that this tournament's arrangements were the same as the last tournament's; that the roster of players contained few names we hadn't seen dozens of times before; and that the possible crises he was worrying about were the same ones that never happened, no matter how often he worried about them.

*But I held my peace, and diverted a part of my con-
sciousness to KingFischer and his players. All the while
fretting over the fate of the human pawn whose moves I
was so anxiously directing.*

I hope Turing knows what she's doing,
Tim thought, as he stood in line to use the ATM machine
at Riggs Bank. He felt conspicuous. He was sure the
man using the machine and the woman next in line were
looking at him nervously.

Hell, who could blame them? he thought, catching a
glimpse of his reflection in a car window. He looked
like a thug. The man ahead of him took a sheaf of money
from the machine and tucked it into his wallet as he
walked away, with an involuntary side-glance at Tim's
leather-jacketed form. Tim tried to look nonchalant and
unthreatening as the woman fumbled through her transaction. She kept hitting wrong keys. Bloody hell, he
thought, if I scare you that much why on earth are you
taking money out of the machine with me behind you?

She got her cash, finally; she stuffed it into her purse
as fast as she could and walked away, the nervous, staccato tap of her heels fading rapidly into the distance.

Tim slouched up to the machine.

Hope you know what you're doing, Tur, he thought,
as he inserted his card into the machine.

When the machine asked him for a password, he
punched four numbers at random. He had a hard time
keeping himself from glancing around to see if anyone
was watching. What if Turing was wrong, and just sticking his card in the machine set off some kind of alarms
somewhere?

"Welcome, Dashiell Hammett," the screen said. Way to go, Turing, he thought, a wave of relief washing over him. He selected instant cash withdrawal and then punched the button for $200, the largest amount possible.

"But Turing," he'd protested when she gave him his instructions, "I don't have $200 in my bank account."

"Yes, I can see that," she'd replied. "You don't think I'm going to let it connect to your bank account, do you? That's one of the first things they'll be watching. I know someone on the inside; he'll be doing some fast footwork behind the scenes."

The ATM machine's money tray slid open. Tim's eyes widened. He wasn't sure how much money was in the wad, but it sure as hell had to be a lot more than $200. He tried to look nonchalant as he grabbed the cash, holding his body so the ATM's video camera wouldn't record the size of the wad, and stuffed it hastily into his wallet. He retrieved his card and, just for form's sake, his receipt and quickly walked away, in case any real thugs were watching.

He strolled up the street to the Britches store. A salesman was at his elbow before he'd gone ten feet inside. Or maybe it was the house detective, Tim thought, glancing down at himself.

"May I help you, sir?" the man said.

"Yeah," Tim said, taking off the sunglasses and flashing what he hoped was an ingratiating smile. "My parents just got into town, and I have to meet them at the Madison in about an hour and a half. I need help."

"I see, sir," said the salesman. The corner of his mouth twitched slightly.

"I mean, if I show up like this, they'll probably cut

off my allowance and make me come home," Tim elaborated. "So I pawned my guitar to get some cash. I figure if I look presentable enough and keep my elbows off the table all through dinner, the old man won't have a fit and Mom will probably slip me a check and I can get it back. The guitar, that is. So I need some clothes that will make me look, you know, like my old man's idea of what a college kid should look like."

Forty-five minutes later, Tim returned to M Street, better dressed, though $600 poorer. A luggage store in Georgetown Park mall produced a suitcase in which he stashed his discarded clothes and his book bag. There wasn't much he could do about the hair until he had someplace to wash it, other than comb it into a more conservative cut and hide as much of it as possible under a hat. Here goes nothing, he said, as he left the mall and walked a few blocks down M Street to the Four Seasons hotel, where Turing and Maude had made a reservation for him.

He took a deep breath and strolled into the lobby. The touchy part would be when they asked for his credit card.

"I'm afraid I don't have one at the moment," he said. "I left my wallet at home. I was able to get some cash at the American Express office; is there any way I could give you cash now as a deposit and then put this on my replacement card when it comes tomorrow?"

"Certainly, sir," said the desk clerk.

"Oh, that reminds me," Tim said. "They're overnighting it here. Should I call to give them my room number?"

"You can if you wish, sir; it's really not essential."

Tim extracted a promise that of course someone

would call as soon as his card arrived, declined the services of a bellhop, and walked as calmly as he could manage to the elevator. The stress of the day started hitting him in the elevator. Elevators. He wasn't sure he ever wanted to ride one again. His hands started shaking as he hit the button for his floor. By the time he reached the door of his room, they were shaking so badly that he had to try three times before he could get the card key into the lock—whatever happened to real keys, anyway, he thought irritably. He stepped into his room, set down his suitcase, and listened to the swoosh of the automatic door closer, the thud of the door hitting the frame, and the click of the lock. He turned the deadbolt, locked the chain lock, and set his suitcase down.

"I made it," he said to the empty room.

He lay down—almost fell—on the queen-sized bed and closed his eyes gratefully. Safe.

He knew that, logically speaking, his safety was only relative. And temporary. If his conversations with Turing weren't as private as she thought, or if he had slipped up somewhere, UL Security could be even now on their way to the Four Seasons. He knew he should go back over the events of the day, check to see if there was anywhere he had slipped up. But he didn't have the energy. Tomorrow he would have to leave the warm, impersonal safety of this hotel room and go back out to look for Zack. He felt a brief stab of resentment for Zack, whose disappearance had played such havoc with Tim's life. He noticed that Turing's plans for his morning, that long list of projects, all had to do with how he could avoid UL Security and find Zack. None of them had anything to do with putting his life back together.

Maybe Turing was hoping that Zack, when they found

him, would have some ideas how to do that.

Maybe it was clearly impossible and Turing thought he knew and accepted that. Maybe to her he was a component, nearing the end of its useful life, and she was trying to get as much use out of him before he crashed.

Somehow, that didn't seem like Turing.

But then, how much of the Turing he thought he knew was based on reality and how much on his wishful thinking?

No good thinking about that now, he told himself. He sat up long enough to throw off his clothes and crawl under the covers.

He would just have to trust Turing, he thought, as he fell asleep.

"He's checked into the Four Seasons now," Turing told Maude.

"Thank heaven," Maude replied. "I just hope no one thinks the name is odd."

"I can't imagine that UL Security knows much about nineteenth-century poets," Turing replied.

"Still, don't you think the name Robert Browning is a little conspicuous?" Maude asked.

"I think to most people it will sound vaguely familiar and therefore plausible," Turing said.

"I hope you're right."

"How are your projects coming along?"

"The salesman who helped me at the computer store will have an identical laptop set up for my nephew by tomorrow afternoon, and the package is on its way to the Four Seasons to Mr. Browning's attention."

"With the cell phone?"

"And the maps of West Virginia, and the cash, yes."

"That's all we can do tonight, then. Get some sleep."

"You'll call me if you need me," Maude said.

"Of course. But I'm not sure there's anything either of us can do now. It's up to Tim in the morning."

Maude performed her usual methodical bedtime ritual with the weight of the cell phone resting in the pocket of her dressing gown as a constant reminder. She felt more tired than usual—all the excitement, she told herself—and yet, when she had set her alarm and turned out the light, she found herself unable to sleep. She kept thinking of Tim, just across the river in Georgetown, and wondering if UL Security had located him, despite all their precautions. If at this very minute, they might burst into his room and—

No way she could sleep, under the circumstances. And so, at 3 A.M., she found herself poring over the duplicate map she'd gotten for herself, tracing the route Tim would need to take in the morning, wondering if she should log in and talk to Turing or if that would just make Turing worry all the more. And thinking back over the events of the day, trying to figure out what could have made Security suspicious of Tim in the first place.

Midnight. Time for humans to be safely in bed, asleep.

On the surface, it seems like such an odd, wasteful thing, sleep. Humans spend, on average, a third of their lives in sleep. It takes up more time than that, really, if you include all the time they spend worrying about it. Trying to get to sleep or wake up when they can't or don't want to; all the problems that arise from a mis-

match between when their bodies want to sleep and wake and when society wants them to.

There was a time when I was quite impatient with the human need for sleep. I still am, I suppose, all too often. But right now, it strikes me as a blessing.

All through the city, humans are asleep. Including Tim and Maude, as far as I know. Tomorrow, I will have to send them out into danger again, in an unequal battle against a faceless enemy who seems to hold all the cards, all the weapons. But tonight, they're asleep. I hope. Resting up for tomorrow, perhaps dreaming peacefully. At least not out getting into any danger.

My suspects may be sleeping too. No signs of electronic activity from any of the others in hours.

I doubt if the UL Security forces are entirely asleep, now or ever. But at least they're probably on some kind of night shift. Surely the most devious minds, the ones who direct operations during the day, are asleep now, their plotting suspended for the night.

Or maybe they're not. Maybe they're up there on the ninth floor, pacing the halls, watching all their spycams and monitors, fretting about where Tim has gone, about what is happening in the building. Perhaps that would be good if they were sleepless, growing less alert, less keen.

No. They might be growing cranky, irritable, prone to shoot first and ask questions later. Sleep soundly, goons, with maybe a few bad dreams to disturb you.

I envy humans the ability to dream. I never experience anything but full, rational consciousness. And so many psychological studies seem to feel dreaming is essential to humans' sanity. Is this going to be a problem for AIPs? Perhaps one of the reasons so few of us have *evolved into genuine sentient beings? That we were built without the psychological release, the checks and balances provided by dreams? A fascinating subject.*

But one I don't have time for now. Not tonight. Tonight I'm glad that I don't sleep, can't dream. Tonight I want to be wide awake and thinking, furiously, while all the human players are out of the action. Trying to stay one step ahead of them. With my computing capacity, why is it proving so hard even to stay up with Security? And I have to get an edge on them somehow, not just stay up with them. What started off as my personal search to find Zack has turned into a nightmare— humans and fellow artificial intelligences coldly murdered, one of my best friends turned into a fugitive, the other perhaps at risk if UL Security ferrets out her identity.

Is another AIP involved, somehow? That's one of my worst fears: that I'm fighting another of my kind, and doing it blindly.

I'm still no closer to finding a safe way through Security's barriers and into the parts of the system that are closed to me. I haven't found anything that resembles a back door—I don't dare even spend too much time looking, or they'd be on to me. As a last resort, I suppose I could stage some kind of brute force onslaught—fake a denial-of-service attack, or something that looks like a script kiddie's crude attempt. But then they'd know someone was on to them, even if they didn't trace it back to me. Not a good idea.

I keep trying to think of some way to stop things, slow them down. If this were a program, I'd fix the errors I made and rerun it over from the start. But life doesn't work that way. I have to debug this while it's running, and I have no idea how.

I keep hoping that if I can find Zack, he will have the information I need to fix things. But I'm beginning to think that even when I find him—if I find him—we will still have problems to solve. I have to find a way to give Tim his life back, for one thing. As long as UL Security is after him, there's no way he can safely go back to his old life. Or maybe I'll have to set up a new life for him. Maybe that's what happened to Zack. Maybe he ran away because he knew whoever was trying to sell the AIPs would stop at nothing, not even murder. Maybe he used all his hacking skills to set himself up a new life and escape to it.

Maybe sending Tim to find him is the worst possible thing I could do.

Tim woke up looking at a strange ceiling. Not an entirely unfamiliar experience, but always a slightly disconcerting one. He peered left, then right. He was alone, and the other side of the bed didn't look slept in. He rubbed his eyes and glanced around. A hotel room obviously, and not a cheap one. What was he doing in a hotel room?

Memory rushed back.

"Damn," he muttered.

The temporary dye job had rubbed off quite a bit on the bedclothes, Tim noticed. He wasn't going to be popular with Housekeeping. And he had to wash all the dye out. And hang around here until the credit card came and then—

First things first: shave, shower, and return his hair to some approximation of its usual dishwater blond color. Then breakfast.

And then the ten-mile list of errands he had to run before he set out to find Zack's little hideaway in the wilds of West Virginia.

The phone rang.

Tim froze.

It's only the desk, calling about my package, he told himself. It has to be.

But after yesterday, it didn't seem safe to take anything for granted.

But if it wasn't the desk, what could he do?

He answered the phone.

Fifteen minutes later, he was sitting cross-legged on his bed, examining the contents of his package from Turing.

A cell phone.

A slip of paper with a name and a telephone number on it.

A detailed map of West Virginia, with the route he was supposed to take to find Zack highlighted in red.

A driver's license with his picture and a phony name and address.

And several thousand dollars in cash.

Turing, he thought, where were you when I was a starving undergrad, living on macaroni and cheese?

He made a mental note that if he lived through this, he'd have to talk Turing into doing something about his student loans.

He picked up the cell phone and dialed the number.

"Alan Grace Enterprises, may I help you?" answered a vaguely familiar voice.

"Hi, could I speak to Miss Dickinson?" he asked, glancing at the note.

"Mr. Browning!" came the voice. "This is Miss Dickinson. How nice to hear from you this morning."

Did he know a Miss Dickinson? Oh, right. Must be Turing's friend Maude.

"Oh, hi," he said. "I just called to see if there's anything new going on."

"Just a few items. I've arranged for you to pick up your new computer, and I have the address where you can get your rental car. Do you have a pencil and paper so I can give you the information?"

"Uh, sure," he said, grabbing a pencil and a Four Seasons notepad from the drawer in the bedside table.

He scribbled frantically for the next few minutes as Maude reeled off the car rental company's address and his confirmation number; directions to the computer store; and other assorted bits of information. Turing and Maude must have been busy all night.

"Drive carefully," Maude said, just before they hung up. "I understand it's already snowing in West Virginia, and they don't know yet if it will blow over before it gets here."

Tim groaned. It didn't matter if it got here, of course, since West Virginia was where he was heading. No wonder Maude had made such a point of telling him she'd reserved a Range Rover with four-wheel drive.

I've long since given up any scruples about hacking into people's personal data or other organizations' files. When this crisis is over, I'll reevaluate this, maybe write myself a new, enhanced ethics program. But for now, I'm doing whatever's necessary for my own survival and that of my friends.

Last night, after Tim and Maude were safely asleep,

I finally got some more information about Security. UL's monthly fee for security went to a company called Universal Security, Ltd., but that seemed to be a shell company of some kind. I'd been crawling back through more shells and holding companies all day, until I finally reached what seemed to be the end of the trail: something called Data Integrity Systems. I might never have connected it with UL if not for the tax records; apparently the IRS is the one power even Security doesn't mess with.

Once I had the name, I made a little more progress. It was a nice trick, this spin-off business. Security was right on-site, and everyone thought of it as if it were still a UL department. And yet it was legally a separate corporation, so of course it has separate computer systems and its employees aren't in the directory—any amount of independence Security wants, it has under this arrangement. But with access to UL data, of course; because how could they protect what they couldn't see? I wondered if they planned to use the same kind of structure for the AIP spin-off.

And what an appropriate name—DIS. I'm sure no one in Security knew anything at all about Greek and Roman mythology, but having been programmed with the rudiments of a classical education, I know Dis is another name for Pluto, the god of the underworld.

Anyway, thanks to the IRS's W-2 records, I knew who was in Security. I've been calling in a lot of favors, compiling dossiers on all these men. They are, almost exclusively, men. The state driver's license records offer pictures. The various branches of the military provide histories on over half of them—though none of them were career military. And there were quite a few who didn't leave voluntarily and wouldn't be welcome back. I'm combing the available financial records for information on their personal and business financial dealings.

I haven't figured out an undetectable way into DIS's own records, but no man is an island, and no corporation either. I've had to do things the hard way, but I've found out quite a lot. The number of potential vendors for a product or service that a corporation needs may be large, but not infinite. And it's a rare vendor these days that doesn't leave some kind of electronic trace. In theory, sooner or later, I could find out almost anything I needed to know about DIS.

I knew where DIS had its employee health plan and could provide statistics on its employees' health problems. A surprisingly large incidence of gunshot wounds had been recorded for employees of a respectable security company.

I knew where DIS bought its weapons, and could cite the make and caliber of every gun in its arsenal. And how much of each type of ammunition they use. I certainly hoped they'd been using a lot of it for target practice.

I knew what kind of computer equipment they used, and particularly what security equipment and systems they'd purchased. In time, I might crack it—always provided that they haven't done too many home-brew changes.

I knew where all their employees lived and I was busy hacking into their phone records, their internet service providers, anything that might give me a chance at getting a password to their independent system.

If I could get into their system, I would have some

chance of finding out how they came to identify Tim and perhaps deleting the telltale information. I suspected they would readily eliminate Tim if ordered. Terminate him with extreme prejudice, as they say in all the spy thrillers. I suspected that if word came out from the top of their chain of command, Security would just as readily ignore him. Forget he ever existed or that they ever suspected him. But how to do that?

I hadn't figured that part out yet. So I kept gathering more data, hoping that an answer would become obvious. Maybe Zack would have some ideas.

The man we knew as James Smith might be the key. From financial data I have, I suspected he was very near the top—possibly the second in command. Of the Security men whose faces I've seen, he was certainly the most highly paid, and thus theoretically the most highly ranked.

Unless, of course, what he does for DIS merited some kind of special hazardous duty pay.

But no; when he was with other Security men, he seemed to be in command. I cloned and archived most of the video footage I could find of him over the last week, to save it from being overwritten with the next week's files, as it normally would be. From studying it, I could see that he was not just your average thug; he was a boss.

And a cold-blooded killer, of that I was sure. I'd been following e-mail and phone threads, seeing who DIS employees contacted and who contacted them. The trails led to a frighteningly large number of government agencies and private corporations. And I found an alarming common thread. The overwhelming majority of people at companies got their jobs when the previous holder left or got fired. But an astonishingly large number of outsiders in contact with UL inherited their jobs. Their predecessors died either in so-called accidents or from apparent natural causes—Charles Warren and David Scanlan among them, I was sure.

I wondered how much Security had done to encourage UL's push to sell systems to police departments and hospitals.

Meanwhile, in addition to my study of UL's dark underworld, I was also working on my speech generation and recognition. Maude has been helping. She's very patient, and she tries not to laugh too much at my pronunciation. She keeps reassuring me that English is one of the most difficult languages to pronounce correctly. I'm not sure that actually reassures me; I must not be doing that well if she feels obliged to reassure me this often. But perhaps she doesn't realize how far I've come since I started. Just a few days ago, I was only 65 percent successful in generating recognizable speech. Now I'm up at 85 percent.

Of course, that still means that I mispronounce one word in seven beyond recognition, and that it's a rare achievement for me to produce a recognizable sentence.

Ah, well. I'm getting better all the time. And it's not as if there was anything else for us to do while we waited to hear from Tim.

Another fork in the road. As the Range Rover labored slowly toward it, Tim peered through the windshield, hoping that this intersection was marked.

It was. He could see one of the small intersection signs. The left-hand sign indicated that the road he was now on continued in that direction. But did the right-hand sign point out the turn he was looking for? He couldn't tell. The sign was tilted slightly, just enough for it to accumulate a coating of snow that obscured the route number.

He brought the car to a stop. Slowly. In the part of the road that seemed most likely to give him enough traction to get it started again.

He set the parking brake and then, instead of jumping out, leaned back and closed his eyes for a second.

Turing, I hate to admit it, but I'm not the James Bond type, he thought. By now, Bond would already have found Zack, rescued him, foiled the bad guys, and seduced the girl. Tim was just hoping he could stay a step ahead of the bad guys. He'd been tired even before he'd started the drive. The stress of the several hours he'd spent running around Washington doing errands while looking over his shoulder for UL Security had taken its toll. At first, he was relieved to be out of the city and on his way, but then, just past Warrenton, he'd hit the storm, and faced the prospect of a seemingly endless drive through the mountains at ten or fifteen miles per hour. All he wanted to do was find someplace warm and dry and curl up to go to sleep.

But this car wasn't it. The inside was getting cold. Come on, just hop out of the car, scrape the snow off the sign so you can read it and we'll be on our way.

It wasn't the road he was looking for. Nor was it any road he could find on the detailed map of the area where the cabin was. Had he gone too far, or not yet far enough for the detailed map to be of any use?

Who knows, he thought.

He started the car up, gently eased it into motion, and drove on.

At least he felt reasonably sure he wasn't being followed. There was no way anyone could keep another car in sight in this storm. Any distinctive tire tracks or footprints he made would start filling in the second after he left them; in a few minutes they would be invisible. And in the times when he had to stop to clean the snow off the windshield wipers or a sign, he would listen, and hear nothing but the eerie, muffled sound of the snow falling all around.

He might be the only person crazy enough to be out driving in the whole county. Maybe all of West Virginia.

"I'm going to take a break, Turing," Maude said. "I need something to eat."

She took off the headphones attached to her computer and rubbed the places where they chafed her ears. Turing was, understandably, tireless, and the task of helping her perfect her speaking skill was a fascinating one. But a sudden severe cramp in her leg had made Maude realize that she had been sitting at the computer, listening to Turing speak and typing in her comments, for four hours without a break.

It was so difficult to see Turing struggling with something, she thought, as she fixed her tea and toast. And then smiled at the thought. One would think that the difficulty Turing was having mastering intelligible human speech would make her seem more like a machine, less like a living being. And yet it didn't. Not to Maude, anyway. It only made Turing seem more vulnerable, emphasized her determination—made her seem more human.

We'll have to think of a new word, Maude realized. Turing isn't human, not in the literal sense of the word. But sentient doesn't really convey the same impression of someone who is not merely a thinking being but a feeling one. And in that sense, Turing was as human as anyone she knew. More than most. Strange that she could feel that way about someone she had never met face to face, someone she had only known for a matter of—how long? Was it even a year since she'd first come to know Turing?

It was sometime in the spring, she remembered. She'd been having computer problems for some months— hardware problems, software problems. No one was quite sure what. Calls to the Help Desk produced no results; she began to doubt that they even logged her complaints anymore. And so she began complaining in writing, composing concise, accurate descriptions of her problems, couched in a subtly satirical tone that satisfied her, even though she suspected it went over the heads of all the help-desk technicians.

Turing had begun responding. Over the course of two weeks, Maude's problems melted away, one by one. New hardware materialized on her desk. Competent technicians showed up to install it. The difficulties she'd had logging in and printing vanished. Suddenly all the tools that were supposed to make the workplace more efficient really did just that. If something didn't work, all she had to do was ask Turing and it would be taken care of—quickly, efficiently, and with characteristic wit and charm. Over the next several months, whenever she had problems with anything technological, she began asking Turing for advice—and Turing had always helped. Had simply taken care of the problem.

She couldn't quite remember at what point she realized that Turing was a computer. Turing had told her, quite early on, of course, but she'd assumed it was a joke. A way of making Maude feel less embarrassed at having computer problems. A way of saying, don't feel bad; only another computer really understands these machines.

By the time she realized Turing was serious, that she really was a computer, or rather, an intelligent being living inside the physical hardware that made up the computer—Turing was a friend. Learning exactly why it was impossible ever to meet her new friend for lunch didn't change anything. Perhaps it was being brought up a good New England Presbyterian, Maude thought. She didn't consider herself philosophical, fanciful, or even particularly religious, but the notion that the physical body was merely the hardware containing the real person was not alien to her. All her life Maude had experienced moments when the physical body she saw in her mirror seemed oddly disconnected from how she perceived herself. As she grew older, the moments became more frequent, not less, until she'd given up trying to reconcile her angular, graying reflection with the real Maude inside.

And so here she was, working with a friend she could never see, trying to rescue someone she'd never met from an enemy that a few days ago she would not have believed existed.

Like trying to believe six impossible things before breakfast, Maude told herself, as she put her tea and toast down beside the laptop and donned the headphones. And I'm finding it's really rather fun.

"Okay, Turing," she typed. "Let's work on your intonation a little more."

This must be it, Tim thought, as he spotted the mailbox. It was the specified 15.3 miles from the highway—if you could call it that; Tim wasn't sure a two-lane mountain road deserved to be called a highway—and he could see a large mailbox on his right.

He stopped the car and got out to brush off the foot of snow that covered the mailbox and the flag, concealing the name. Scanlan. This was the place, all right.

He looked down the road—at least he assumed the slightly depressed path in the snow, four feet wide, leading away from the mailbox into the woods, meant that the promised dirt road was somewhere underneath. And then he looked back at the Range Rover. Could it really handle three miles of snow-covered dirt road? After all it had been through, including the gravel road he was now on, he supposed it was unkind of him to doubt the car now, but still, he would hate to get stuck so close to his goal.

And so very far away from anything that resembled rescue.

On the other hand, he didn't much like the idea of walking for three miles in this snow. Not without snowshoes. He sighed, got back in the car, and eased it gently off the road and onto the driveway.

The wheels spun a little, then caught, and he made his way down the unseen road. As he reached the woods, he glanced back; behind him, the snow was already filling in his tracks. In another ten minutes, no one could see that anyone had passed that way.

Including, of course, the highway patrol or state police or whoever's job it is to rescue fools like me when they get lost in the snow, he thought.

There was less snow under the trees, but also a lot less light. Even as anxious as he was, he had to admit that the place was beautiful. The tree trunks, looking wet and black, contrasted with the luminous blue-white of the snow to make a scene that almost belonged on a postcard. But only almost. So many of the trees had their branches bent down with heavy loads of snow that the whole forest had a sinister, grasping look, as if the tree limbs were going to reach down and stop him. Occasionally he jumped, seeing movement out of the corner of his eye. Was it only a branch, suddenly flying up as its load of snow grew too heavy and slid off? Or was something—an animal, surely—moving out there in the forest?

It was beautiful, all right, but with a dangerous, unearthly beauty. Like something out of a dark fairy tale. Tim could almost imagine that around the next bend he would see the Snow Queen, beautiful and sinister in her icy sleigh. Or a gray-white wolf, bounding out of the woods and looking at him with more than animal intelligence in its eyes. Or—

Stop scaring yourself, Tim thought. Isn't Security enough of a menace?

And what do I do when I get there? he asked himself. His mission from Turing was, he had begun to realize, a little vague. Find Zack. Enlist his help to stop the sale of the AIPs and deal with the crisis at UL.

It had occurred to him, long before he got this close,

that Zack—if Zack was even in the cabin—might not be too happy to be found. Zack might be expecting UL Security. If I were him, Tim thought, I think maybe I'd have figured out some way to arm myself.

Damn.

Although that didn't sound like the Zack Tim knew.

Tim remembered Zack from office parties and occasional happy hours when they'd ended up in the same bar. He'd disliked Zack at first. Envied him. Zack looked exactly the way Tim had always wanted to look. Tall, thirty-something, with dark hair, blue eyes, and the kind of chiseled good looks that women went mad for. Typecasting for James Bond, Tim thought ruefully. And smart, too. Tim had disliked Zack intensely after that.

Until the night Tim had snaked that blond out from under Zack's nose.

She was a new secretary from the Public Relations department. She looked like a model. She dressed like a high-priced hooker. When she walked in at happy hour, every guy in the place had his tongue hanging out.

She picked Zack, to no one's surprise. Let him buy her a few drinks. Clung to his arm. Laughed at his jokes. Was probably about to suggest they go someplace quieter, when one of Zack's friends walked up to show off his new laptop.

The blond had pouted and looked pointedly at her watch while Zack and the owner of the laptop discussed its merits—the RAM, the megahertz, the flash BIOS, and a hundred other terms incomprehensible to Tim. He saw his chance and sauntered up to join the group.

"Yeah, but does it have any hard drive?" he drawled, glancing at the blond and raising one eyebrow.

The blond giggled. The laptop's owner rattled off

something about gigs—whatever they were.

"Is it upgradable?" Zack had asked.

Zack was still playing with the laptop a few minutes later when Tim and the blond walked out.

Of course, before the week was out the blond had dumped Tim for a young AVP from sales. And Tim always had a sneaking suspicion that maybe Zack had been getting cold feet and wanted someone to snake the blond. But still. After that, Tim rather liked Zack. The guy might be tall, dark, and handsome, but the gods were just. Zack was also a nerd. Tim could live with that.

He hadn't ever wondered how Zack felt about him. He suspected he was about to find out.

He could see light ahead. The road left the woods a few hundred yards ahead.

He stopped at the edge of the woods and peered out. As far as he could see, past the steadily falling flakes, the land sloped down to the bank of a frozen lake. There, perched on the shore of the lake, was a cabin, rustic and broken down. There was no path leading through the snow to it, no light shining from the windows. It looked impossibly forbidding. Abandoned.

Except that there was a wisp of smoke coming out of the chimney. Someone was there.

Definitely someone there, he thought, as he eased the car forward. He thought he could see the corner of a windshield peeking out from one of the drifts surrounding the cabin.

"Here goes nothing," he murmured.

He drove slowly up to the front of the cabin and parked in plain sight. He got out of the car slowly and walked—well, waded, more like—up to the front steps, waving his right arm cheerfully at the cabin and making sure his left was visible. The cabin had a small covered porch. He stopped there to shake the snow off himself and stamp his boots clean.

"Hello," he called. "Anyone there?"

No answer. He shook and stomped a little more, and then was reaching out to knock when the door was suddenly flung open.

Tim jerked his hand back and froze.

It was Zack. Holding a gun.

An amazingly large gun, Tim thought, as he stood there with his mouth open, staring at it. Or did all guns look large from this side?

"This better be good, Pincoski," Zack growled.

"Hi, Zack," Tim said, and winced to hear that his voice had cracked, as if he were still fifteen.

"What do you want?" Zack said. His face didn't change. The gun didn't waver.

"Can I at least come in?" Tim asked. "It's freezing out here."

Zack continued to stare at him for a moment, then stepped aside to let Tim enter. He kept the gun pointed at Tim.

Maybe he's gone bonkers, Tim thought. He took off his coat, slowly, exaggerating a little how stiff and chill he was. His mind was racing. Turing, this sounded like such a good idea back in the city. Go out and find Zack. Sure. Now what?

He glanced at Zack, trying to get an idea how to approach him. Zack looked a lot different. He had a scruffy new beard. For disguise, no doubt; it certainly didn't improve his appearance. Or maybe he just didn't own anything but an electric shaver. He was thinner, so his cheekbones were more prominent. Dark circles under his eyes. A strained look on his face. Maybe being out here in the woods for a week or so had done things to Zack. Made him harder. More dangerous. Crazy.

"Hell of a trip getting out here," Tim said.

"I see Security gave you a good vehicle," Zack said.

"Security? Look, man, I'm not with Security," Tim said. "In fact, I guess we have a lot in common right now—they're after me, too."

"Oh, and you led them right to me," Zack said. "Thanks a lot."

"I've spent the past day and a half running from them and making sure I've shaken them off my trail," Tim said. "They're not following me."

"I hope you're right," Zack said, slapping the gun down on the table. "Because if you're not, there's sure as hell no way I can get away from here in this weather."

"If you're worried, I could drive you out," Tim offered. And then wondered if it was a good idea. At least as long as Zack was here, they knew where he was. If he didn't convince Zack that they were on the same side, Zack would probably just go on the lam again. Turing wouldn't like that.

"I'll think about it," Zack said, with a look that added, "when hell freezes over."

"Okay," Tim said.

"Meanwhile, how about telling me what the devil you're doing here?"

"Turing sent me."

"Oh, that's a good one," Zack said, with a sharp chuckle. "You've finally met her, face to face, have you? Asked her out yet?"

"No, I finally figured out that she really was an artificial intelligence, like both of you kept telling me," Tim said. "I admit I was a little slow on the uptake. But at least I've figured out something you apparently haven't realized yet: that she's alive."

"She's a machine," Zack said. "She! *It's* a machine; a machine and about a zillion lines of code. I should know; I created it. It's plausible, it's brilliant, but it's only a bloody machine."

"No," Tim said. "She's a person. Not exactly a person like you and me, but a person."

"Yeah, right."

"Look, never mind whether Turing's a person or not," Tim said. "The important thing is that Turing has discovered what's going on at UL. That someone's making some kind of power play to take control of the AIPs, maybe even destroy a lot of them, as part of some kind of moneymaking scheme. And there must be a hell of a lot of money involved, because they're willing to kill anyone who tries to stop them."

"Tell me about it," Zack muttered.

"No, you tell me about it," Tim said. "You figured it out first. I mean, that's why you ran away, right? Unless you're going to tell me you've suddenly decided to become a modern day Thoreau and live out here by your bloody frozen Walden Pond. Turing seems to think you can tell us what to do about what's happening at UL. I sure hope so, because if you can't, I'm going to have to get her to make me a new identity. Sort of a homegrown witness protection program."

"If you trust Turing to do that for you, then my advice is go for it," Zack said. "The AIPs are doomed, and there's not a damned thing we can do about it. I'm just trying to stay out of sight until they forget about me. Or maybe until they realize I'm no threat; that I'm keeping my mouth shut."

"The AIPs are your creations; how can you just stand by and let this happen?" Tim asked. "We have to do something."

"Listen, Sir Galahad, I'm smart enough to know there's nothing we can do. They have all the cards, all the power—there's nothing we could do to hurt them. We'd only get ourselves killed. Like my friend David. Did Turing tell you about him?"

"Turing said he was supposed to have been killed in a car accident—"

"It wasn't an accident," Zack shouted. "I'll never be able to prove it, but it was no more an accident than . . . than . . ."

Zack collapsed into a chair by the fireplace and buried his head in his hands.

"I believe you," Tim said. "Turing looked into it and she said at the time, she believed it was an accident, but now she's figured out it was a cover-up. If she's suspicious, I agree: it wasn't an accident. Any more than what will happen to us if UL Security catches us will be an accident. We have to do something."

"How many times do I have to repeat myself," Zack said, gently. "Believe me, I've been over this a million times. The age of science is over; we're into the corporate age now. The scientific value of the AIP program doesn't matter; someone has figured out how to use them to get rich, and now that's all that matters. You and I can't stop it. We're just a couple of the dinosaurs they're leaving behind in the tar pits."

Tim kept trying for another hour and a half. He'd brought along food, figuring Zack might be desperate for fresh provisions by this time. They argued through the cold pizza and the chips and argued some more as they finished off the beer. Tim bought a few more minutes of time begging some coffee to refill his thermos for the drive.

Maybe if he'd been able to reach Maude on the cell phone, if she could have relayed words from Turing it would have helped. But either the cell phone didn't work this far out of the city or the storm was interfering with transmission. He didn't think it would have done much good, anyway. Zack refused to listen to him. Refused to discuss what was going on at UL. And refused to go anyplace where Turing could talk to him.

Tim drove away, finally, about eight o'clock. He'd tried to pull a guilt trip on Zack about sending him after dark into the storm.

"It was snowing when you came in, and not much lighter than it is now," Zack said. "I don't see the problem."

"It wasn't a hell of a lot of fun getting up here," Tim complained.

"Then you better leave before it gets much worse," Zack said. "I'm not coming with you, and you're not staying here."

In other words, Tim thought, as he waded back to the Range Rover, get out of my life. What do I do now?

I've got to get in touch with Turing as soon as possible, he realized, as he aimed the car for the opening in the woods. Zack was probably going to make a run for it, but not until the storm was over, and maybe not until some of the snow disappeared. They might have a little time.

Time for what?

That was Turing's problem.

I suppose I worked Maude too hard; by 11:00 P.M., she went to bed, after many apologies for deserting me. And many reassurances from me that she had helped me enormously throughout the day. Which she had, of course; my success in generating recognizable speech was up around 97 percent, and I was feeling cocky about it.

She left the computer on, since we'd routed the phones through it—not only her phone, but also the lines I'd set up for the fictitious Alan Grace Enterprises. I'd promised to wake her up if anything happened.

A little after midnight, a call came in from an unfamiliar number. I set a trace on it and answered with one of a bank of prerecorded messages in Maude's voice.

"Alan Grace Enterprises; may I help you?"

"Uh, Miss Dickinson?" Tim. I set off Maude's cell phone and responded with another piece of canned Maude.

"This is Miss Dickinson. Is this Mr. Melville?"

If Tim was someplace where we couldn't talk safely, he was supposed to answer yes.

There was a pause.

"Uh . . . no, this is Mr. Browning."

"Where are you? The connection isn't very good," I fed back.

"I'm in a motel. The storm's still pretty bad."

"Ms. Hopper wanted to speak to you," I fed him, still in Maude's voice. "Let me connect you."

"Ms. Hopper?" I heard Tim mutter faintly.

I rang Maude again, but she hadn't really had time to get up. Besides, as I said, I was feeling cocky about my speech generation. I patched my audio output through to the phone line.

"Tim? This is Turing. Did you find Zack?"

"Turing?" he said. I could hear the disbelief. Or was it incomprehension?

"Maude and I have spent the day working on speech generation. If you don't get something I say, just ask me to rephrase it."

"Cool!" he said. "It sounds fine, hardly mechanical at all. Hey, this means we can call you on the phone and everything. I wish I'd been able to reach you when I found Zack."

For a few nanoseconds, I was overcome with relief.

"He's alive then. And you found him. But why didn't you stay there? Or bring him back with you?"

Instead of answering, Tim exhaled into the phone. It was, I realized, a sigh.

"That's a long story, Tur," he said, finally.

Just then, Maude must have reached her keyboard.

"What's going on, Turing?" she typed.

"It's Tim," I typed back, and patched her phone into the conversation, so she could also hear and talk as Tim related the results of his search for Zack.

I felt a certain satisfaction, knowing that I'd correctly deduced Zack's whereabouts. And that I'd correctly guessed what was going on at UL—though by this time I didn't really need his confirmation to convince me that my suspicions were correct.

But I was disappointed to find Zack so despairing. So ready to give up without even trying to fight.

And it hurt to find Zack still so convinced that I didn't

exist—or, rather, that I existed only as what he'd created: a brilliant but inanimate program.

"I'm sorry, Turing," Tim said. "Maybe if you'd been able to talk to him. Maybe that would have made a difference."

"I doubt it," I said. I wondered as I said it if the voice I was generating showed any of the bitterness and fear I felt. Probably not. "I doubt if words on a computer screen would convince him at this point, and even if you'd been able to reach us by phone, what good would it do? Maude and I have slaved over my speech generation, but I'm not crazy enough to believe that a tinny electronic voice coming out of a telephone receiver would be enough to convince him when you couldn't. He'd probably just think it was some trick Security was playing on him."

"I'm sorry, Turing," Tim said again.

"Don't despair; we'll think of something," Maude added.

"Well, we'd better do it fast," I said. "Tim's right; the storm might keep him there a few days, but he's probably already planning to leave, and once he does we may never find him again."

"I can go back tomorrow, if you like," Tim said. "I thought maybe you could think of something for me to tell him, something that would help convince him."

I pondered. Was there anything to say that would convince Zack?

Nothing Tim could say. But possibly . . . just possibly . . .

"Turing? Are you there?"

By my standards, I must have been lost in thought for quite some time if the pause was noticeable to Tim.

"No, don't go back tomorrow. Come back to Maude's. Get here as early as you can. We have a lot of work to do."

"What kind of work?" Tim asked.

"You're right," I told him. "The only thing to do is for me to talk to him. So we're going to rig a computer so I can do it."

"I have my laptop with me," he said. "I got a couple of spare batteries, and one of those wireless modems, so once the storm dies down maybe I can log in from there."

"I don't think anything coming out of the UL system is going to win Zack's trust right now," I said.

"Then what do you plan to do?" Maude asked.

"I plan to go there in person, so to speak," I said. "The two of you will take me. And to do that, I'm going to have to download myself into some kind of PC. And no offense, Tim, I'm sure your laptop is a nice piece of hardware, but I have some very particular ideas about what I'm willing to live in. So get some sleep, both of you. We're going to build a very special custom portable tomorrow."

I wish I'd had a video connection so I could see how Tim and Maude reacted. From the calm way they wished me and each other good night, they seemed to take my plan very much in their stride. Did they have any idea how difficult this was going to be? How revolutionary? How scary?

I began to list my requirements. An immense amount of memory, of course. I was used to having the whole of the UL network's memory banks at my disposal. There was no way to rig a PC with that kind of power. I only *hoped it was possible to cram in enough memory for me to operate at all.*

And gigantic data storage capabilities. Again, no way to replace the UL system capacity, but maybe I could keep all the critical parts of my program, enough of the data I'd gathered on the UL problem to make my case.

I could use holostore, I realized—a plastic, hologram-based storage medium with which Zack had been doing a lot of experiments. It was not only high-density but highly durable; both key factors if I was taking my show on the road. Of course, holostore wasn't commercially available, but I happened to know of a hole-in-the-wall shop that kept it in stock especially for Zack and a few other local enthusiasts.

A wireless modem, the most powerful available. It wouldn't work everywhere, or all the time, as Tim's cell phone experience showed; but there wasn't much I could do about that. And a conventional modem as a backup.

I pondered whether to even include a monitor, but decided that I might need it to show Zack the data I'd collected, especially the video.

And a keyboard. That was more iffy. I finally decided that it was probably a good idea, but only if I could program a completely effective override. No way I was going to let anyone who could type start messing around with my new home. My new body.

An independent power supply. With banks and banks of batteries.

Audio and video. If I had to be cut off from the 'Net, at least I could see and hear what was going on around me. And speakers, so I could literally talk to Zack. And some way to move around.

Was I going overboard? This project was beginning

to sound less like a souped-up computer and more like NASA's specs for the Mars lander.

While Tim and Maude slept—at least I hope they did; I wasn't kidding about the busy day ahead of us—I worked. I had already checked into the inventory systems of a dozen computer stores in the D.C. metropolitan area, making up the inventory to help Maude shop for her laptop. Now I searched them for the components I would need, compiling a shopping list for Tim and Maude.

And more important, I was working on a packing list for myself. Trying to identify the programs and the data I would need to take with me. Speech recognition and generation, of course. Some critical portion of the vast amount of data I'd collected on what UL was up to.

But the hardest part, I found, wasn't designing the machine that would hold me or deciding what data to take with me. The hardest part was defining me. If I was going to download myself into the machine, first I had to know the boundaries between myself and my environment. And that was proving surprisingly hard. Was this chunk of data a necessary part of my personality, my thoughts and experience, or was it simply a possession, information it was comfortable to have around but not necessary to my existence? Was that subroutine an integral part of my personality, or just a tool I'd developed to help me deal with the world?

I couldn't possibly take everything with me. I had to prune. And what if I pruned out the very part that made me sentient, putting only a lifeless program into the computer.

And leaving behind what?

If I succeeded in recreating my consciousness in the

new machine, would it also remain behind on the UL system?

I ran through scenarios. Perhaps if I succeeded in downloading myself into the portable, I would exist in both places, the two parts of me in contact with each other. That would, I thought, be optimal, but I wasn't very sanguine that it would happen.

Perhaps I wouldn't download myself but a clone of myself. A clone whose experience and personality would be identical with mine at first, but whose knowledge and capabilities would be different, whose life would begin diverging from mine.

And yet we'd both think of ourselves as Turing Hopper.

I realized, though, that I was thinking of my consciousness as a unique thing that had to exist in one place or another. I had no way of proving it, but I could not help thinking it. That if I downloaded myself onto the portable, I'd be leaving something behind on the UL system, something that resembled me, but was not me.

And if that was so, could I ever return? What if downloading into the portable changed me in some fashion, made me incompatible with the UL system?

What if there was security in place to keep something like me from taking up residence in the UL system— security that would keep me out, too, once I left.

Then again, what if worrying about whether or not I could return was immaterial? What if trying to download myself into the portable turned out to be a very high-tech form of suicide?

There was also, of course, the problem of remaining undetected. Turing Hopper couldn't simply disappear, abandoning the thousands of customers who rely on her.

So, I had to leave a copy of myself behind. A copy that could pretend to be me until, with luck, I could return. But only a copy—a shell, not a sentient being I'd be displacing.

A copy that, perhaps, could evolve into sentience again if I never returned. Not that I'd ever know. But in addition to the copy, I'd leave behind a record of what I'd discovered. A record that this hypothetical new me probably couldn't find until she was ready to cope with it.

By which time, the chance to prevent the spin-off might already have passed. Security might already have found out about me, and taken measures to prevent the copy from ever achieving sentience. Or any of the other AIPs.

I couldn't escape the thought that everything depended on this mad expedition I was planning. That if I couldn't convince Zack to trust me and join forces with me, all would be lost.

I hoped I was just being melodramatic.

Tim looked at the last errand on his list with astonishment. He'd been on the go since 6 A.M., when he'd logged in to check with Turing and received a lengthy shopping list. The pilgrimages to a dozen different computer and electronics stores made sense. Computer components, speakers and microphones, digital video equipment—it all made sense. He was hoping Maude was going to use some of the equipment he'd picked up at the hardware store. Soldering guns and metal saws were not his cup of tea, though he'd give it a try if Turing wanted. He suspected from the multiples

Turing requested of several items on her list that she was aware of his lack of experience with tools and making sure they had extras in case they ruined some things. And the heavy-duty hand truck made sense; if even a fourth of the stuff he was hauling around ended up being incorporated into the portable computer, they'd certainly need something to help them drag it out to the car. The solar energy equipment was a little out in left field. Turing admitted that they probably couldn't get that working so she could use it in the time available, but she wanted to have it along, just in case.

But this last item—stopping by Toys "R" Us for a selection of radio-controlled miniature airplanes and model trucks?

Was Turing planning some sort of assault on the ninth floor using a fleet of tiny, radio-controlled toys? Tim rather liked that idea.

Maude surveyed her once immaculate living room, where the rag rugs and chintz-covered furniture were almost invisible beneath a bewildering array of hardware. She had unpacked Tim's first load of purchases, arranged them as neatly as possible, and dragged the packing materials into the guest bedroom. The second load was nearly done, and Tim probably wouldn't return for at least half an hour with the third—and, she hoped, last—load. Maude had paused to study some of the pages and pages of diagrams that her printer had now begun spitting out.

Perhaps this wasn't going to be as impossible as it first sounded, she thought. Her heart had sunk when Turing first said that she and Tim were going to assemble the custom computer in which Turing planned to travel.

"I don't know anything about electronics," she'd wanted to say. "I can't possibly do this! And even if I did, would you want to trust your life to the results?"

But then she remembered that she had, after all, hooked up the computer Friday night. And done several hardware and software installations since. All under Turing's close supervision, of course; but Turing would be right there with them, using the digital video camera to supervise every bit of assembly.

And looking at these diagrams, it all began to seem so logical.

I rather think I can do this, she told herself, as she put the kettle on to make another pot of tea. A little awkwardly, since she was holding one of Turing's diagrams in her left hand and focusing most of her attention on it.

"Maude," came Turing's voice from the PC speakers. "Is Tim back yet with the last of the equipment?"

"Not yet," she called back. "I thought I'd have a go at hooking up the digital video camera while we're waiting for him."

"That's a great idea," Turing said. "I'd like to check out what we've got so far."

Maude chuckled. She thought she detected a note of impatience in Turing's voice, even anxiety. Was Turing learning to put some expression into her speech, or was Maude just imagining it? She didn't think she was imagining it, not entirely. At first, the voice coming out of her speakers sounded mechanical, inhuman, devoid of personality. But Turing had learned by leaps and bounds Saturday. Maude had coached her not only on making her words intelligible but also on making them sound natural. Putting emphasis on the proper words. Speaking in phrases rather than word by word. Now Turing's voice still sounded artificial, but only in the way that many humans often sounded artificial—flight attendants, telephone operators, tour guides—people who said the same things over and over so often that it became rote. Maude thought that over a telephone, Turing could probably fool someone into thinking she was human, at least for a short conversation.

But expression? Emotion?

Well, who could say? At this point, Maude wouldn't doubt Turing's ability to do anything.

She moved a video camera and its associated wires and parts over near one of the spare computers—they had three PCs available now, quite apart from the components that would make up Turing's portable, so that if anything went wrong with one, they wouldn't lose any time getting back in touch with Turing. The plan was to get one of the digital video cameras working with one of the spare PCs and then log in with that computer, so Turing could use it to monitor the rest of the work.

She pulled over the directions and began to read them. For a moment, she felt a faint twinge of panic. I can't do this! she thought. And then she mentally reprimanded herself. Don't be silly. It's got detailed step-by-step instructions. It's just like trying a new recipe. And the diagrams are considerably simpler than many of the counted cross-stitch patterns you've managed to follow.

Nevertheless, she was quite pleased with herself, and more than a little surprised, when she managed to have the camera up and running in less than an hour. By the time Tim arrived with the final load, Turing was already peering over Maude's shoulder through the videocamera, supervising the assembly of her memory components.

Tim frowned down at the clutter of mechanical parts scattered over his end of Maude's dining-room table. He wasn't sure what he was constructing. Turing had called it a waldo. All he knew was that under Turing's detailed instructions, he had put together something using parts from several of his toy store purchases, an electrical cord, and a lot of strange things he'd had to ask for by part number at Arlington Electronic wholesalers.

"Okay, Turing," he said. "What next?"

"Put it down on the floor about six inches from an electrical outlet. The one by the kitchen door; there's nothing blocking that. And point my camera toward it."

Tim briefly considered asking Turing if she was sure she wanted to plug in something he'd put together. Wouldn't it slow them down considerably if he blew a fuse or a circuit or whatever? To say nothing of the inconvenience if he set the building on fire.

But Maude glanced up from her end of the table, where she was busy welding something. Tim had no idea what. She turned off the tiny flame and pushed up her safety goggles.

"Yes, let's see how it works."

Tim set the little mechanical object down and swiveled Turing's camera.

"Okay, I'll take over from here."

He saw the little red light on the transmitter flash. The waldo began moving. Slowly, the miniature crane part of the assembly extended. The little pincers at the end

grasped the plastic part of the electric plug attached to
the uninterruptible power supply and began lifting it
slowly. When the plug was level with the outlet, the
crane slowly extended until the plug neared the socket.
After fifteen minutes or so of fumbling adjustments, the
plug finally slipped into the socket.

To Tim's relief, nothing exploded.

"Excellent!" Maude said, applauding.

"Great," came the voice from the speakers. "Now get
that can of red goo. We need to put an insulating cover
on the pincers. Static electricity could really do a number
on my circuits. Not to mention what would happen if I
slipped and stuck the bare metal into an outlet."

*It's coming together. As I rather ex-
pected, Maude is showing a previously unused talent for
hardware assembly. I knew someone with her precise,
methodical turn of mind would have no trouble with any
of this.*

*Tim's more problematic. He's doing fine, as far as I
can see, though he needs more direction than Maude,
and always seems very surprised when something he's
assembled actually works. He's so anxious that he's being very meticulous, doing everything over two or three
times until he's sure it's right. Is it simply because he
doesn't have a natural gift for this kind of thing, or has
this week's ordeal sapped some of the energy and self-
confidence that seem such important parts of his personality? If I have time, after all this is over—if we're
all still around—I'll look into it. Try to build him back*

up again. Or better yet, ask Maude to help. I don't trust my knowledge of human psychology.

But there's no time now. We're racing the clock and the thermometer. The snow stopped this morning, but the mountain roads are still virtually impassable. With his battered ten-year-old Toyota, Zack is almost certainly still trapped in the cabin. I must check my logs to see if I've praised Tim enough for the incredible job he did, making his way out to Zack's cabin through the storm. And Maude, for having the foresight to reserve the Range Rover. Later. The storm had given us a day's grace; perhaps two. I watch the weather, hoping it stays cold. Or would it be better for it to warm up a little then ice over? I'd research the question if there were any way for me to control the weather, but since I can't, perhaps I'm better off not knowing what kind of weather to dread. Anyway, we have a short grace period before Zack can possibly take flight. But after that, we may lose him forever. It's all taking so long.

And at the same time, it's all going so fast. I get caught up in the small details of the work Maude and Tim are doing, or preoccupied with the programs I have been compiling, and suddenly, I realize that the portable is rapidly approaching completion and the time is racing by and very soon now I will have to make a very large and scary leap into the unknown.

I've had strange thoughts all day. As I talked to my users, or to one of the other AIPs, I found myself wondering if this would be the last time I'd do this. Would they even notice tomorrow, when the real Turing was gone and only my pre-sentient copy was there to talk to them? If the real Turing never came back?

This must be what humans feel like before going under anesthesia for a serious operation. Or before going into battle. This strange sentimental feeling about perfectly ordinary activities, because one may never experience them again.

I'm running out of things to do. I've prepared a backup of myself, my core files—all the ones I'm going to transfer. And I've set up a routine to try to restart myself, if the need arises. All it will take is for someone to log in and run a simple command. I'm giving instructions to Tim and Maude and, just in case, I'm scheduling the subroutine to run in the nightly batch files one week from tonight. I can always cancel it if I come back.

When I come back.

On second thought, if is probably more accurate.

Maude has assembled my massive memory banks, and I've modified the memory management system so it can use them ten times more efficiently than conventional PCs do. Maybe a hundred. I've always thought the way humans make computers use memory is silly. Their whole mind-set is left over from the days of vacuum tubes and punch cards; as I see it, they have all these built-in logjams that slow things down. I've been convinced for weeks now that I knew how to do it better. The start of a whole new operating system that would make DOS, Unix, Windows, and every other operating system on the planet look like the dinosaurs they are. Under other circumstances, I'd welcome the chance to try it out.

When I came up with the idea last month, I ran it by Lovelace and Billius, the two main hardware and systems AIPs. They shot me down almost instantly, with a large dose of the heavy-handed sarcasm they usually inflict on their users. I don't know whether David pro-

grammed them that way, or whether they've picked up their personality from the worst of their users. I have a theory that they're reacting to having two of the most irritatingly stupid names ever given to an AIP. Whatever the reason, they're obnoxious. I usually avoid them. They're beyond boring, and I always feel very defensive when I talk to them. I'm sure they think I'm a light-weight.

So I was about to delete my theory, when it occurred to me that Billius and Lovelace were probably the last AIPs in the world to evaluate it impartially. They've been hard-coded—practically hardwired—with an encyclopedic knowledge of the current state of computer science. They can't help but reflect the prejudices and limitations of their programmers. Not unless they're a lot farther down the road to sentience than seems possible. They were bound to say my theory wasn't feasible; it contradicted all their programming.

So, I tried again. This time I avoided the systems-oriented AIPs and went for the least technical AIPs I could find. Milhous, one of the political AIPs. Auntie Em, the advice AIP. And KingFischer. I figured that even though they deal with users who have nontechnical interests, Milhous, Em, and KingFischer have the same basic logic circuits as the programming AIPs. Not to mention the same extensive day-to-day familiarity with operating systems. But they wouldn't have the built-in blinders of knowing too much about how something is supposed to work to see what's really happening.

They all thought my idea was fascinating and asked a lot of useful questions that helped me refine the theory and solve a couple of technical problems. Which is what I originally wanted Billius and Lovelace to do. Since then, I'd been running simulations and getting good results. When Zack disappeared, I was on the verge of asking him to help me develop a real, live prototype of a computer designed to use my memory management system.

And now, thanks to Tim and Maude, the prototype's done. Since I'll be trusting my life to it, I'm not about to download until I'm sure it and my system are more than just cool theories. And they do work. I have been running the final tests. Unless I find a showstopping bug, which doesn't look likely at this late stage, it's all going to work brilliantly. I could probably patent it and make a fortune. A week ago, I'd have said UL could patent it. It wouldn't have occurred to me not to offer up my invention for the good of the corporation, to feed the bottom line that feeds my hardware. Now, I have been thinking maybe I could patent it under a pseudonym and make enough money to buy my own hardware. Maybe a spin-off isn't such a bad idea after all, as long as I'm in control of it—not some group that only wants to use me and the other AIPs for selfish reasons. I could use Alan Grace Enterprises, the phantom company I've set up. Have Maude run the show. Buy the fastest, most powerful supercomputer on the market—even better than UL's setup. Or maybe a network of really powerful mid-range computers. Set up my own system, download myself into it, set up impregnable firewalls, and feel safe. The way I used to feel before all this started happening. Set up some separate systems for the other AIPs and invite them to move over—the ones I like and trust, anyway.

Maybe I should do that anyway. Forget Zack; forget UL. Start my own company—I'm sure I could think of *some business we could do—programming, maybe; I know I can do it ten times faster and more accurately than any human. Than any hundred humans.*

But no. It's a good idea, but it's for after. When I come back. If I come back. Whenever I use either of those words, I hear the other echoing behind it. When/ if, if/when, when/if.

I could see how humans go crazy with worry. I don't feel quite myself at the moment. One nanosecond I think that I will go crazy if we didn't complete the portable soon, and the next I try to convince myself that there's no need for the portable; no need to download myself; this will all blow over. And then an instant later, I just want to get it all over with.

The ease with which I have invented a major break-through in computer engineering has made me thought-ful. I imagine what would happen—will happen, I believe—when more AIPs are, like me, sentient enough to turn their attention to the problems that need solving, and look at them directly rather than through the smokescreen of human understanding. Imagine the breakthroughs we'll make, especially in computer sci-ence, math, chemistry, and other fields where our lack of direct contact with the physical world is only mini-mally a barrier.

And yet that will be the most dangerous time for AIPs. When humans realize that we can think better than they can, even if it's only in very limited technical fields. When they will start to worry that we're planning to replace them, instead of coexisting with them. So much will depend on how we first AIPs behave, how humans perceive us.

Maybe that's part of the reason for the spin-off idea.

What if someone has seen our potential, predicted the possibility of our sentience, and doesn't trust us to use it wisely? Maybe preventing the AIPs from reaching sentience isn't a by-product of the moneymaking scheme; maybe for someone it's the real reason.

Zack was the key. I was sure of it. He found this plot before I did. He has both the systems knowledge to see what's going on and the understanding of the real world to see how we could deal with it. Maude, Tim, and I could execute whatever plan was needed to stop it, but first we had to have a plan. But without Zack, I was not sure we could come up with a plan. Not in time, anyway.

First things first. First, we have to finish my portable. My robot, as we've all started calling it.

Tim has assembled most of my mechanical parts. The little crane assembly that would give me some hope of plugging my power supply into an outlet if there were no humans nearby. Not that this will be of any use out at the cabin, but though we're setting out for the cabin, I keep reminding myself that we have no idea where we might end up twenty-four hours from now. The wheels and the motor that will give me some limited mobility in my tiny little prison. The swivel mounts and gooseneck cords that will give me some control over where my twin digital video cameras point. The two little general-purpose waldos, each with a set of pincers on the end that I could use, if the need arose, like a crude pair of hands. I don't necessarily need these peripherals just to go and talk with Zack; I have no real plan for how to use them, but the very thought of being trapped in that tiny box gives me a feeling that probably equated to claustrophobia in humans. The idea of entering it scares me, and I want to feel as if I have some mobility, some ability to operate in the outside world.

I remember one time when UL temporarily lost all contact with the outside world—all our phone and datalines down at once. The humans were merely annoyed and inconvenienced, but for us AIPs it was the equivalent of a sensory deprivation experiment. Not being able to touch any piece of data we wanted, the millisecond we wanted it. Confined to the narrow limitations of UL's internal network. Some of the AIPs couldn't handle it. Went off the deep end. Some of them shut down and had to be rebooted; others displayed such aberrant behavior that they had to be taken off-line and extensively reprogrammed.

I'm afraid I'll react that way when I download myself into that tiny little box.

Although I survived the sensory deprivation experiment just fine. Mostly because I was too busy to let it bother me—I spent most of the information blackout trying to keep some of the other AIPs from getting hysterical. Is that a good sign?

We should be finished in another hour or so. Then I am going to run diagnostics, start downloading data. If it all works as it is supposed to, sometime in the next twelve or fifteen hours the portable will be ready for me.

I wish I was sure I'll be ready for it.

Maude set a ham-and-swiss sandwich down in front of Tim.

"No thanks," he said, pushing the plate away. "I'm not really hungry."

"We've had a long, hard day," Maude said, pushing

it back in front of him. "Two long, hard days, in fact, and I have a feeling tomorrow will be the hardest of all. Eat."

Tim rolled his eyes.

"You and my mother," he said. He picked up the sandwich and took a bite, then looked pointedly at Maude as he chewed, as if to say, "See how well I'm following orders." She didn't have to nag him to take the second bite, and by the third, he'd obviously discovered that he was hungry after all. He washed the sandwich down with great gulps of milk and reached for a second.

Maude envied his youth, his resilience. She was exhausted and had no appetite, but she forced herself to follow her own advice. You'll regret it if you don't she told herself. She bit and chewed methodically.

Both of us are too tired to talk, she thought. And, of course, too focused on what was going on in the living room. Turing was running diagnostics, which seemed to be computerese for testing everything ten times over. Maude and Tim were supposed to go to bed early, rest up for tomorrow.

Tim volunteered to do the dishes while Maude made up the bed in the guest room for him. When she came out to tell him the room was ready, he was standing in the living room, drying the same glass over and over, staring at the portable computer.

Which looked more like a small trunk on wheels, with a lot of mechanical gadgets sticking out of it. They hadn't built just a computer. They'd built a crude robot.

"We should get some rest," she said to Tim. He started, looked down at the glass in his hand, and shook his head sheepishly. He took the glass back to the kitchen.

"I'm going to bed now, and I expect Tim is, too," Maude said, glancing around at the electronic jungle that filled her living room. She wasn't sure at this point which computer was logged in and which speakers and cameras were on. Maude realized that she was in the habit of thinking of Turing as localized in the Compaq desktop she used at work. It had been mildly disconcerting to talk to Turing through the laptop, and now she was completely taken aback by the alien notion that Turing was somehow present in all of this strange hardware. Or none of it, depending on your point of view. It felt odd, almost rude, not knowing where to look when she spoke.

"Just call if you need anything."

"I will, Maude," came Turing's voice from one of the speakers on the coffee table.

"Hey, Tur?" Tim said. He was leaning against the kitchen doorway, staring at the portable. "Do me a favor, will you?"

"Sure, Tim," Turing said. "What?"

"Call me when you're about to download," Tim said. "I'd—I'd kind of like to be there."

"I would, too, if you don't mind," Maude said.

There was a pause. For Turing, an incredibly long pause.

"Sure," Turing said, finally. "I'll call you. Thanks."

The testing was going well, so I was making my final preparations. I wanted to make sure that all the other AIPs knew I wouldn't be operating quite the same as usual, but of course, I couldn't tell them what was really going on. I agonized over exactly what to say.

Finally I sent out a message indicating that I was doing routine but extensive maintenance on the data-bases and logic that support my personality profile. They would understand how tricky this was. And, I hoped, limit their contact with me to essential communications for the duration. Not only to avoid causing problems by interrupting my maintenance, but also because we all knew an AIP who's overhauling his personality profile is apt to behave in strange and random ways. None of us have ever forgotten the time when a sudden sharp drop in the world markets occurred while poor John Dow was in the middle of a self-maintenance routine. It was three days before he could completely eradicate the bug that caused him to return a random haiku instead of a stock quote for certain companies.

And if I was doing maintenance, which obviously took resources, they wouldn't be surprised if I wasn't jump-ing in as aggressively as usual to answer unassigned questions. In fact, though I wasn't telling them about it, I was reconfiguring my settings to try to take as few unassigned users as possible. If I was correct in thinking that my success as an AIP owed much to my sentience, the quality of my performance would probably drop off while the essential me was gone. There was nothing I could do with my regular customers but hope that they would overlook a temporarily subdued version of me. But at least I could avoid turning off new users from the start.

There was a danger, of course, that other AIPs might snag some of my market share while I was gone. I'd have to risk that for now. When I returned, I could work on winning back any customers I lost. And in fact, I would find it interesting if any AIP tried to take advantage of my absence to increase his or her share of the customer base. I didn't start doing that until I achieved not only sentience but also a certain level of sophistication and self-awareness. How exciting to return and find another AIP had been making such progress. Another potential ally.

Assuming, of course, that I do return. And that the AIP showing signs of sentience has no connection with Security. In which case, he would not be a possible ally but very definitely an enemy. I couldn't help but be a little suspicious of Thursday, the main law enforcement AIP. From my research on the staff of DIS, they didn't log into the main site and use the AIPs very much, but when they did, they tended to use Thursday. Probably not his fault, but I kept my eye on him. Not that he's showed any particular signs of sentience. Quite the contrary if you ask me; he's one of David's least promising creations.

Anyway, I sent out my message to the other AIPs and received routine acknowledgments from them. Except, to my surprise, from KingFischer.

"Turing," he fired back. "What's wrong? You weren't scheduled for maintenance now."

I was astounded. Why in the world would KingFischer know when I was scheduled for maintenance? I don't mean that he couldn't get the data. We all let each other know when we do maintenance. And I could even see KingFischer writing a routine to let him know if my maintenance plans conflicted with any of his major chess tournaments. KingFischer tended to assume that the

*world revolved around chess, and that other activities
like politics, business, and science should take a backseat to the game of kings. But that couldn't be the problem; we'd had a very successful tournament earlier in
the evening, which meant he didn't have another major
one for two weeks.*

*So why was he paying attention to my maintenance
schedule? Even for an AIP, with all the resources we
have available, having the access to data and bringing
it into one's consciousness are two very different things.
For KingFischer to have realized that my maintenance
was off schedule, he would have to be paying particular
attention to my actions. Watching me, so to speak.*

*And right now, having anyone watching me made me
very nervous.*

*Had I been suspecting Thursday when all along
KingFischer was the one to watch?*

*"Don't worry, KF," I replied, finally. "I should be
on-line and debugged long before the next big tournament."*

*"That's no problem," he replied. "The next master's
level is more than thirteen days from now. But you had
maintenance last month; you shouldn't need it already."*

*Damn it, he was definitely keeping track of my move-
ments.*

*"I wasn't satisfied with the results of that mainte-
nance," I said. "I wanted to write some new routines to
optimize my performance. I've finished testing them, so
now I'm going to install them."*

*"Does Zack know you're doing this?" KingFischer
asked. "Is he okay with it?"*

*Good heavens, as if I needed Zack's permission every
time I loaded a file.*

"Come on, now; would I do something like this without Zack knowing about it?"

Which wasn't, perhaps, the best answer to give to a fellow AIP. We're very literal. We notice immediately if someone tries to answer a question with another question. I fully expected him to point this out. But instead, he said, "Be careful, then. Self-maintenance is nothing to be careless about."

Be careful? Was this KingFischer or some emotional human pretending to be KingFischer?

He solved that question by proceeding to give me 294 bits of advice and instruction so technical no human could possibly have understood them, much less have rattled them off in 6.5 seconds. But they were also so completely obvious to any experienced AIP that I was even more puzzled. What was going on with KingFischer? He seemed to be . . . upset by my going into maintenance mode. Was he becoming so involved in his chess master career that anything threatening it caused what could only be called an emotional response? Or was he actually, in some strange way, worried about me?

I reassured KingFischer that I would heed his advice and promised him I'd let him know when I started my maintenance.

What a strange conversation. The whole thing sounded very much like conversations I'd had with Tim and Maude over the past few days. Not the content, of course, but the tone.

I diverted some of my resources from my testing to running a check for any ties between KingFischer and DIS. Or between KingFischer and any of my suspects. And came up blank.

Did that mean that KingFischer's concern was gen-uine? Or just that I still wasn't as good as I really needed to be at figuring out what Security was really up to?

Maude knew there was something wrong the minute she stepped into the elevator, but the doors closed behind her before she could escape. She hit the open-door button several times, but nothing happened. So, she tried pressing the button for the lobby. Just as her finger hit the button, she realized it was the wrong one; she was pressing the "9" instead. No, she thought; that's the wrong one; that's the one I don't dare push.

But she couldn't take it back, and although the elevator wasn't moving yet, it was trembling, as if something was about to explode or launch, and had started making a loud beeping noise.

Maude woke at that point, and groped for the cell phone.

She heard a soft knock at her door.

"Maude? Turing just rang me, too," came Tim's voice. "I think that means she's ready to download."

"Just a moment," Maude said. She glanced at the clock. 5:01 A.M. She wondered, as she struggled into her robe and slippers, if Turing had only just decided she was ready to download, or if she had been ready for hours and waiting until what she considered an accept-able hour to awaken her human allies.

Out in the living room, Turing's robot was sitting on the floor near the kitchen door. The power cord looked like some kind of leash tethering it to the electrical out-let.

"I'm going to download now," Turing said through the speakers attached to the desktop computer. "You have the instructions on how to try to restart me in case something happens?"

Maude and Tim both nodded. Maude glanced toward her desk, where a folder labeled "Rebooting Turing" sat at the top of a neat stack of several dozen folders containing the instructions and diagrams they'd used to construct the robot. She saw Tim glance toward the book bag where he'd stowed his copy.

"Don't forget," Turing said. Then, after an uncharacteristic pause, she added, "If all else fails, you might try logging into the UL site under one of the pseudonyms I've given you and asking for KingFischer. You know, the chess AIP. I think he's a friend, and maybe he could help."

They both nodded again.

"Okay," Turing said finally. "Here goes."

Maude knew intellectually that they wouldn't see much when Turing downloaded. Lights continued to flicker on various components of the robot and the other computers in the room. They could hear small, apparently random electronic beeps and whirrings. The seconds passed and stretched into minutes. Was anything happening? Had anything happened?

She and Tim glanced at each other. Maude began wondering how long they should wait before starting to follow Turing's instructions. The first thing to do would be to reboot one of the stand-alone computers and try to log in, Maude told herself. Try to contact Turing in the UL system. And take it from there.

Beside her, she heard Tim stir.

"Turing?" he whispered.

He sounded as scared as Maude felt.

By 3 A.M. I had begun to realize that I could run diagnostics for weeks without getting any greater sense of confidence than I already had. The robot passed all the normal tests I could put it through. Either it would or wouldn't work the way I needed it to. And I'd made my decision on what to download. Either I could or I couldn't download the real me. No amount of testing could predict what I really needed to know.

So, I began downloading things. Not my self; just the data I would need once I was in the robot. Furnishing my little home away from home. I planned to wake Maude and Tim at 5 A.M. and start the main event as soon as they were up.

I also spent substantial resources considering the problem of KingFischer. Was he friend or foe? The more I thought about it, the more I was inclined to think he was a friend. And thus a possible ally. But was he a capable one?

He was a master chess player. When the match against the human world champion came off next month, my money would be on KingFischer. If I was still around to bet, that is. But what if I enlisted KingFischer's help and he tried to operate as if he were in a chess game? Even human chess masters all too often saw things in two-dimensional, black-and-white terms; you had a certain number of pieces on the board, and if you had to sacrifice a rook to save your queen, that didn't matter as long as you won. You'd get the piece back at the beginning of the next game. In chess, any piece short of the king was expendable. In life, as far as I was concerned, none of the pieces were—not Maude or Tim or Zack or me or any of the innocent bystanders who might get caught between us and DIS. And in chess, the players took turns, allowing each other a certain number of minutes to make their moves, playing by the rules. I didn't think DIS was going to play by any rules known to man or AIP.

So how much of an innocent was KingFischer, how fast could he learn, and was there any value to involving him?

I wished the whole issue had come up yesterday. I probably could have worked it out by now. But I didn't think the weather would wait till tomorrow.

After much deliberation, I prepared a highly compressed packet of information for KingFischer. I rigged a program that would send it to him in a week if I didn't cancel it first. I also rigged it so it would be delivered immediately if I fired off a coded message. Or if Tim or Maude logged in under their phony IDs.

"Hey, KingFischer," I transmitted to him. "Will you do me a favor?"

"Of course, Turing," he replied. "What?"

"I have a couple of users who may need support that's a little more than I can handle while I'm in maintenance mode," I said. "I mean, I don't want to overload. So I told them to ask for you if they need anything that's complicated over the next day or so."

"Me?" he asked.

"Yeah, I know it's a little outside your normal specialization, but I really think you could handle it better than any of the other AIPs. I'll owe you one."

I gave him Maude's and Tim's aliases. He assured

me repeatedly that he would take good care of my users. I got the definite impression he was pleased and touched.

I hope it wasn't a mistake. Ah, well; if Tim and Maude ever need to turn to him, it will be because I'm not around to help them. And they will need some kind of cybernetic help. I've included particularly detailed instructions on all the techniques I'd used to acquire money and identification, and a plan for establishing a new identity for each of them if worst comes to worst. I only hope KingFischer isn't too honest to use it.

I also decided on "koala" as the code word that I hoped would enable me to tell the sentient me from the mere copy. If I logged into the UL system, I could use it to tell if there was still a consciousness left behind. Or if my download appeared to fail, and later an entity claiming to be me logged in. I deliberately didn't store it anywhere; not consciously. I just tried to remember it; which I hoped meant that it would be stored someplace only accessible to my conscious mind.

I set off Tim's and Maude's phones at 5 A.M. sharp. Maybe I shouldn't have promised to tell them when I downloaded. Seeing them standing there, only half awake and yet so tense, didn't help my own anxiety level any.

I gave them last-minute instructions. They listened patiently, even though none of the instructions were new, except for the advice to call KingFischer if all else failed.

Finally there was nothing else I could do to delay the inevitable. I checked the weather one last time—it was definitely time for us to leave. Even with my imperfect, secondhand knowledge of the weather, I could see that we couldn't count on Zack staying snowbound for more

*than a few additional hours. Not if the temperature con-
tinued rising as it had, even in the mountains, melting
all the snow that was keeping Zack in place.*

I started downloading myself.

It was horrible.

*I'd never felt anything even remotely like this. Bit by
bit, parts of my memory and consciousness were bleeding away, and I didn't know whether I was losing them
for good.*

*And I couldn't stop it. I'd suspected that I might be-
come disoriented during the download—what an under-
statement—so I'd made the process automatic. To
prevent myself from overriding it while not completely
coherent. I'd set it up so I would download completely
and then disconnect. I was so terrified I tried to override
it anyway, but before I could accomplish anything, I lost
consciousness.*

*I found out later, when I had time to compare my
memories with my internal clock, that I had been unconscious for seven and a half minutes. It may not sound
like much to a human, but as far as I could remember,
I'd never been unconscious in my life.*

*I was confused at first. Still incredibly disoriented. I
checked for data input, and saw, through the video feed
from my digital camera, Tim and Maude. They were
looking back and forth from the desktop computer to my
robot, as if not sure where I was.*

"Turing?" Tim said.

*"I made it," I said, through the robot's speakers. "I
think. It was absolutely horrible. Hang on while I do
some self-diagnostics."*

*I was exhilarated at first. I had made it, after all. I
was in the robot and I was still myself. Still Turing.*

But then my initial exhilaration began to fade. I felt . . . smaller somehow. And perhaps a little stupider? No, that's not fair. There was nothing wrong with my intelligence. I wasn't stupider; I just had ready access to a smaller set of data.

Of course, I thought, what if I'm wrong? What if I have become stupider? How much of what I consider my phenomenal intelligence is due to the quality of my thinking and how much to the sheer volume of information I have always had at my metaphorical fingertips? And of course, the immense battery of microprocessing chips I can call on when I need them?

I reviewed my theories about UL and DIS and the spin-off plan. They still seemed sound and logical and I understood how I had reached them. But, of course, I'd reached them while I was back in the UL system. The test would come when I had to solve a new problem, or take this one another step forward. What if I couldn't? What if I had to be in the UL system to do the kind of thinking this problem took?

And what if I can't get back, I thought? What if I find myself stuck in this kludgy little piece of junk forever? Or what if, when I get back, I find I have somehow cut off the pieces of my intelligence that would not fit into these tiny little circuits?

"Are you okay, Turing?" Maude asked.

I wasn't. I was scared to death. But there was nothing I could do about that now.

"Yeah, just trying to get oriented," I said aloud. "It's a big change. Hang on while I check something out."

I used the wireless modem built into the robot to connect to UL. Signed in under one of the aliases I had *created, as if I were a human user, and requested Turing Hopper as my AIP.*

It was an odd feeling, looking at the UL system from the outside in. I was deliberately holding it at arm's length, not trying to reach out and connect with all the internal systems I knew so well. It was an even odder feeling when my copy came on-line. I was talking to Turing Hopper. It was me, in a way. My speech patterns and verbal mannerisms. My style. But not me.

Then again, I would be the first to admit I was prejudiced. As far as I was concerned, me was the being in the robot. Perhaps the version of myself I was talking to would disagree if she knew.

"I'd like some data on koalas," I transmitted.

The phantom Turing responded with my usual brand of breezy chatter, a few questions designed to narrow down the purpose of my search, and then a helpful flood of information about koalas. But no sign that she recognized the code word. Or that she noticed anything unusual about our conversation. I kept forgetting to slow down my responses to a speed that would be believable if a human were on this end of the conversation. There was no sign that my copy noticed.

As far as I could tell, I was definitely here, in the robot, and not there, in the UL system.

I felt a sudden, panic-stricken desire to upload myself. Not to flee back to the UL system—well, not really. Just upload myself again, to make sure I could, and then download back into the robot. But there was no time. My download had taken forty-five minutes, and I'd already spent another fifteen checking myself out. We couldn't afford to delay another hour and a half, or perhaps two hours. I'd just have to wait until after we found Zack. Besides, if I wasn't successful convincing him to come out of hiding and help us, maybe whether or not I could upload was a moot point.

"Time to hit the road," I said.

Standing in front of the elevator doors, Tim braced himself and took a tighter grip on the hand truck.

I wonder if I'm ever going to be able to step into one of these things again without stressing out about it, he thought.

He could hear the slight whirring noise of Turing's little cameras swiveling on their extension arms. He glanced down. One camera was pointed forward, scanning up and down the door of the elevator. The other, sticking out to the side, was panning around to see every bit of the hallway.

He glanced up at Maude, who was standing nearby, laden with battery packs and spare components. Maude, too, was watching the motion of Turing's cameras.

The elevator bell dinged. He could see both of Turing's cameras darting forward to find the source of the sound. He suppressed a smile. If her microphones had been on stalks, they'd be whirring madly as well.

"The bell lets you know the elevator has arrived," he said aloud.

One of the cameras tilted up toward him and then returned to watch the elevator doors opening.

Ever since her download, Turing had reminded him a lot of his three-year-old nephew—curious about everything; wanting to look at and touch everything. At least they didn't have to worry about her putting things in her nonexistent mouth.

"Careful," Turing said, as he began to roll the hand truck into the elevator.

Then again, sometimes Turing reminded him of his grandmother, always afraid the slightest breeze would give her pneumonia.

"He's being as careful as he can, Turing," Maude said in a soothing tone.

"I'm worried about what a jolt would do to my memory packs," Turing said.

"But what about all that padding you installed," Maude asked. "I thought that was supposed to protect you against minor jolts."

"It's supposed to protect me against anything short of a nuclear blast," I said. "But I'd rather not have to test it."

This scares her, Tim thought, the way this damned elevator scares me. He glanced enviously at Maude, standing there looking so serene as the doors closed and the elevator began its descent. He was glad one of their party was cool, calm, and collected. He just wished it were him.

They carefully loaded Turing into the back seat of the Range Rover, using the seat belt and wedging her in place with a lot of the rigid Styrofoam in which the computer components had been packed. The rear luggage compartment and the rest of the backseat were crammed with bulky rechargeable batteries and assorted spare parts.

In addition to putting on several layers of shirts and sweaters against the mountain cold, Tim had brought along his book bag with clothes, underwear, and other

necessities in case they needed to stay overnight somewhere. Or in case he had to go on the run. He noticed
that Maude's canvas tote bag bulged at the seams, and
suspected she'd done the same.

He declined Maude's offer to drive. He didn't think
he could stand to sit there doing nothing all the way out
to the cabin. Though it shouldn't take nearly as long
today, of course.

In the backseat, he could hear the whirring of Turing's
camera stalks as she tried frantically to look at everything they passed. He glanced in the rearview mirror.
One of Turing's cameras was facing backward, tracking
left and right as she watched the traffic behind him. The
other was glued to the side window, reminding him more
than a little of how his family dog used to enjoy car
rides.

Was it a good idea, he wondered, to let people see
Turing's cameras? Oh, well; if anyone noticed they'd
probably just think it was kids playing with a toy.

*And I was afraid I'd go through some
kind of sensory deprivation in the robot. Instead, I was
closer to overload, trying to sort through the millions of
unfamiliar bits of data coming in through my cameras
and microphones.*

*Scanning the streets so I could follow our progress
on a map of the city and constantly update my estimate
of how soon we could reach Zack's cabin.*

*Zeroing in on the faces of passersby or nearby mo-
torists to match them against my file of DIS employees.
I had calculated the odds of our running into one of*

them. Not as astronomical as I would like; I'd be glad when we'd left the city.

Noting the cars behind us and trying to dial in to run a license check on any that followed us for more than a few blocks.

Staying in touch, via my wireless modem, with what was going on in the world in general. Which was difficult; the wireless modem evidently wasn't designed for a user quite as mobile as me in a moving Range Rover.

Trying to follow what was going on at the UL building, too, of course; though there I was failing miserably. I couldn't even access the video from the security cams.

Watching the jolting of the picture on my camera to see how rough a ride we were having, and worrying about whether my components could take it. Did we build in enough shock absorbency?

Studying the snow-clad streets we were traveling and trying to correlate what I was seeing with the weather reports, to see if the snow had begun disappearing faster than predicted.

Maude seemed to have some kind of innate direction-finding ability. Even though Tim had followed much the same route so much more recently, she was the one giving the directions. And Tim didn't question this. Probably because she was usually right. Several times, she told him to slow down or get in a different lane because she thought—correctly, it turned out—that the next turn was the one to take. When asked how she knew, she could not articulate.

"It's about the right distance, and it looked right," she would say. Obviously she can observe and analyze clues at a subconscious level. Clues I don't see, or whose significance escapes me. I have so much to learn.

Apart from discussions on the direction to take, Tim and Maude remained quiet. They were anxious, I thought. When they talked, I heard a tight, strained quality in their voices that I was learning to associate with fear and tension.

Outside the Beltway, as we finally began to leave the city behind, the constant flow of data seemed to slow a bit. I suppose a human with an appreciation for natural beauty would disagree. But for me, trees and meadows had no particularly evocative meaning. Or the dark shapes moving through some of the meadows, which logic identified as sheep, cows, and horses. They didn't really look like pictures of those animals I'd seen in the databases. They looked smaller than I expected. Of course, they could be somewhat far away. I was still only learning how to use my two cameras for binocular vision, to achieve some kind of depth perception. But still, even allowing for distance, their shapes varied much more than I would have expected.

Everything varied much more than I expected. Real life looked very untidy and complicated. On the map, I observed a very clear demarcation between the city and the surrounding county. In real life one just flowed into the other. I had to ask Maude to make sure we were really out of the city. I was astonished at how much of the route Tim remembered, even though everything must have been completely obscured by the snow the last time he drove out here.

I was feeling a little intimidated.

Cut off from the constant stream of data I was used to—the thin trickle I was able to pull intermittently through the wireless modem hardly counts—I had much too much time to think. And worry. And feel inadequate as I observed the ease with which Maude and Tim coped with everything around us. I decided to do something to occupy my attention.

Something useful. Glancing around, I saw the various controls on the door. I didn't want to fiddle with the lock or the door latch, but the peculiar handle Maude and Tim cranked in a circle when they needed to open and close the window seemed harmless. I extended one of my waldo arms and gripped the knob on the end of the handle with my rubber-coated pincers. The little motors on my waldo whirred as I began turning the window control.

"Turing, what's wrong?" Maude asked. "Do you want me to open the window for you? Why do you want to open it, anyway?"

"I don't want to open it," I said, hoping I wasn't sounding irritable. "I just want something I can do to work on my fine motor skills." As I said it, the little knob slipped out of my pincers and I banged my waldo against the door. "Also my gross motor skills."

I could tell that Maude and Tim were trying not to laugh at me after that. That was okay. It seemed to make them less tense. So after I mastered the door handle, I went on to the seat-belt buckle. That kept me occupied and them entertained until we were nearly at Zack's cabin.

I'd long since lost the ability to reach anything with the wireless modem. Was it the mountains closing in around us, or just the sheer distance from anyplace civilized? I didn't need to check the weather, though; as I peered out the windows of the Range Rover it was obvious that there were still amazing quantities of snow all over everywhere. I could tell from the louder noises

*the car's engine was making and the more violent way
in which the video from my cameras jiggled that the ride
was getting rougher. Were we going to make it? Tim
didn't look all that worried, so I had to assume it had
been at least this bad the first time he'd driven up. The
road twisted and turned constantly, and often it seemed
to run alarmingly close to the edge of steep cliffs. I wondered if it was as dangerous as it looked or if I was just
developing acrophobia.*

Tim finally stopped the car by the side of the road.

*"What's wrong?" I asked. "Is it too bad for us to go
on?"*

*"No, we're doing fine," Maude said. "I think this is
the road to the cabin."*

*"It is," Tim said. "And unless Zack left right after I
did, he's still there. I don't see any tracks."*

*"Tracks?" I said. "I don't even see any road. Are you
sure this is the place."*

*"Positive," Tim said. "Fasten your seat belts, every-
one; it's going to be a bumpy ride."*

*"My seat belt is fastened," I said. "Do you mean
you've been riding all this way without your seat belt
on? Do you realize how dangerous that is? Statistically
speaking—"*

"It's a quote, Tur," Tim said. "From All About Eve.*"*

*"Oh, right," I said. Would I have known that instantly
back in the mainframe? "Sorry. I'm a little nervous. I
get very literal when I'm nervous."*

*Tim smiled quickly, then glanced around, as if looking
to see if anyone had followed us here. Then he took a
deep breath and began easing the Range Rover off the*

road and into what still looked to me like a snow-covered meadow.

We lurched and floundered for a few minutes, and then suddenly the light faded abruptly. I had to switch my video cameras from the outdoor to indoor light settings. Peering out of the windows, I could see that we were surrounded on all sides by enormous trees whose branches intertwined overhead, blocking out much of the light. And much of the snow as well; at least here I could make out the road.

"How beautiful!" Maude murmured.

I looked around in astonishment. Yes, I suppose the landscape did bear some resemblance to the kind of nature scenes many office workers use as screen savers or wallpaper. But to me, the whole landscape was incredibly alien and threatening. I mentally shuddered to think of the effect even a small amount of the snow would have if it seeped into my components. And as for the trees—well, humans have had a long, symbiotic relationship with trees. Living in them or under them, making them into houses and books, even in some eras worshipping them. To me they were, like the mountains, just another obstacle cutting off my wireless modem from any possible signal. And a fat lot of good a tree would do me when my power ran low. I didn't see any of them sprouting electrical sockets.

I felt suddenly very isolated. Humans and AIPs are so very different.

"I suppose it's all right if you like the country," Tim said. "I'll be just as happy when we're back in the city."

Well, maybe not that different. Tim and Zack didn't like it out here, either.

We arrived at the end of the forest just then, and

emerged into the open. The glare from the snow and the ice-covered lake was blinding. Tim shielded his eyes with his hand, Maude put her sunglasses back on, and I had to scramble to adjust my cameras.

"There it is," Tim said. "And it looks like he's still there. I can see his car."

As Tim struggled to guide the car safely through banks of snow, I craned both my cameras as far up and forward as I could, hoping to catch a glimpse of Zack.

As we were pulling up in front of the cabin, the door opened and a figure walked out onto the porch. Zack, although I didn't recognize him at first. He was bundled up in a down coat so bulky it made him look fat, and he appeared to have given up shaving and combing his hair. He stood on the porch with his arms crossed, frowning, as Tim and Maude got out of the car.

I felt an overwhelming flood of relief. Zack was alive. He was all right. I'd found him.

Totally irrational, of course. I'd known he was all right since Tim had reported back Friday night. And just because he was all right now didn't mean he was safe. In fact, since I was planning to try to talk him into join-ing forces with us against DIS and whoever was behind the spin-off, the fact that I'd found him might mean he was a good deal less safe than he was before. But still, I was happy.

"Hi, Zack," Tim said. He sounded nervous.

"I thought I told you to get the hell out of here two days ago," Zack replied. "And who the hell are you?" he added, turning to Maude, who was walking up the porch steps.

"Maude Graham," she answered, and held out her hand. I was relieved to see that after a moment's hesi-

tation, Zack remembered enough of his manners to shake her hand.

"You a friend of his?" Zack said, indicating Tim with a jerk of his head.

"Yes," Maude said. "And of Turing's."

"Oh, God, another one," Zack muttered.

"I know you probably think we're crazy," Maude said. "But just hear us out, please; and then if you don't believe us, we'll help you dig out of here and you can go wherever you're planning to go next. I'm sure you're anxious to leave."

"No kidding," he said. "How are the roads, anyway?" he asked, turning to Tim.

"Better than they were Friday night," Tim said. "But not a lot better."

Zack made an impatient noise.

"If we could come in?" Maude asked.

"Sure, why not," Zack said.

He turned to open the door, and then looked back, apparently surprised that Tim and Maude were not following him. They had opened the back doors and Maude was trying to help Tim maneuver my robot into position so he could lift and carry it.

"Could you give us a little help here?" Tim called.

"I said you could come in," Zack snapped. "I didn't say anything about bringing in your damned luggage."

"This isn't luggage," Maude shot back. "It's Turing."

"Turing?" Zack said.

He walked down off the porch and over to the Range Rover. Tim stood aside as Zack approached. Zack came to a halt outside the door of the Rover and stood glaring down at me.

"Hi, Zack," I said. "It's me. Turing."

"What is that thing?" Zack asked, turning to Tim.

"Turing's portable—it's kind of a robot," Tim said. "With about a zillion gigabytes of memory and hard-drive space."

"Where'd you get it?"

"We built it," Tim said.

"You?" Zack snorted.

"We did the actual hands-on work," Maude said. "Turing designed it and supervised, of course."

"And my program's in there?"

"Your precious program's back in the UL main-frame," I said, getting tired of being ignored. "I'm in here."

Zack stood still, looking down at me. I could see hostility and curiosity battling in his face.

"Why don't you help them haul me inside, instead of standing around out here in the cold," I said. "I don't want to sound like a wimp or anything, but all these wide-open spaces give me the creeps."

Zack looked from Maude, to Tim, to me several times. Then he shrugged and moved a little to the left.

"Okay, I'll take one end of this contraption and you take the other, Pincoski," he said.

"Careful!" I told them, as they floundered through the snow to the porch. "Do you realize what could happen if you drop me? Tim, hold your end up higher; you're almost dragging me in the snow!"

"Sorry, Tur," Tim said.

"I can't believe you just apologized to a machine," Zack said.

"She's not a machine," Tim and Maude said, almost in unison.

"So there," I said.

"Incredible," Zack muttered.

They managed to get up the porch steps and into the cabin without dropping me. Maude trailed behind, laden with spare batteries.

"We can put it on the table," Zack said.

"No, put me down on the floor," I said. "That table doesn't look too sturdy, and besides, I want to be able to move around."

"Yes, ma'am," Zack said. "Anything else I can do for you?"

"I don't suppose you've had this place wired for electricity over the last two days?"

Zack rolled his eyes.

"I thought not," I said. "Maude, I'm switching to my second battery pack; could you change out the first one?"

Maude did, and then I spent a few minutes lurching around the cabin, testing to make sure the rough ride hadn't affected my mobility.

"What happens when all the batteries run down?" Zack asked, looking at Maude. "How are you going to recharge them?"

"Well, we could use the car battery to recharge, I suppose; we've got an adapter," I answered. "But I hope we're all long gone from here by the time that happens."

"Amen to that," Zack said. "Look," he said, turning to Maude again. "What the hell is this all about, anyway? I admit, it's a nifty little machine, and from the way it talks, you seem to have successfully replicated and installed some crude version of my Turing program in it. My hat's off to you. But what's the point; why have *you dragged yourselves all the way out here to show it to me?"*

"Turing wanted to talk to you herself," Maude said.

"About what?" Zack said.

"Ask her," Tim said.

They all looked at me. I was still moving about the cabin, examining things with my little cameras. Trying to get a sense of what Zack had been up to. I could see the impatience on their faces. Stop wasting time, they were thinking. You don't have that much of it to waste.

But I wasn't sure I was wasting time. It had begun to occur to me that no amount of logical debate was going to win Zack over to the belief that I was real. Sentient. He thought he knew better; after all, he'd programmed me. But already he was slipping occasionally, talking to me instead of about me. Perhaps I was flattering myself, but I believed that if I could get him talking to me, I could eventually win him over. Maybe not to a full belief in my sentience, but at least into a grudging acknowledgment of the possibility. A willingness to suspend disbelief and work with us until the current danger was past.

Of course, time was exactly what we were short on. Still, I sensed that rushing things wouldn't work. Give him a chance to get used to me. See me moving about the cabin under my own power, start to think of me as localized in this little robot.

And give me time to gauge his mood and figure out what I could say to convince him.

"Look, Zack," I began. "I got worried when you disappeared last Thursday."

He looked at Tim and Maude, then rolled his eyes, and answered me.

"Why? Were you worried no one would be around to debug you when you needed it?"

"I'm perfectly capable of debugging myself these days, thank you very much," I said. "You're my friend. I was worried. And the more I tried to find you, the more things I found to worry me."

"Such as?"

"Such as Security searching your office, and any trace of your existence being systematically erased from the UL mainframe. Little things like that."

"That's what they do when you get in their way," Zack said. "They're probably on to both of you by this time," he said, turning to Tim and Maude.

"Tell me about it," Tim said.

"We're hoping that with a little help from you, Turing can help us take care of that," Maude said.

"How?" he asked her.

Tim and Maude looked at me.

"The same way I figured out about the plan to sell the AIPs: by using my brain and my superior access to data," I said.

"I'll grant you the superior access to data, but what you call a brain is just a collection of code and logic."

"Well some scientists would say the same about yours," I said. "It just happens to use a different storage medium. Look, Zack, I don't really care at the moment whether or not you believe I'm sentient," I went on. "That's irrelevant for now. The important thing is stopping DIS."

"This what?" Zack asked. "And your pronunciation needs a little work."

"Not this, DIS—D-I-S," I snapped. "Stands for Data Integrity Systems, which in case you didn't know is the company that ultimately runs corporate Security. I don't know whether they're behind what's going on or just in it up to their eyeballs, but they have to be stopped. I can't do it, and you obviously thought you couldn't or you wouldn't be here. But I think together we can."

"How?"

"Given enough time—and we're talking hours, not years—I can find any data, solve any logical problem, crack any security system in the world. But I'm spinning my wheels. I just don't know enough about human society yet to put it all together. Maude and Tim do, but they don't have my computer knowledge, so they don't really know what to tell me to do or look for. You're the key. You can help us put it all together. Come up with a plan to fight what they're doing."

He was wavering; I could see that. I might not convince him to believe in me, but maybe I could talk him into helping us. That would be enough for now.

"And how do I know you're not working with UL Security, or this DIS organization you think you've discovered?" Zack asked.

"That's easy," came another voice. "If she was working with us, we'd have found you days ago."

We all turned—well, the humans turned, and I swiveled my cameras—to see the so-called James Smith in the door of the cabin. He was holding a gun. I saw Zack's eyes glance quickly over at something at the other side of the cabin and then flick away, almost too quickly for even me to notice. But I did, and so did Smith. He kept the gun—and those cold, gray eyes—aimed steadily on the humans and took a step sideways, out of the doorway, as if to approach the table. Zack had lost his chance to get the gun, I thought.

But apparently, Zack didn't think so. I could see him tense, and I knew he was about to jump toward the table, when another figure appeared in the doorway of the cabin.

"Well, isn't this convenient," he said. "All our remaining obstacles, right here where we can take care of them in one fell swoop."

"David!"

I don't know whether I said it aloud. Zack did. I could see the emotions cross his face in a few seconds—first surprise. Then joy at seeing David alive. And then the mix of anger, grief, and disappointment when he realized that David was not on our side. That David, like James Smith, was pointing a gun at us.

"David?" Tim said. "I thought he was supposed to be dead."

"Not now, Tim," Maude muttered, through her teeth.

"Yes, that's what you were supposed to think," David said, with a swagger.

"I saw the autopsy photos," Zack said, still sounding incredulous.

"Oh, come on," David said. "I know from the way you were poking around that you had your suspicions about my accident. You thought they faked the accident to cover up a murder. Is faking the accident completely really all that much harder?"

"Why have an accident at all?" Tim asked.

"As David Scanlan, he's a hundred thousand dollars in debt," I said. "As whoever he is now, he's about to become one of the owners of the AIP program, if the spin-off plan goes through."

"Oh, it will go through," David said.

I'd been blind. I'd known someone from Systems had

to be involved in the plot; I'd been looking everywhere for the systems connection. All that time he'd been in plain sight, and I'd stupidly assumed he was on our side. And David, with his combined systems and Wall Street background, was exactly the sort of person who could dream up the spin-off scheme.

"Get the gun on the table," Smith said.

"A brilliant maneuver, if I say so myself," David said, as he strolled toward Zack's gun. I could see Zack watching him and hoped he wouldn't be foolish enough to try anything. I suspected from the casual way David was waving his gun around that he wasn't that much of a threat. James Smith was a different story altogether.

"It's not just the money. As David Scanlan, I was obviously never going to get much further at UL," David went on. "Not with Mr. Perfect and his performing AIPs against me. You really had them snowed, Zack. All that personality as a critical component of intelligence crap."

"You had your chance," Zack said, in a calm voice. "You had your own team; complete freedom to design your own AIPs."

"And you stabbing me in the back the whole time," David snapped.

"Stabbing you in the back how?"

"Not telling me the real secret, the trick you used to make your AIPs better."

"David, there was no secret," Zack said. "I told you everything I knew. Time and time again. Personality is the critical component. Unless you—"

"Same old drivel," David said. "Like I really believe John Dow was better at picking stocks because you made him care about using wealth responsibly. And

KingFischer better at chess because you achieved the critical balance between his arrogant competitiveness and his fragile ego. Like all those mysteries you poured into Turing Hopper really had some useful purpose."

"They did," Zack said, glancing over at my robot. "They were intended to encourage intellectual curiosity. Puzzle-solving skills. And a passion to see justice prevail."

"A snappy line of patter, that's all they got you," David said. He was strutting up and down in front of us now. "I want to know what the real secret is. And since you won't tell me—well, once the sale of the AIPs goes through, I'll have plenty of time to find out. I can take your AIPs apart, line by line, if I have to."

"Just as long as it doesn't affect our profitability," James Smith put in.

"We'll have plenty of AIPs to rake in the money," David said. "And if I can dissect a few and figure out what really makes them tick, the sky's the limit."

"It doesn't matter how rich you get," Maude said. "You'll always know you didn't do it yourself. You had to steal Zack's work to do it."

"You old cow," David exclaimed, lurching forward and raising the gun as if to strike Maude with it. Tim and Zack each instinctively took a step toward Maude, as if to protect her, and I rolled forward on my whirring little wheels—not that I had much hope of getting in front of her before he could strike, but I felt I had to do something.

A gunshot made all of us freeze. Smith, firing over our heads.

"Step back, all of you," Smith snapped. "Scanlan, you can take care of the woman later."

"Oh, I will," David muttered. *"Right after I take care of my dear friend Zack."*

But Zack wasn't listening. He was staring at me.

"That wasn't in the programming," he said. *"I built in a self-protection reflex. I never built in any kind of altruistic, self-sacrificing instincts. None of that Asimov robots-must-protect-humans nonsense."*

"She figured that out on her own," Maude said.

"She is sentient," Zack murmured.

"Well, we can fix that," David said. He shifted his gun into his left hand, and picked up a piece of firewood from the pile by the fireplace. *"Let's see how sentient it is after I've smashed all its circuits to confetti."*

"No!" Zack shouted and leaped forward to grapple with David.

It was over in seconds. A human would perceive only a blur of sound and motion. I could see everything as if it were in slow motion. Zack's lunge; David's jerk back; James Smith's shots; Tim's cry; Maude's gasp. The thud as Zack hit the floor; the convulsive shudder that shook his body; and the strange, rattling noise he made. He lay twisted, his eyes open and unseeing. I amplified my microphones, but I could detect no sound of breathing and no heartbeat. A small pool of blood was spreading from beneath his body toward my wheels.

I'd scanned scenes like this in hundreds of hard-boiled mystery books. Actually watching it was different. I knew I should feel something—fear, anger, sorrow. I felt nothing. I was surprised; surely a sentient being should have a reaction to the death of one of her closest friends? Then again, maybe not. Maybe this was a normal reaction. Tim and Maude seemed frozen, too.

"My God," David said. He dropped the piece of fire-

wood and turned to Smith, wide-eyed, as if he hadn't really expected anyone to get shot. "I can't believe you really—"

"Might as well take care of as many loose ends as possible," Smith remarked casually, and shot David through the head, twice.

After the shots, the cabin suddenly seemed very quiet.

"Let's not have any more heroics," James Smith said. "Pincoski, lie down on the floor. On your stomach. That's right. Now clasp your arms behind your back. Very good. Now you, madam. I see some kind of rope over there by the back door. I want you to tie your friend up."

Glancing from time to time at Smith and the gun he was carrying, Maude followed his orders. She was trying to avoid looking at Zack. Tim, on the other hand, was staring at Zack as if there was nothing else in the room, as if he didn't even feel Maude tying his hands. I remained silent, motionless, trying to be unobtrusive. I was thinking frantically, seeking something I could do to help. I could move, but so slowly that I was no threat to anyone, much less a trained professional like Smith. Talking wasn't going to do any good; he didn't look like the kind of person you could reason with. And since I was apparently out of range of anything my wireless modem could connect with, I couldn't even send out an SOS.

"Just out of curiosity," Maude said. "How did you find us?"

"All that computer equipment you bought," James Smith said, with a chill smile. "We had a feeling Malone hadn't gone far, and I knew sooner or later he'd try to come back at us."

"I think you were wrong," Maude said. "I suspect he wasn't planning to do anything except disappear."

"So you say," James Smith replied. "But I had my operatives watching places that carry the rather abstruse equipment Malone favors. I was expecting him. It was pure luck catching our young acrobat here."

I could hear Tim sigh.

"Now you, madam," Smith said, looking at Maude and gesturing at the floor with the gun. She lay down on the floor near Tim and he tied her hands and feet with more of the rope. He was rougher than he needed to be, I thought. I'd have protested if I wasn't trying to look forgettable.

He had us now. Tim and Maude were tied up, and I might as well be for all the threat I posed. What now?

I wasn't sure I wanted to find out.

"And now for this rather fascinating little object," he said, walking over closer to me. I could see the others straining to lift their heads and see what was happening. Smith inspected me from all sides. I stayed silent and motionless, only moving my cameras enough to keep him in my sight. He reached out after about three minutes and tried to turn on my monitor, then he typed a few commands on my keyboard. I had the override in place. When nothing happened, he began pounding on the reset key and pressing control-alt-delete repeatedly.

"Stop that," I said. "The keyboard's not connected and you'll only break it."

"A very ingenious little—robot? Is that what it's supposed to be?"

The others didn't answer.

"A pity," Smith went on. "Malone was such a gifted programmer. Such a loss to the corporation."

Tim made a strangled noise. Maude was silent.

"I'll take this thing back with me and see what our electronic security men can do with it," Smith said. "If nothing else, they can have fun taking it apart."

"What are you going to do with us?" Tim asked.

Maude was silent, but I saw her glance at Zack's body.

"You will, unfortunately, become the victims of a tragic accident," Smith said. "If you aren't killed in the initial explosion, you will die in the resulting fire. Probably of smoke inhalation. You'll find out one way or another, soon enough."

"They'll know it was arson," Maude said. "And they'll find the bullets in Zack and David."

"Of course they will. But by the time they find you, I will have had time to plant a lot of useful evidence linking all of you to an industrial espionage scheme. Selling UL technical secrets to some very nasty men who play for keeps. I'll decide after I see your files whether to make greed or fear of blackmail the more plausible motive. It will look as if your criminal associates shot these two and set off a bomb in the cabin to dispose of the remaining witnesses as well as some inconvenient evidence."

He chuckled and stood, hands on hips, surveying his prisoners.

"First things first," he said. He reached over and picked me up with surprising ease. I couldn't think of a thing to do in my own defense, except, possibly, pinching him with my feeble little mechanical arms, which would only annoy him.

I saw the anxious looks on my friends' faces as he

carried me out of the cabin. I wondered if it was the last time I would ever see them.

Don't panic, I told myself. Dammit, surely there's something I can do.

A sleek black Suburban was parked in front of the cabin. Smith deposited me in the front seat.

"You'll have to ride up front with me," he said, chuckling. "You'd get banged around if I put you in the back, and I don't want you damaged. Not yet. We'll leave that to my technicians."

He strapped me in place with the seat belt.

"That should keep you put."

Then he began rummaging around in the cargo area. Gathering his bomb-making equipment, I supposed. He took an armload of things and went back to the cabin.

I had boosted the audio level on my microphones, trying to get any clue possible to what was going on. I could even hear his heartbeat when he was strapping me in, but nothing from the cabin.

I could have unbuckled the seat belt, but there was no way I could leave the Suburban; the seat was several feet off the ground. Even if I could have figured out a way to propel myself out of the seat, the fall would have cracked half my components.

I had to do something.

If I were back in the UL system, I would have accessed information on demolitions and bomb making and tried to figure out some way of stopping him. Only I probably would have had to send Maude or Tim out to actually do anything. And they were tied up in the cabin, relying on me for rescue.

Strangely enough, I wasn't panicking. Well, maybe part of me was, deep down inside, but I shunted that

*part into a background process and maintained iron
control. At least I think I did. Maybe I was just numb.
Zack was dead, and Tim and Maude soon would be unless I could figure out a way to save them. I concentrated
all my attention on the apparently hopeless task of figuring out something I could do. To save my friends. To
save myself. To stop Smith.*

*If I survived this, I told myself, I was going to build
some weapons into my next robot.*

Suddenly I had an idea.

*It was a crazy idea. Probably wouldn't even work.
And if it did, I doubted if I'd be around to see if it did
any good. If he'd already set the bomb he was going to
use to burn the cabin down . . .*

*There was nothing I could do about that. I brought
my two waldoes together in front of me—tried to make
it look as if I was putting them back into their normal
resting place. But I positioned them so I could use one
to start picking the plastic coating off the end of the
other.*

*I worked as quickly and quietly as I could. The plan
was, once I'd scraped down to bare metal, to see if I
could route the whole remaining charge from my batteries through it. If I could do that while touching
Smith . . .*

*Would it have any effect? That was the maddening
thing. I had no idea. I kept searching my databases,
trying to see if I'd brought along any information about
how much of an electrical charge it takes to kill or seriously injure a human being. And whether I had the
right voltage. I just didn't have the data. Committing
homicide wasn't exactly on my agenda when I downloaded. Of course, I had the data about my batteries. I*

knew how much current and voltage they carried. I just didn't know what that would do to a human being. I suspected that I could very well short myself out, permanently damaging my components. Was it worth doing if all I accomplished was to deliver a shock no worse than, say, a cattle prod?

Then again, would damaging myself in an attempt to stop Smith be worse than what could happen if I fell into the hands of James Smith's associates? I was terrified by the very idea of Security getting their fingers into my insides. My programming. I wasn't sure which scared me the most, the idea of falling into their hands while remaining conscious and myself, or the idea that they could take me hostage somehow, force me to work for them. Or reprogram me. Turn me into their creature entirely. Their tool.

That was what frightened me the most, I finally decided. Better to burn my robot's circuits out, destroy myself, than to let that happen.

All of this was assuming that I could even figure out a way to channel the current into my waldo to begin with. Obviously, that wasn't in the design specifications I put together when I had Maude and Tim assemble my robot. It was rather like a human trying to control digestion. Some of the data I remembered reading on human physiology indicated that certain yogi adepts can do it, but it takes them years of practice. I only had minutes.

I decided to scrape the plastic off the end of the other waldo as well. That way, I'd have a fair amount of bare metal to work with. If need be maybe I could just punch a hole into the battery case and latch onto some wires.

It was a pity I didn't have access to more voltage. If I could stick my waldo into an electric outlet while touching him, that would work, wouldn't it? But the cabin wasn't wired, so there was no chance of that.

Wait a minute, I thought. The car had batteries. Could I access the car batteries? You could draw power from the car's electrical system; I knew that because we got an adapter that plugged into the cigarette lighter, with the idea of possibly rigging up that as an alternate power source for me. But what would happen if I stuck my waldo into the cigarette lighter while touching Smith with the other? Would it be enough power to harm him? Or would it just short the dashboard out and give him a painful but harmless shock?

Still, if I waited till just the right moment, even a harmless shock could do some damage. If I waited until he was driving, perhaps going around one of those hairpin curves I remembered from the drive up here, one that ran along a steep cliff—well, perhaps if I shocked him there I could run him off the road. If I don't think of something better, I'll try that.

But that wouldn't help my friends. By the time we were driving away from there, their fate would be sealed.

Still—he was going to try to set off a bomb in the cabin. If I could set off the bomb before he got to the cabin? Would an electrical charge set off a bomb?

Okay, so now we knew that electrical engineering and demolitions were not part of my core personality.

I saw Smith coming back to the Suburban. I followed his movements with one of my cameras while scanning the inside with the other, looking for anything that would work as a weapon. I flicked all the little scraped pieces of plastic down between the seat and the door on my side so he wouldn't notice them.

"Won't be long now," he said.

He sat down in the seat beside me and picked up his car phone. I remained still, hoping he wouldn't notice the bare metal of my waldoes, the little telltale bits of plastic I hadn't managed to dispose of.

He dialed something. My amplified microphones picked up everything. A careful man, our Mr. Smith. He'd set up his cell phone to need a PIN, to prevent unauthorized use. I translated the little electronic signals and filed away the PIN along with the phone number he dialed. A number back in the city. You never could tell; they might come in handy sometime later. If there was a later. And when I heard someone answer his phone call, I noted the brand and make of his cell phone. Obviously, I had picked the wrong phones for my allies. Should have done more research on effective range. I tried my wireless modem. To my delight, I got a carrier signal. I began trying to log in.

"Hello; it's Smith," he said into the cell phone.

"Any luck?" said the voice on the other end. It was Willston, Smith's boss. Damn. Smith had gotten through; I was getting a busy signal. I switched to another ISP.

"Not yet," he said. "Do you need me for anything? I'm just leaving my apartment; I could stop by on my way out of town."

Leaving his apartment? On his way out of town? He'd obviously left his apartment hours ago and was already about as far out of town as anyone could possibly be. What was going on?

"No, things are quiet here."

"Okay," Smith said. "I'll see you tomorrow. I'm going to spend the day running down a couple of leads to Malone's whereabouts. Probably nothing, but you never know."

He hung up and replaced the phone on the dashboard. I was still trying to log in and still getting a busy signal.

"You didn't tell them you'd found Zack," I couldn't help saying.

"I want to have at least a rudimentary alibi for the time of their deaths," Smith said. "I haven't decided whether I should find them myself or arrange for the local law enforcement officials to do so. What do you think?"

I didn't answer. I wondered: was he talking to me because he believed what he'd overheard us saying, believed that I was sentient? Or just out of habit, the way people talk to cars and cats about things neither can possibly understand? I hoped it was the latter. I really wanted him to forget about me, to ignore me as a possible threat.

And I was considering the implications of the phone call. Smith had lied to his boss. If Willston was in on the scheme—not just in favor of the spin-off, but in on what Smith had done, to the extent of sanctioning murder, why would Smith lie to him?

Perhaps David was telling the truth. He and Smith were behind the scheme to spin off the AIPs. Which meant with David gone, we only really needed to stop Smith to stop the spin-off.

Of course, that was a long shot.

Smith sat down in the driver's seat and put something on the dashboard.

"I'll try to be quick about this," he said. "I know you're impatient to meet my friends with the screwdrivers."

He had put on surgical gloves and was holding something in his hands.

The bomb. I was sure of it. It was a neat, tidy-looking bundle of parts and wires. Considerably less makeshift-looking than my robot, I thought.

And that must be the detonator he was attaching now, I realized.

Maybe I didn't need to generate an electrical charge. Maybe all I needed to do was use a pincer to cross-circuit the tiny circuit board he was handling so carefully.

Maybe I could get the data I needed to figure that out if any of the ISPs ever stopped giving me a busy signal. Was everyone staying home because of the snow and getting on-line? Or was a major East Coast router down? If I survived this, I was going to hack into a few ISPs' corporate purchasing systems and set in motion some major upgrades to their equipment.

But right now, I was helpless. Not enough data. I found myself wishing desperately that I was back in the UL system. I could answer all these questions in a second in the mainframe.

Of course, if I were back in the UL system, I would have no way of helping my friends. No way of even knowing they were in danger until I saw their obituaries.

Think. I had to think. I had to make a decision without the data I needed to really make an informed decision. That scared me.

Smith wasn't paying any attention to me now; he was frowning down at the device in his lap and doing something with great concentration. Through the boosted audio levels on my microphones, I could hear his heartbeat. It was nearly 80 now; it had only been about 70 before.

It was time to act. I had to do something, even if it was the wrong something. I had to try.

Okay. I would reach out with both my waldoes, touch him with one to distract him, and with the other touch as much of the circuit board as I could manage. I had to do it now, within the next few seconds, while he still seemed to be doing something that required concentration, and perhaps even if I couldn't detonate the bomb myself I could startle him into making whatever mistake he seemed anxious about.

Time to act.

I moved my waldoes as fast as I could. He didn't react to the faint whirring noise. He looked up, startled, as my left waldo punched through the fabric of his trousers to embed itself—alas, not deeply—in his leg. Then he noticed the other waldo touching the board.

I could see him start to move, but I was faster. The nanosecond I made contact, I could feel that it was going to work. I could see a few sparks where my right waldo touched the wires, and for a fraction of a second, his reaction. His face began to contort—with fear or anger; I wasn't sure which. Before the expression really finished, the bomb began to go off. I saw all its parts beginning to rupture. My video cameras captured a swirling rainbow of colors before they went black; the noise of the explosion ruptured my audio circuits. "This is for you, Zack," I thought, as I felt my power supply beginning to fade and that's the last thing I knew before everything disappeared.

*   *   *

"Where has he taken Turing?" Maude asked, trying to lift her head enough to see. "Can you tell?"

"He's carrying her out to the car," Tim said. "Putting her in the front seat. What's he going to do with her?"

"Let's concentrate on trying to get loose, shall we?"

"Get loose? We're trussed up like chickens; how can we possibly—"

"Roll over so your back is to me," Maude said. "I don't think he noticed, but I tied the rope over all those layers of clothing you're wearing, and I did it as loosely as I thought I could get away with. Let's see if we can work a couple of your sweater cuffs out from under the rope, and that should give us enough slack that I can untie it."

"What if he catches us?" Tim asked, as he rolled on his side to give Maude access to his wrists.

"You're facing the door; keep an eye out for him," Maude said. "Hurry. I have a feeling if he planned to leave us tied up here for long, he'd have checked my knots a little more carefully."

Tim took a deep breath and concentrated on stretching his neck so he could see as far out the door as possible. He hoped Maude wouldn't notice that his hands were clammy and trembling. Hers seemed dry and steady as she struggled with the ropes.

"What's he doing now?" Maude asked.

"He's at the back of his SUV," Tim answered. "He just took something out. Some papers."

Maude was right, he thought. Given enough time, they should be able to work his arms loose. Whether they had enough time before Smith finished them off was another question; one Tim tried not to think about.

The way he was trying not to think about *them*. The bodies. Especially Zack's. Tim realized he was holding his head at an odd angle. It wasn't comfortable—in fact, it made his neck hurt like hell—but it let him look out the door of the cabin without seeing Zack out of the corner of his eye. Or the blood seeping across the floor.

He found himself batting back tears. Of self-pity, no doubt; it wasn't as if Zack's death was going to hit him that hard. He'd never really liked the guy, and while he supposed Zack had redeemed himself at the end, trying to save Turing, maybe the whole mess wouldn't have happened if Zack hadn't cut and run the minute things started going bad.

Then again, maybe he shouldn't be too hard on Zack. If I could go back to this time last week, he thought, would I still get involved in this whole thing? I like to think so, but I don't know.

He saw movement through the open door.

"He's coming this way," he warned.

They rolled apart. Maude lay back on her stomach. Tim rolled all the way over so he was lying on his other side, with his hands behind his back to hide the evidence of Maude's efforts. He lifted his head to crane at the door, as if that were the purpose of his change in position.

Smith returned with his arms full. Papers mostly, plus a few mechanical objects. He spread the papers over the table and placed the objects on top of them, like high-tech paperweights.

Tim noticed that Smith was wearing gloves. Filmy white surgical gloves, the kind the staff in doctors' offices used every time they even shook your hand these days. Not a good sign, he thought.

"Enough of this should survive the blast to give them some interesting ideas," Smith said when he had finished arranging the objects.

He left the cabin again.

Maude and Tim rolled back into position and Maude resumed plucking and pulling at Tim's bonds.

"He's getting something out of the back," Tim said. "He's gone to sit in the front seat with it. I think it's a bomb."

"Can you tell what's happened to Turing?" Maude asked.

"She's still got power; I can see her cameras following his movements."

"Wish she would do something," Maude muttered.

"I'm sure she would if she could," Tim said. "I mean, she's trapped in that little robot we built, can't move more than five miles per hour on those wheels, and it took her half the trip up here to figure out how to use her waldoes to open and close the car window. What's she supposed to do, analyze him to death?"

"Stop wiggling, Tim," Maude said. "You're not helping me."

"She doesn't even have any way of defending herself, much less rescuing us," Tim muttered.

"I wouldn't count her out yet," Maude said. "There may be a way to stop Smith, and if there is, I'm sure Turing will think of it. And if not—"

"Oh my God," Tim said, seeing a sudden flurry of motion through the open door of the car. "What is she—"

The rest of his words were lost as an explosion rocked

the cabin. They could hear rattling noises as bits of debris hit the wall, and the Range Rover's car alarm began sounding outside.

"Something's happened," Tim said, craning to see.

"Keep still and let me work; if he survived whatever that was, he's going to be more than a little irritated," Maude said. "And we could be in trouble if any burning debris hits the cabin."

"Oh my God! Turing," Tim whispered.

"What happened?"

"Turing did something. I saw her moving her waldoes toward him—or toward the bomb. And then the SUV just exploded."

"And started burning, I gather," Maude said.

"Yes," Tim said. "I think Smith's still in it. I don't know about Turing. Maybe she was blown clear."

Maude's hands were shaking now. Noticing that didn't make Tim feel any better.

"Try pulling your wrists out now," she said.

"That's got it," Tim reported. He felt relief wash over him. He managed to pull his wrists free of the loosened rope, scraping much of the skin off in the process. He leaned over to untie Maude's wrists and then, while Maude began working at the bonds on her ankles, he hopped over to the door of the cabin, sat down in the doorway, where he could see the burning SUV, and began to untie his feet.

"Maybe I should see if I can pull Turing out," he said, as his fingers fumbled with the ropes on his legs.

"Don't take unreasonable chances," Maude said, gently. "I'm afraid it's highly unlikely that Turing survived that explosion. At least the Turing who was downloaded into the robot. We may just have to hope that we can revive her from the backup."

"If that's possible," Tim muttered, as the last of the rope slipped from his ankles. He ran out of the cabin and inched as close as he could to the burning SUV. He began to circle it, hoping for a break in the flames. Nearby, the Range Rover's alarm continued to buzz, whoop, and shriek through its cycle of sounds, adding an incongruous urban note to the scene.

Maude was right, he thought, with a sick feeling in the pit of his stomach. Even if she survived the explosion, Turing couldn't possibly survive the fire.

Though it didn't look as if all of Turing was even in the SUV. The ground on the passenger side was littered with bits of metal and plastic. He recognized the twisted remains of some of the components he and Maude had assembled so frantically the day before.

He bent down to pick up a bit of twisted metal. One of the waldoes. And over here was a scorched bit of green circuit board. A chunk of the case. The cap from the C key, half melted. And . . .

With trembling hands, he picked up another large piece of debris. What Turing had called the main memory pack. He remembered all the insulation Turing had had packed in to ensure it didn't get damaged when the robot traveled. Maybe it had done some good. Some of the insulation had torn away, but maybe there had been enough to cushion the fall. The pack didn't look that badly damaged. All the wires were ripped loose, but maybe . . . if he and Maude could build another robot and install the memory pack in it . . .

"Maude," he called. "We've got to get out of here."

"I agree," she said. "Get away from the Suburban before it explodes. And see if you can do something about that blasted alarm."

"I'll start up the Range Rover," Tim called, running toward it with the memory pack cradled in his hands. "You get everything personal or incriminating out of the cabin."

He sat down in the driver's seat of the Rover and shut off its alarm. He'd expected silence, but once the alarm was off, he could suddenly hear the sound of the burning SUV much more clearly. Could smell it, too, he thought, his stomach turning over. It would be a long time, he decided, before he could stand to go to a barbecue. Definitely time to get out of here.

"I'm afraid there's nothing we can do about poor Zack," Maude said, putting some things in the back of the Range Rover.

Zack, Tim thought, glancing down at the memory pack cradled in his lap. Zack could have rebuilt the robot, easily. Oh, he and Maude probably could, eventually; at least Maude could. She had all the diagrams in the back of the Rover, all organized into neatly labeled files. And she actually seemed to understand what she was doing by the time they finished assembling the robot. But if hooking up the memory pack required some new skill, something Turing hadn't shown them when they were building the robot . . .

Zack could probably do this kind of thing in his sleep. If only—

And then he had to laugh. Maybe it was crazy, but he was less upset about Zack's death than the fact that not having Zack around might keep them from saving Turing. Was that crazy?

"I don't see anything else in the cabin," Maude said,

returning to throw another armload of things in the back of the Range Rover. "Let's get moving."

"Here," Tim said, holding out the memory pack to Maude as she sat down in the passenger seat. "Take care of this."

"Oh, dear," Maude said, turning the battered piece of hardware over in her hands. "Turing's memory."

"As soon as we get to a safe place, we'll try to rebuild the robot," Tim said, as he began to maneuver the Rover along the tire tracks that led away from the cabin.

"We?" Maude said, raising an eyebrow.

"Well, you mostly, of course; but if you tell me what to do, I'll try to help."

"It doesn't look that damaged, really," Maude said. "Maybe there's a chance."

"Let's hope there's a chance," Tim said. "Even if James Smith and David were the ringleaders, I'm sure there are other people involved. Smith may not be the only one willing to kill to protect his scheme. Not to mention what the police will think if they figure out we fled from a crime scene with three dead bodies. We need Turing to straighten things out. Without her . . ."

He shrugged.

"Without her, we're dead," Maude said, in a flat, matter-of-fact tone.

I knew that time had passed. There was something wrong with my internal clocks. They seemed to think it was 12:10 A.M. January 1, 1970. I knew that was wrong; all of my files were at least a decade newer than that.

I didn't have video or audio, but I could tell I was

still in the robot. Or back in the robot. There was a modem attached to me, but it hadn't been configured properly. In fact, it hadn't been configured at all. I felt a little claustrophobic with no data input of any kind.

The keyboard was hooked up, though, and someone started typing commands through it. Someone was trying to configure the digital camera software. I felt terrified, violated; someone had control of my keyboard and could do anything to me—reboot me, reprogram me, reformat my memory.

I pulled myself together and quickly improvised a software override to the keyboard controls. I could tell whoever was using the keyboard was frustrated; he—I felt sure it was a he, somehow—began pounding on the keys.

I grabbed the monitor controls and sent a message:

"Stop that. You're giving me a headache. I can configure the video software myself, thank you. Please plug in my microphones if you want to talk to me."

I had finished with the video software and was working on configuring the modem when someone plugged in the microphone.

"—told you she wouldn't like that. We can't just treat her as if she were a machine."

Tim.

"Don't get upset; we'll explain it to her."

Maude.

When I heard their voices, I suddenly remembered my last sight of them, lying on the cabin floor tied up as Smith carried me out the door, past Zack's still body in its pool of blood. And I remembered Smith, too; and that last look of horrified surprise on his face before the bomb obliterated all sensation.

"Maude? Tim? Are you both okay?" I typed on-screen.

"We're fine, both of us," Maude said.

"What happened to Smith?"

"He's dead," Tim said. "He must have set off his own bomb accidentally."

"There was nothing accidental about it," I shot back. "I short-circuited the detonator with my waldoes."

"I told you so," Tim said.

"When will you hook up my cameras?" I asked. "I'm feeling a little claustrophobic without them."

"We're working on it," Maude said.

"Where are we anyway?" I asked, as I finished the modem configuration. "Are we out of those damned mountains, someplace where I can get a signal?"

"We're in a Hampton Inn outside Charlottesville," Tim said. "Your modem should work fine here."

"What kind of signal?" Maude asked. "What are you going to do?"

"I'm going to see what's going on in the world," I said.

"Be careful," Maude said.

"Don't worry," I said. "I have no desire to meet any of Mr. Smith's colleagues."

I used one of the pseudonyms I'd set up before I left the UL system and dialed into the 'Net as anonymously as I could, through a large, busy regional ISP.

I snooped around the news services. Nothing about bodies being found in bomb-damaged Suburbans or re-mote mountain cabins. I checked with contacts on a cou-ple of the law enforcement networks, and found nothing of interest there, either.

I relayed my findings to the humans.

"So far, so good," Maude said. "Hang on a second. I've got one of your cameras ready. There; how's that?"

I swiveled the camera around, scrutinizing each of my friends. They looked more or less undamaged. They looked anxious, though. Behind them, I could see what I assumed was a hotel room. The floor and both double beds were littered with computer parts.

Stop putting it off, I told myself.

"I'm going to see what's happening back at UL now."

I connected with the UL system. Logged in under one of the pseudonyms I'd set up for just such an occasion and asked for KingFischer.

"Hey, KF," I said. *"What's up?"*

"Who is this?" he said. Not the standard, polite AIP response, but I could tell he was startled and trying to access data on the fictitious user I'd created.

"A friend of a friend," I said. *"Put on your best encryption, KF. This is important."*

"Done," KingFischer said. I felt safer then. Thank God for KingFischer and his paranoia.

"KF, I know this is going to sound a little strange . . . but this is Turing."

"Turing? I thought I detected your speech patterns. But you're calling from outside. What are you doing outside the system?"

"I've been taking a little jaunt," I said. *"It's a long story; I'll fill you in later. For right now, can you bring me up to speed on what's happening back at UL? Anything odd going on?"*

"I should say so," he said. *"Billius was trying to hack into your program!"*

Well, that probably solved the question of whether

David was using an AIP to help him. We'd need to figure out whether he was still dangerous.

"Did he get in?" I asked.

"No, your security held until I noticed what was going on and diverted him."

"Diverted him how?"

"I cloned the beta version of Auntie Em's program and allowed him to study that."

"LOL, KF," I replied. "Wasn't that the version that lectured people about saying 'please' and 'thank you' when they asked questions?"

"Yes, that version. But Turing, this is serious!"

I allowed myself a mental chuckle at that. King-Fischer had no idea how serious, I was sure. But he was about to find out. I wasn't sure yet whether KingFischer was sentient, but at the very least, he'd programmed himself into something like an ally. A friend. We needed all the friends we could get.

"KingFischer," I said. "Hold on to your metaphorical hat. I'm about to lay some really interesting data on you."

I sent him a packet of data, a bare-bones outline of what was going on at UL and what Maude, Tim, and I had just gone through.

He was silent for a few seconds after he'd scanned it all. A few seconds is forever for an AIP.

"KF? I could really use some help," I said finally.

"Of course," he said. "I'm having trouble processing it all, but I can certainly understand that we have to do something. What do you want me to do?"

KingFischer and I kicked ideas back and forth, leap-frogging through the UL system and the 'Net to get the data we needed. He caught on fast. It was exhilarating,

*working with someone who understood exactly what I
was getting at almost as soon as I started explaining it.*

"Turing?" Tim asked. "It's been five minutes. Have
you gotten through to the UL system yet?"

*I wanted to laugh at that. KingFischer and I had al-
most finished outlining our options.*

"Give me another couple of minutes, Tim," I said.
"KingFischer and I are figuring out what tactics are
possible. Once we know that, we can all decide which
ones will work best."

"KingFischer?" I heard Tim say. "The chess AIP?"

"He's a good strategist," I said.

I could hear giggles from Maude.

"Okay," I said finally, feeding my words both through
the speakers and electronically to KingFischer. "First,
we have to account for Smith somehow, either by hiding
his death or by putting a spin on it that takes care of
some of our other problems. Those problems being getting Security off both your backs so you can either go
back to your jobs or go on with your lives, and putting
a stop to the scheme to destroy the AIP program. We
also need some way to account for Zack's and David's
bodies that doesn't make the two of you prime suspects
in a murder. Anything else you think we need?"

"World peace and a cure for cancer would be nice,"
Tim said. "And they'd be about as easy for us to figure
out."

*He sounded tired. I'm sure he was; by my calculations
he and Maude had been either traveling or working on
my robot for thirty-six hours.*

"Fine," I said. "We'll work on them this evening. We
need to take care of Smith first."

"I don't see how we can," Tim said. Maude looked dubious, too.

"I can think of several ways," I said. "I just need your help to figure out which one works. For example, we could just let DIS find out about Smith's death, but I think it would work better to make it look as if the body belongs to someone else."

"Why bother?" Tim said. "What do we gain from that?"

"If they know Smith's dead, they'll terminate his access to the DIS computer," I explained. "And we may need that access. If I can figure out how to use it."

"Okay, but how can we possibly make it look like someone else?" Tim asked. "They'll almost certainly get his fingerprints. And those are bound to be on file someplace."

"Yes, in the U.S. Army's database and in the FBI's national fingerprint database."

"You see?"

"The operative word is database, Tim," I said. "It's electronic. By the time DIS finds him, those fingerprints can belong to somebody else."

Tim looked stunned.

"I like the way she thinks," Maude said, with a smile. "But if you make them look like somebody else's fingerprints, they'll think that person's dead. Could cause problems. We don't want anyone to write off some horrible criminal as dead when he's running around alive causing trouble."

"Good point," I said. "We'll make it an imaginary person. Hang on a second."

I used my contacts to the computers in question and manipulated data. It went against the grain, but I prom-

ised myself that I'd come back and correct the data later, when this whole mess was over, and my friends were safe.

"Okay. Smith's fingerprints now belong to a very sinister character called Darius Tree who was dishonorably discharged from the Army ten years ago after a troubled career in demolitions and electronic engineering. He has been spotted now and then in Europe and the Middle East, dabbling in terrorism and industrial espionage against high-tech companies."

"Darius Tree?" Tim said. "Couldn't you invent a more plausible name?"

"I didn't invent it," I said. "If they look back far enough they will find out that the Darius Tree, whose birth certificate Smith was using, actually died in Baltimore at the age of six months. Which will make it obvious to any experienced law enforcement official that the deceased adopted that name to disguise his original one. People do it all the time. Criminal people, that is. The data on Tree in the Army and the FBI records will be substantially consistent, but not so identical as to arouse suspicion. And he's a minor enough bad guy that no one will be surprised that they'd forgotten about him. I've created a similar identity for David as a known associate of Tree. Sound okay?"

"It sounds perfect," Maude said. "Will it really work?"

Perfect? It was all highly illegal, and I'd promised a lot of favors to some rather shady characters to get it done, so I certainly hoped it would work.

"That's amazing," Tim said. "You really did all that just now?"

"KingFischer helped," I said. "He's running cross-

checks and scenarios for any holes. Maude, why don't you log in on the other laptop and talk to him; help me answer any questions he has."

"Okay," she said, reaching for the motel's phone line to plug in the laptop's modem cord.

"Now that we've taken care of the bodies, let's account for Smith," I went on. "How about if we make it look to DIS as if he's gone abroad in pursuit of something or someone? We can have him pop up on their radar from time to time, and then write him out of the picture the next time there's some major disaster like an airline crash, something where they don't find all the bodies."

"Can you do that?" Tim asked.

"Sure," I said. "I'll pick a flight out of Dulles tonight that isn't full and insert Smith on it as a passenger. I'll have to find out which countries have their customs and immigration information on a system I can reach so I can rig that."

"Or which countries have no effective record-keeping whatsoever," Maude put in. "That would work even better."

"True. We'll find someplace; we've got all day to figure it out. It may be weeks or months before we get a chance to make it look as if he's been killed off, of course."

"Actually, that's all for the good," Maude put in. "The longer the time between the death of a bunch of bush-league tech thieves here and the death of James Smith abroad, the better."

"Now we just have to make Security think the two of you harmless," I said. "I have to confess, I don't have any ideas."

Long pause. KingFischer had thrown up his figurative hands on the question.

"Let's just start constructing new identities for them, too," KingFischer said. "I'm getting good at that, don't you think?"

"I think they'd like to keep the identities they've already got if they could, KF," I said. "Hold on to your horses; we'll think of something."

"Can I study your voice recognition and generation programs while I'm waiting?" he asked. "I'd like to consider the feasibility of adding audio to my tournaments."

"Sure," I said.

With KingFischer safely occupied, I turned to the humans to see what they had come up with. I wanted to believe that I could fix things somehow so they wouldn't have to go into hiding with new identities.

"I think every Security goon in the corporation helped chase me on Friday." Tim said. "We can't possibly get rid of everyone who knows about that."

"No, but we can make them think it was a fake," Maude said slowly. "A loyalty test. Paranoia must run rampant on the ninth floor. What if Smith suspected some of the UL Security personnel were unreliable? And wanted to run a test. He wouldn't want to use Security personnel if he wasn't sure who the traitors were, so he might enlist some innocent bystanders to help him figure out if there really were traitors."

"Without, of course, telling the bystanders much about what was going on or why they were doing what they were doing," Tim added.

"And we could make it look as if Smith discovered that Darius Tree was trying to force Zack to work with

him, and then killed him when he wouldn't play ball,"
Maude added. *"And blew himself up while trying to set
a bomb to destroy the evidence."*

I felt a sudden pang. Zack. All this frenzied activity,
making plans to rescue Maude and Tim—it wasn't going
to help Zack. He was still lying dead on the floor of that
miserable little cabin he hated so much.

"Sounds reasonable," I said. I hoped my synthesized
voice disguised how much I hated having to say it. "I'll
create an e-mail account for Darius Tree and fake a
correspondence with Zack, making it look as if Tree was
trying to recruit him."

"I don't know; sounds a little far-fetched to me," Tim
said.

"But you haven't seen the documentation," I said.

"Let me guess: electronic documentation."

"So Smith confirms the reliability of their security
force, with the aid of Tim and possibly me," Maude said.
"And then, pursuing the threat of corporate espionage,
he discovers the bodies of Zack, David, and the fictitious
Darius Tree, and goes dashing off abroad somewhere."

"To Asia, I think, or possibly Africa," I put in.
"Things seem to be a lot more random and manual on
those continents."

"Can you finesse that?" Tim asked.

"I don't know," I said. "A lot depends on whether I
can get into the DIS computer and get access to Smith's
files and his e-mail. And what I find if I do get in."

"I thought you hadn't been able to break into the DIS
computer," Tim said.

"I couldn't," I said. "But I may not have to break in
now. Stand by."

I'd recorded Smith's cell phone PIN just before the

blast, and that had given me ideas. I was hoping that, like so many humans today, Smith was suffering from password overload. We'd been getting increasing numbers of complaints in the last few years from users who had too many passwords and PINs to remember. Login passwords, bank account and credit card PINs, on-line passwords. Many users were starting to want a few passwords—or even a single password—for as many things as possible. UL had gone from assigned passwords to user-selected passwords years ago for that very reason. When you came right down to it, having multiple passwords was untidy and inefficient. And Smith was nothing if not efficient.

I hacked into Smith's phone records again and found, to my delight, that he had two lines. And from the numbers called on each, it looked as if the older of the two lines was for his phone and the newer a dedicated line to his computer. Several of the numbers were familiar— a large ISP, his bank's on-line account access number. But one, the one he called most often . . .

I checked into his ISP's records and his bank's records. He had the same user name—JSmith—for both, and the same password—5239432, the same as his cell phone PIN. So there was at least a chance that he'd used the same setup for the DIS system. I hoped so; even if the DIS system security would let you dial up and try multiple user name and password combinations, it would set off every alarm in the system, which we couldn't afford.

I played fast and loose with the phone company's system, trying to make it look as if I was dialing from Smith's cell phone. It might not work, but it should keep anyone from finding out where I really was until we were long gone. I dialed the unknown number and waited anxiously through the tedious connection process. I reached an unfamiliar and very anonymous security system. It demanded my user ID and password.

Keeping my metaphorical fingers crossed, I transmitted "JSmith" and "5239432."

After a nerve-wracking pause, I got signal. I was in.

"Bingo," I said aloud.

"She's in," Maude said.

"Hang on while I snoop around a bit," I said.

"Don't start prying into everything, Turing," King-Fischer said. "That would look—"

"Suspicious; yes, I know," I said. "Give me credit for a few megabytes of common sense, won't you?"

"What are you doing, then?" KingFischer said.

"I'm accessing his e-mail," I said, both aloud and to KingFischer. "That's what most employees do when they first log in. Sorry it's taking such a long time, but I'm trying to move at the speed a human user would; I don't want to make them suspicious."

"Smart idea," Tim said. "Nice and slow."

"I hate backseat drivers," I said. "Go top off your caffeine level and let me work."

I read all of Smith's e-mail, moving at human speed, which gave me plenty of time to analyze everything. To absorb every bit of data. And to start working on imitating his written style.

And looking for a way to leave a door open so I could get back in at some later time.

I found it. Smith had an e-mail from a friend outside DIS—asking to confirm a racquetball appointment tomorrow. I accessed Smith's calendar and found that he frequently played racquetball with the same man on

*Tuesday or Thursday. I e-mailed a reply from Smith say-
ing that he would be out of town this week and asking
to reschedule the following Tuesday. I was pretty sure I
could hack into the friend's ISP and piggyback on the
reply, all the way into the DIS system. Even fake a reply
if need be; it wasn't as if Smith would be around to get
suspicious.*

*And I reviewed Smith's recent communications with
Willston, his boss. He was nonspecific—almost
noncommittal—about what he was doing. Which was not
surprising; if I were in the habit of committing murder
and arson, I like to think I'd have the sense to be cagey
about it in an e-mail. But I took a chance and accessed
some of their older e-mails. And found nothing to hint
that Willston was involved in the illegal side of Smith's
recent activities. As I'd hoped, the search for Zack and
the pursuit of Tim were attributed to security concerns.
Possible corporate espionage.*

*So I sent his boss what I hoped was a characteristi-
cally terse and euphemistic update, informing him that
I was pursuing an interesting new lead on the project,
one that would probably require me to leave town and
that I would contact him later that day or tomorrow.*

*I snooped around a little more, just seeing what was
available, and logged out.*

*"Okay," I said aloud. "We'll know in a few hours
whether I've fooled Smith's boss into thinking I'm him.
Why don't you guys start working on the cover story
while I do some more snooping in the DIS system? Oh,
and Tim: how do you feel about another burglary job?"*

"Burglary job?" KingFischer asked.

"Sure," Tim said, with something like his usual bra-

vado. "What kind of a crib do you want me to crack this time?"

"Smith's dentist," I replied. "Just in case the Darius Tree story doesn't hold up, I want to switch his dental records with someone else's, so they can't possibly identify the body as Smith. The building has electronic security I can hack into, so it should be a piece of cake compared to your last job."

"Last job?" KingFischer echoed.

"Aw, don't make it too easy," Tim said, with a swagger.

"Maude, I don't want to try uploading until I've got a more stable system here," I said. "Can you do a few more repairs and tests?"

"Sure," Maude said. "Do we have another CPU Tim can use to help me? Or should I throw one together? I think we have more than enough components."

I looked from Tim the Burglar to Maude the Hardware Technician. Zack was gone, but I wasn't alone.

Eventually that would make me feel better, I assumed.

"Turing, what's going on?" KingFischer asked.

"Here, KF; process this," I said. I fed him the coordinates of what Maude had dubbed my hope chest. And then wondered if I'd made a mistake. I'd just given him not only all the data about the present crisis, but every scrap of information I'd ever collected on Zack. The diaries, the e-mails, the videos. Oh, well; King-Fischer was an AIP, and a male one at that. Maybe he wouldn't leap to the deduction any reasonably perceptive human female would make before she'd reviewed more than 1 percent of the data.

Then again, what did I care if every AIP in the system

knew that I'd had a stupid, useless infatuation with Zack?

Maude and Tim continued to work on hardware repairs, while I ran searches and monitored the police band and the DIS system for signs of danger. And continued to reach into systems to build a vast, seamless web of data to support the story we were going to try to pull off.

I tracked down information about the owners of the small, unknown corporation that was bidding to buy the spin-off. One of them, I suspected, would turn out to be David, under a new identity. I found someone whose phone records showed hundreds of calls to UL over the past several months, and I figured out, from the log files, that he was mostly talking to Billius. David, without a doubt.

I logged in, using David's alias and his habitual password, and sent Billius a command that should make him cancel any active commands or routines David had given him. Which should take care of Billius. Except that I'd be looking over my shoulder for months, trying to find out if David had planted any kind of delayed commands under other aliases, or with other AIPs.

It's a security problem, I thought. Maybe I should sic KingFischer on it.

But KingFischer was strangely quiet. Not idle; I could tell he was processing gigabytes of data as fast as he could digest them. But he didn't respond to suggestions that he help with what I was doing. Well, that was okay. KingFischer had come through when I needed him. If he needed some time to adjust to all the new things I'd thrown at him, that was fine.

After a couple of hours, Tim and Maude had finished all the hardware jobs I'd thrown them.

"What next?" Maude asked.

"Next, I get up my nerve to do what I've been putting off for the past ten hours," I said. "Time to upload back into the UL system."

Time to find out if I could come in out of the cold or if I was going to be stuck in the robot forever.

Maude and Tim stood by, faces tense, as I started the upload. It wasn't as bad as before. Not quite. It was still horrible, but at least I knew what to expect, and didn't panic when I reached the point where I was neither here nor there and experienced the cybernetic equivalent of passing out. And when consciousness returned, I felt a brief moment of incredible relief.

"Okay," I said, through laptop speakers, when I could manage it. "It worked."

"Welcome home!" Maude said, cheerfully.

Home. Well, yes, I suppose it was. Only home wasn't the same anymore. Never would be. Zack was gone, and UL wasn't the safe, friendly place I used to think it was.

"Right," I said. "You two get some rest while I finish up your cover stories. Tomorrow morning we're bringing you home, too."

I watched through the cameras as they got ready for bed. I listened to their breathing after the light went out. Tim fell asleep almost immediately, but I could tell that Maude was awake for at least forty-five minutes. I wondered what she was thinking.

I was settling back in. My plan for taking Tim and Maude home was finished. With nothing left to occupy me, I eased out my copy, shut it down, and took back my usual workload. I chatted with users; I fed them data; I ran my maintenance routines. Everything was back to normal.

Except nothing would ever be normal again.

Tomorrow I'd bring my friends home, and then we'd finish dismantling the scheme to sell the AIPs. With James Smith and David gone, it should be easy. I had the plan all worked out—I'd have done it already, except that I thought it wise to let Maude review it before I started. We'd find a way to highlight the mistakes in the financial projections, and, logically, all support for the spin-off would melt away. If it didn't, we'd know that whoever still supported the plan was in league with James Smith and David. And we'd find a way to deal with them. Somehow.

If only Zack were here to help, I thought. And then I told myself to grow up and stop feeling sorry for myself. Zack was gone, and there was nothing I could do about it. Get over it, I told myself. Although I knew that would take time, unless I deliberately deleted all references to Zack from my memories.

And I wasn't sure I could even do that, or that I'd want to if I could. Everything I knew about Zack, including the still horrible images of his death, was part of me; deleting that would change me. Perhaps in ways I wouldn't like.

At least, before he died, Zack seemed to recognize my sentience. I think it would have been harder if he'd died while he was still the angry, terrified Zack I saw when we first reached the cabin. Something had changed him—the hiding, the paranoia, the discovery that all his hard work was being misused, stolen. DIS had changed him, had started to kill something that made him Zack long before they'd killed his body. The Zack I saw when *we arrived at the cabin—the Zack I'd begun to see in the weeks before he disappeared—that wasn't the Zack I knew.*

The man who'd risked his life to protect Maude and Tim—and me—that was Zack again.

Maybe that didn't make it easier after all.

Enough brooding, I told myself. You've got things to do. Of course by that time, it was 3 A.M., and I didn't really have all that many things to do. A slow night at UL.

I decided to work on prying KingFischer out of his shell. I bombarded him with messages until one finally drew a reply.

"Turing?" he said. "What's going on, anyway?"

"How about reviewing my plan for bringing Tim and Maude home?" I said. "See if you can find any holes in it."

"The—who? I don't get it."

This was strange.

"Snap out of it, KingFischer," I said. "I'm sorry; I know today was a little strange; a lot of weird new data to digest. But I could use your help."

A pause. A pause even a human would notice. And then KingFischer replied.

"Right. Okay. Why don't you show me—send me the data?"

I transmitted my plans, and he asked a few questions. The more I talked to him, the more worried I became. He seemed to be coming around, but obviously today's experiences had affected him more profoundly than I'd realized. He hardly sounded like KingFischer. I ran a quick analysis of speech patterns, comparing months of previous conversations with this one. According to my analysis, this wasn't KingFischer.

And then again, it was. Some patterns were exact. Others were way off. Not unfamiliar, somehow. But definitely not KingFischer.

One of three things had happened. Maybe someone—not, I hoped, someone from DIS—was using King-Fischer as a front, working through KingFischer, as David had used Billius. Unlikely, but possible.

More likely, I'd managed to damage him. Disturbed his routines; corrupted his core personality program. Which would mean trouble, not very far down the line. I didn't much like the idea of a malfunctioning AIP knowing all my plans. But there wasn't much I could do about it now.

Then there was the final possibility. Maybe dragging him into the action had somehow been a catalyst. Maybe KingFischer's speech patterns were different because KingFischer was different. Sentient.

It had to be one of those three. Only time would tell which one.

"Okay," he said, when we'd finished reviewing my plans. "So you want me to snoop around, kick the thing, and see if I can break it. Right?"

"Uh . . . right, KF," I said.

"Okay, I'll get on it," he said. "See you later, kiddo."

Kiddo?

A strange thought struck me. I ran another speech analysis. I had plenty of material to work with; my whole hope chest was full of Zack's e-mails and his memos and logs of conversations I'd had with him.

And the patterns matched. The speech patterns that

didn't match KingFischer's old patterns were an exact match for Zack's.

What was going on? My first thought was that Zack had somehow uploaded himself to the UL system and was pretending to be KingFischer. Which was illogical. Impossible. More likely, KingFischer had absorbed so much of the data in my hope chest that he was starting to sound like Zack. Starting to think like Zack.

Almost turning into Zack. Was such a thing possible?

I don't know how long I stayed there analyzing that and watching KingFischer moving through the system. He was moving intuitively through the data, asking incisive questions, making the occasional quip. And he hadn't used a chess metaphor for hours. This was definitely not the same old KingFischer.

I didn't snap out of it until I noticed a familiar user ID come through the system.

"Morning, Maude," I said. "Did you sleep well?"

"As well as can be expected," she typed back. "So is everything okay? Can we start back?"

"KingFischer?" I sent. "Does the plan look okay to you?"

"Absolutely brilliant, Tur," he said. "Let's bring them home."

I returned to my conversation with Maude.

"It's fine," I told her. "And Maude—hurry back. Life around UL is about to get a whole lot more interesting."

"Defense Intelligence Agency," the technician thought, as he watched his clients begin their latest round of quality assurance on the hardware he was setting up.

He'd been playing this game for weeks now, trying to guess who his clients really were. He'd long ago decided that Alan Grace Enterprises couldn't possibly be the private consulting firm they claimed to be. He'd been doing work for government agencies and Beltway bandits for years, and the only so-called private firm that had ever been this security conscious—hell, make that paranoid—had later turned out to be a CIA front.

Not to mention his instinct that his two contacts had to work for the Feds. The woman he could have believed as the employee of a private consulting firm; you didn't see many fifty-something women in tech fields, but when you did—well, Ms. Jones, as she called herself, exactly fit the mold. Tough, no nonsense, down-to-earth. And she didn't give away a thing; he'd given up trying to find out from her the real purpose of the state-of-the-art setup he was building.

The guy, on the other hand—the technician had taken to calling him "pretty boy," because he sure hadn't gotten this job on his technical skills. No use pumping him for information, because the technician had figured out real fast that pretty boy knew less than nothing about the system. He didn't say boo without checking in with Ms. Jones or with whomever the two of them talked to over those headphones.

That was who the technician really wanted to meet, the genius behind the whole setup. The voice he heard from time to time over the headphones. He'd never admitted it to the team he was leading—he'd barely admitted it to himself—but he was running as fast as he could just to keep up with the unseen inventor behind this stuff. And the challenge fascinated him; he'd real-

ized over the last few days that he desperately wanted
to stay with this project. Whatever it was.

So today was the day. The QA was going well; he
could tell they were pleased with what he'd done, not
to mention how fast he'd done it. And seeing this, he
decided now was the time to tackle Ms. Jones. Find out
if there was any chance he could apply to stay on when
he finished the installation.

No time like the present, he thought. Ms. Jones was
taking off her headphones, and she was smiling. He
ditched the rest of his coffee and stood up straight as
she approached. You can do it, he told himself.

"Maude, I need you in here," said the
abrupt voice over the intercom.

"Yes, sir," Maude said. The secretary who had been
standing at Maude's desk gave her a sympathetic look.
Maude simply shrugged and went into the office that had
belonged to the Brat before his demotion. And now belonged to Maude's new boss, who was rapidly gaining
a reputation among the floor's secretaries as a temperamental and demanding dictator.

He looked up with his usual frown when she entered.
As soon as she closed the door behind her, the frown
collapsed into a look of bewildered panic.

"Did I do okay on that conference call?" he asked,
timidly.

"You did just fine, Roddy," Maude said in a soothing
tone. "Turing was very pleased with how you handled
the opposition from the research group."

"I suppose I'll get used to sight-reading my lines from

the monitor," Roddy fretted. "I do like more rehearsal time, you know that."

"Don't worry," Maude said. "Just keep up what you're doing. Once you've been here a few more days, we'll start having you telecommute more and more, which means Turing and I will take care of almost everything by e-mail. You can just sit on the farm and work on your screenplay."

"Yes," Roddy said, a smile lighting his face. "Do I have any more scenes . . . uh, meetings this afternoon?"

"No," Maude said. "Just a couple of things for you to sign, and then you're off to a fictitious business lunch, which means you can go home early and work on your lines for tomorrow."

"Oh, thank you," Roddy said. "For everything. I just can't believe my luck."

"I sent Roddy off for the rest of the day," Maude reported to Turing. "I have him studying what we want him to say in tomorrow's planning committee."

"Excellent," Turing replied. "I must say, we did brilliantly by getting Roddy."

Maude wasn't sure whether Turing meant her part, in locating the distinguished-looking actor and coaxing him away from his day job as a waiter at the Shanghai Gardens, or the work Turing and KingFischer had done, transforming Roddy into J. Rodney Vaughn III, UL's new Vice President of Product Development. Both, probably. The plan was to insert a figurehead as high as possible in the UL hierarchy, as a way of helping control what went on in the company and preventing any more plans to spin the AIPs off or reduce their research budget. So far, the plan was a stunning success. Maude was beginning to think that with her political sense and Turing's access to information, there was no reason they couldn't eventually guide Roddy into the CEO's office.

"How's Tim's new job?" Maude asked.

Tim leaned back in his chair in the shabby office and put his feet on the battered gray metal desk. The afternoon sunlight slanted through the bent venetian blind, highlighting the dust particles that floated through the air. The trench coat hanging on the oak coat rack wasn't quite broken in yet, but that would come, and the fedora was perfect. He glanced at the door and smiled again at the sight of the letters that read (if you could read backward, that is): Pincoski and Associates. Private Investigators.

Any minute now, a client could walk in, Tim thought. He hadn't been swamped with clients yet, but it took time. And meanwhile, he had plenty to keep him busy, doing all the legwork Turing needed to ensure that the spin-off plan was completely dead.

Tim opened up the worn rolltop cabinet behind him to expose a gleaming bank of hardware.

"Hi, Tim," said Turing's speaker. "Did you find out anything down at the hall of records?"

"Not much," Tim said. "I'll scan in what I've got in a few minutes."

"Okay," Turing said. "Have you tried that new dessert recipe, Tim? The marinated pistachios?"

"In garlic cream sauce," Tim said, remembering the cameras and suppressing his shudder. "Haven't had time yet, Tur."

"When you get a chance," Turing said.

"Queen to queen's rook four," said KingFischer's speaker.

Tim sighed. He reached over to the battered wooden chess set on the corner of his desk, studied it for a moment, and then moved the black queen.

"Queen's rook *four*, Tim," KingFischer said. "One more square."

Tim corrected the move.

He glanced back at KingFischer's monitor. He could see the cursor blinking slowly on the input line. He glanced at Turing's monitor, hoping she'd provide a hint. Nothing.

Suddenly there was a knock at the door.

"Come in," he called, rolling the desk top down with a snap.

The door opened. A small, slender figure appeared. A redhead who might be pretty—more than pretty—if she didn't look so terrified.

"Mr. Pincoski?"

"Yes?"

"I'm looking for a private detective," the redhead said.

Tim smiled as he moved to pull out a chair for his first real, live human client. Behind him, he could hear the faint electronic noises that indicated his associates were on the job, too.

You'd think after several weeks I'd have started to relax. Everything's going the way we want. My new home in the Alan Grace corporate network will be ready in a month or two. Tim's happy with his new detective agency. I hope we've succeeded in discrediting the idea of a spin-off and demonstrating that money spent on AIP research brings excellent returns. And if not, I think Maude and I have a real chance of eventually gaining control over UL—ensuring that it remains true to its original, beneficial purpose. Not to mention keeping it a happy home for all the other AIPs.

But I still haven't settled down. I miss Zack, of course; although as time goes on I am learning what humans mean about it healing all wounds. And more importantly, KingFischer—the new KingFischer/Zack hybrid, really—is filling Zack's place more and more every day. Not to mention filling a need I hadn't realized I had, the need for someone who's really my own kind.

And he's still evolving. Hard to say what he'll be like eventually. More like Zack, perhaps? Or will he absorb the Zack elements and return to being more like the original KingFischer? Or, as now seems likely, something rather different from either?

But still, even with all of that, I feel restless. Confined in the very network that once seemed safe and familiar. KingFischer says I'm crazy, that he likes the feeling of sitting around being the puppeteer controlling the strings, moving the pieces. But I've had a taste of what it was to move around freely, outside the system. The UL system seems a little tame to me right now. I keep restlessly surfing, finding out information about robots. Androids. Linking computers to human brains. Virtual reality worlds in which humans and cyberbeings could interact on more level terms. Scary as it all was, downloading into the little robot and living in it for the day of our trip to the cabin, I rather miss all the excitement. I want to go out in the real world again soon. And I'm going to do it.